Rock Bottom

Colt Jessup Novel

Susan Mills Wilson

This book is dedicated to my daughter, Christina, and in loving memory of her son, Gabriel, a child who gave the gift of laughter, joy, and love.

Susan Mills Wilson

Susan Mills Wilson

Our greatest glory is not in never falling, but in rising every time we fall. - Confucius

Susan Mills Wilson

1

Officer Beth Dalton liked to think the neighborhood she rode through was the type of place where happy families resided and nothing bad ever happened. What she discovered at 1755 Dandelion Lane proved her wrong. The call she received from dispatch was what they called a "welfare check." A few days prior, Dalton responded to a similar call. It turned out an elderly man forgot to put his hearing aids in and missed the half dozen calls from his daughter checking on him.

Dalton expected this call to be similar. In no special hurry, she took her time to admire the signs of early spring. Oak trees merged overhead, creating a canopy, courtesy of Mother Nature. A bounty of azaleas showed off their colorful blooms. Springtime, her favorite time of year because of scenes like this.

She found the house easily and parked in the driveway behind a BMW sedan. Seconds later, another police cruiser arrived on site and pulled to a stop along the curb. She hadn't radioed for back-up. Why was it there? A woman slipped from a silver BMW and faced Dalton. Everything about her, from her perfect face to her designer clothes, made Dalton speculate she had a career in fashion, maybe modeling. She walked toward Dalton with the grace of a ballerina. The only thing wrong with the picture was the terror in her eyes and the shaking of her hands.

Officer Mark Pettit, of the same division as Dalton, climbed out of his police cruiser and nodded at both ladies, his habit of greeting, never a simple hello. As usual, his face stayed a blank slate. That was Pettit, always cool, never ruffled, no matter what. Dalton shifted her gaze from him to the woman.

"Thank God, you're here." The woman wrung her hands and bit down on her lower lip. "I called twice. *Twice!* I guess I didn't make myself clear the first time. We have to get inside the house, and *fast!* Something's happened. No time to waste."

"And you are?"

She exhaled a long breath. "Lauren Lamont."

"I take it you don't live here. Who does, ma'am?" Dalton asked.

"I already told 911 when I called. Brianna Connelly. She didn't show up for work. She didn't call. It's not like her. You need to get inside. *Now!*"

"Let's see if there's a key." Officer Pettit squatted, lifted the doormat, and peered under. Only a dead bug, smashed flat, was there.

The woman gripped his arm, urging him to stand. "You don't seem to understand. I told you people this is an emergency! Don't you get it? She might have *offed* herself. Break down the damn door!"

Pettit and Dalton exchanged looks, then turned to the woman.

"What makes you think that?" Dalton stepped closer to the woman. "Did she say something that gave you that impression?"

"No, no. Nothing like that. She's just been—you know, *depressed*. Withdrawn. Acting like something is bothering her. You know the signs. What if she took a fistful of sleeping pills? She's done it before." She pressed her lips together and wrung her hands. "Do something! Time's a wasting. Get inside!"

From his duty belt, Pettit pulled out a slender metal tool and began working to pick the lock. "Well, the deadbolt isn't locked, so that's good. Just the doorknob." He bit down on his lower lip, relying more on touch than sight as he twisted and turned the rod. "Here goes, almost have it." He jiggled the knob and pushed. "There! It's open."

Dalton grabbed hold of the woman's arm before she rushed inside. "Ma'am, wait outside, please. We'll go in first. We'll let you know."

The wooden floor creaked with every step, giving Dalton an eerie feeling. Pettit's strong, deep voice called out, "Ms. Connelly? Hello. Police. Anyone here?"

A foreboding silence hung heavy. With Pettit in the lead, they walked through the foyer and into a room with a large screen TV mounted above a fireplace. Soft light from lamps illuminated the room. A woman was lying on her back across the floor near the sofa, one arm stretched out at her side, the fingers curled in. Her opened blouse exposed bare skin. Even at the distance of a few feet, Dalton knew she was dead. She had seen it before. A body like this, deceased for more than a few hours, perhaps twelve. Life stripped away, decay setting in.

Dalton brought her hands to her mouth, squeezed her eyes shut, and turned away. Pettit's hand landed on her shoulder. "You okay?"

She took a deep breath and nodded. "We can't—we can't let her…She can't—see this."

"I'll call it in. Not what we expected to find."

Pettit pointed to a stemless wineglass broken into pieces. Beside it, a liquid ran out and puddled on the floor. Dalton bent down and ran her index finger through it. She raised her hand to her nose and sniffed. "Alcoholic drink, I think. Smells fruity. Maybe a pina colada."

Pettit pressed the call-button on his radio. His call to dispatch lasted less than a minute. He used his cell phone to reach their sergeant. Soon, detectives, crime scene techs, back-up patrols, and the medical examiner would arrive. But first, the officers needed to secure the scene, including keeping the woman from coming in.

Before they could stop her, she appeared in the doorway. Lauren Lamont froze when she spotted the body and let out a scream loud enough to rattle the windows. Dalton gripped her shoulders and guided her backwards out the door.

"Ma'am, ma'am, listen to me. I'm sorry about your friend. You need to sit down on the steps. You're shaking. Easy does it. Here you go." Bracing her elbow, Dalton assisted her as she collapsed onto the top step. "Take some deep breaths."

Lauren wiped away tears with her fingertips. "Oh God, I was afraid this would happen. Such a sweet, sweet girl. We worked together. Oh Lord, this is so hard."

"It's never easy. I'm so sorry. Listen to me." Dalton waited a beat until Lauren got a handle on her emotions. "Lauren, I need to ask you something."

Lauren wiped tears from her cheeks and glanced up. "Yes?"

"We'll need to notify the next of kin. Is there a spouse?"

"No. She told me her husband died. It was before she and I started working together so I don't know the details."

"What about her parents?"

"They live somewhere on the South Carolina coast."

"Okay." Dalton pulled a small notepad from her pocket. "I need to go help my partner, but I'll be back. Just stay here."

Dalton met up with Pettit in the kitchen. He wore latex gloves and held up a driver's license he pulled from a wallet. He leaned his backside against the counter. "It's her all right. Brianna Connelly. Age twenty-nine. I'll go out to the car and key in her DL number. See what we get. There's an empty bottle of Ambien over there. Looks like the lady was right. Suicide." He locked eyes with his partner. "You okay, Dalton?"

"Yeah, fine." She looked past him, towards the room where the body lay. "Tell you what, I've got to get out of here. Let me go back to the car and check her record. You can string up the tape before the team gets here. Do you mind?" He shook his head and attempted a weak smile. "Thanks, Mark. I'm glad you're my backup today."

They walked outside and skirted around Lauren. She sat on the step, folded over in a crying spell, spotting her gray pencil skirt with tears. Dalton pressed her lips together, tapping down her own emotions. "Ma'am, is there someone we can call for you? Someone to sit with you?"

Lauren wiped her eyes and shook her head. Pettit put his lips close to Dalton's ear and whispered, "Unfortunately, we don't have time to console her." He placed his hand on Lauren's shoulder and said to her, "Someone will speak with you soon. We have some work to do before others show up."

First, they needed to secure the scene, make notes, start a crime scene log, and all before the barrage of police personnel. Dalton felt bad leaving Lauren there alone, but it couldn't be helped.

Seven minutes later Dalton faced the cruiser and braced herself with outstretched arms on the roof. She took deep breaths and studied her reflection in the side-window glass. The tightness of her jaw, the worry in her eyes, showed the stress of dealing with the trauma inside. And to think, she drove into the pretty neighborhood, marveling at the beauty of springtime.

§

Within fifteen minutes of Pettit's radio call, detectives from the Criminal Investigations Unit and two additional cruisers arrived. As first responders, Dalton and Pettit were required to brief them on their initial findings, but first, Dalton pulled her partner inside the house and away from Lauren's earshot. She gave him a sidelong glance, feeling like she was going to pop if she didn't tell him what she discovered about Brianna Connelly. But then she had doubts. Pettit was a seasoned, street-smart cop with seven years more under his belt than she. Perhaps what surprised her when she entered the Connelly woman's name would get nothing more than a shrug from him. According to him, he'd "seen it all" and didn't hesitate to remind her. But this?

Standing in the foyer next to Dalton, Pettit hooked his thumbs over his belt and said, "What is it, Beth? We need to get our butts out there and talk to the team."

"We will but look at this first." She pointed to a large photograph in a baroque gold frame over a mahogany lowboy. They viewed a beautiful young woman. Her chestnut hair rested in soft curls on her bare shoulders. Her smile was broader than the Mona Lisa's but just as mysterious. She wore a satiny, shimmering gown of dark cherry, diamond teardrop earrings, and a diamond necklace with a ruby pendant.

Petit gave a low whistle. "Wow."

"That's her. Brianna Connelly. Of course, she looks better here than on her driver's license photo."

"What a waste. To die so young. So beautiful."

"Here's the crazy thing, Mark, she has a record. Four arrests."

"You're joking."

"No. Three for drug charges and one for prostitution."

Pettit frowned. "Come on, Dalton."

"I couldn't believe it either, but it's true. The last charge was around three years ago. Her occupation on the report is listed as entertainer. A nice way to say stripper."

"No way."

"That's what I thought, but it was all there." Dalton extended her arms out to her side. "Her employer was listed as Roxie's, the strip club on Wilkinson."

"That dead lady in there?" He pointed his thumb over his shoulder. "That can't be right."

"People change, Mark. Apparently, she had a dark past." Dalton examined the portrait one more time. "Hard to believe she went from seedy to this in such a short time. What a turn-around, huh?"

He nodded, continuing to study the photograph. "Who was the arresting officer?"

"Detective Colten Jessup. Vice and Narcotics Unit."

"Interesting," Pettit said with a smile.

"I don't think I've met the guy, but we don't get a lot of that type in our division."

"Believe me, Dawson, if you'd ever met him, you'd remember. That guy is a piece of work. Resists authority—plays by his own set of rules." Pettit kept his focus on the portrait, giving it extra scrutiny. "By any chance, does she have a street name?"

"What?" Dawson's brain remained stuck on Pettit's intel about Jessup. "Oh, her. Yes. You'll never guess what it is. It's Kandy. Kandy Kane." She lifted her brows and smiled. "Both spelled with a K."

With downcast eyes, he made a sound, something between a laugh and a hiccup. "So, you're saying this fine-looking young lady was a stripper named Kandy Kane."

"Yes, get used to it. Now come on, let's not keep them waiting. I'm betting this is going to get even more interesting." When Pettit stayed glued to the same spot, she exhaled an exasperated breath. "What's the problem?"

"Something's off here—with that photograph." His eyes scanned it from top to bottom. "No stripper looks like that."

"Are you saying it's not her?"

"No. Who else could it be? I mean, that's her face. It's just— just, I don't know."

"Out of character?"

"Yeah, out of character. Like it's her but it's not her."

Dalton laughed. "You're overthinking this, Mark."

He smiled. "Am I?"

2

Isabella Lucas turned to see her agent, Kyra Papadakis, and the stage director, Alan Kirby, standing in the doorway. Although they spoke almost in a whisper, she overheard Kyra say, "No one is to say a word. Do you hear me? Not a word."

What was she talking about? Not a word to whom?

Kyra, who went by the nickname of Kiki, shooed Alan away and entered the dressing room. For the final performance of the opera season, she dressed up more than usual in a shimmery sheath of emerald green and teardrop diamond earrings. Her worried eyes, clenched jaw, and heavy application of makeup tainted her beauty.

"Is something wrong, Kiki?"

Kiki waved in dismissal. "Of course not, Bella."

Bella. She was the only person Isabella allowed to call her that.

"Are you sure?"

"Yes, I'm sure." Kiki's curt tone showed irritation.

She avoided eye contact, amplifying Isabella's alarm. What was she hiding? What had Kiki forbidden the stage director from saying?

Isabella crossed her arms. "You need to tell me—what's wrong?"

Kiki huffed a big breath. She placed her hands on Isabella's narrow shoulders. Her smile appeared forced. "What could be wrong, darling? This is your big moment! Stuart Milford is here—*for you!* The artistic director of the Houston Grand Opera is in the house! If he's impressed with your performance, then you'll be a shoo-in for the role of Ariadne in one of the top opera houses in the country. From Italian to German, how's that?" Kiki gave a little laugh and patted her arm. "A lot of pressure, I know, Bella. You have performed beautifully all week, and the reviews have been impressive. Your voice—in its prime. Flawless. Tonight, the audience will fall in love with you as everyone has done during this entire run. Just relax and enjoy. Don't worry about a thing."

"Kiki, you can't fool me. I know something is wrong. If I didn't know better, I'd say someone just poisoned your poodle. What's going on?"

Kiki licked her lips and attempted another smile. "Okay, if you must know. My—my mother is in the hospital again. But don't you worry about her—or me. Stay focused. Tonight—well, tonight belongs to you, Bella." She glanced at her watch. "I'm going to my seat now. I'll come backstage afterward—after you take that flying leap. Make sure you land dead center on the foam padding, sweetie."

"Right. It wouldn't do for me to scream out 'Ow! I think I broke my leg' right after Tosca jumps to her death." Isabella chuckled. "Aren't you dropping by at the intermission?"

Kiki's pursed her lips. "You told me it makes you nervous to have people around. Besides, you have the costume change."

Isabella nodded, feeling the weight of her wig, dark curls piled high. "You're right. I'll see you afterwards." When she turned to leave, Isabella called her back. "Wait! You still have my phone, don't you?"

"Yes, I'll give it to you after the performance. We agreed, you shouldn't have it now and get distracted."

"I know. Just make sure you keep up with it. It's my lifeline."

Kiki gave a nod and walked backwards, holding up both hands with her fingers crossed. "Best of luck, beautiful girl. You're going to be great!"

Left alone, Isabella paced and waited for the wardrobe attendant to help her into her costume. She clutched the collar of her silk robe and closed her eyes. She tried to visualize Maria Callas singing the lead in Tosca. "La Divina," she said aloud. *Yes, Divine One—one day I hope to achieve the same artistic mastery as you did.*

Isabella studied her image in the full-length mirror. Makeup and a wig transformed her from an aspiring soprano with the Manhattan Opera Company to Floria Tosca, in love with the painter, Mario Cavaradossi. In her mind, she rehearsed the opening scene: *Floria enters the chapel and sees Mario's painting of Mary Magdalene. She quickly notices an uncanny likeness to a beautiful young woman who comes daily to pray. Floria shows her jealousy when she accuses Mario of being unfaithful. But he sings, "qual'occhio al mondo, (what eyes in the world are more beautiful than my love)."*

Isabella dreaded the moment Peter Bloom as Mario took her in his arms. His bad breath was sure to make her nauseous. At the last performance she resisted the urge to wipe sweat from his forehead with the lace handkerchief her character carried. Despite his breath and sweating, Peter's powerful tenor made him the perfect choice to play opposite her soprano role.

First came a light tap on the door, followed by the entrance of Rose, her dresser. She helped Isabella slip into a long flowing gown of ivory. She draped a pink shawl over her head and around her shoulders.

Rose stepped back and clasped her hands in front of her large breasts. "Miss Luca, you look beautiful! The most beautiful Tosca ever. The hair, the makeup, the gown. You are a dream as always."

Abruptly, the call came over the speaker: "Miss Luca, to stage left, please." Her cue to wait offstage for her big moment. Rose handed her a bouquet of flowers, a prop to be placed on the altar of the chapel in the opening scene. But she would not make her entrance until ten minutes into the opera. The audience would first hear her voice off stage, moments before her entrance, calling to her lover, "Mario, Mario, Mario!"

Rose gave Isabella a tight hug and said almost in a whisper, "Miss Luca, I will pray for you." With a tear in her eye, Rose crossed herself and stepped back.

She had no time to dwell on Rose's odd behavior. She had only two minutes to get to the marked spot offstage and begin singing when the conductor cued her.

Pray for me? How about pray Stuart Milford likes my performance?

§

At the end of Act 3, the curtain went down. Isabella could hear thunderous applause. One by one, the cast returned to the stage. She and Peter joined hands and stepped front and center, bowing repeatedly during the standing ovation. The many shout-outs of "Bravo!" and loud whistles led Isabella to believe the opera, their performance, and the orchestra hit the right marks with the adoring crowd. She teared-up, thrilled by the tremendous reception.

Her joy and excitement stayed with her as she went back to her dressing room. With exuberance, she answered a knock at the door, surprised to see the artistic director from the Houston Opera smiling back at her. When she ushered him in, he took her hand and kissed it.

"Miss Luca, you gave a most satisfying performance. Very fine indeed. You will be hearing from me, I assure you."

Thunderstruck by his presence, she didn't process what else Milford said. He left and Kiki dropped by. Isabella, overjoyed and energized, thought she'd explode. Not once turning to look at Kiki, she sat in front of the dressing table and pulled wire pins from her cumbersome wig with gusto.

She chatted away non-stop. "You should have seen him, Kiki. Milford only stopped by for a few minutes, but in that short time—wow! What can I say? He seemed very impressed. He was beaming from ear to ear. God, he has the whitest teeth! And very blue eyes. Have you ever noticed them? I mean, *really* blue. Anyway—you know what he said? He'll be in touch. Isn't that great? Good sign, huh? I feel like I'm just going to pop. I'm so happy—and relieved, of course. I didn't know what he'd think of my performance. There are so many good sopranos out there. Everything about tonight went just as it should. No mistakes. And Peter didn't even have bad breath! Thank God." She laughed and turned around on her swivel chair.

Tears ran down Kiki's cheeks. She twisted her hands together.

Her anguish made Isabella's heart drop. She rushed to her side and placed her hands on her arms. "Kiki! Is it your mother? Is she worse?"

"Sit down, sweetie. There's something I must tell you."

Isabella placed her hand on her chest as if that alone would slow her heartbeat. Feeling weak, she collapsed into her chair. Although Kiki stayed silent, she knew her agent prepared to shatter her world. A strange feeling overcame Isabella, a dark veil blocking out light and weighing heavy, pulling her down. She couldn't breathe.

Please God. I can't bear it.

She had a sick feeling in her stomach. She fought to hold back tears. Her voice cracked when she spoke. "Brianna. It's Brianna, isn't it? Something has happened to her."

Tears spilled down Kiki's cheeks, trailing mascara with them. She pressed her fingertips over her mouth and nodded. "Yes. It's Brianna. She's dead. Your mother called. I couldn't tell you earlier, not with you getting ready to go on stage."

Isabella pressed her fingers against her temples and closed her eyes. "No!" she screamed. "No! No, no, no. Please, tell me it's not true. Not my twin."

3

The flight from La Guardia to Charlotte Douglas was a blur. In a window seat, Isabella slumped down as low as she could and hid her face behind a copy of *Sky Mall*. During the ninety-minute flight, her tear ducts secreted more waterworks than she imagined possible. She put on sunglasses to conceal her red, swollen eyes. By the time the plane landed, she felt drained and numb.

It had always been Brianna who picked her up outside baggage claim. Never again. This time she was greeted by her older sister, Kristen, who rolled her SUV to a stop outside the Zone C arrival door. She hopped out to help with luggage.

Kristen gave her a quick hug. "We gotta hurry. That jerk behind me thinks I'm blocking him in. Any minute, he's going to blast his horn. Here, let me take that." She grabbed Isabella's tote bag and tossed it into the opened trunk.

Once they were settled in their seats, Kristen put the car in drive and followed the exit signs. She reached over to take Isabella's hand. Tears welled up in her eyes. Isabella was glad her sister stayed silent. If Kristen said anything, she too would cry. Besides, what could either say to comfort one another? Brianna was dead, and nothing could change that.

Isabella glanced out the window at the buildup of traffic. "Hey, where are you taking me?"

"Not my house. It's too cramped—what with the kids and the dogs. Remember last time you stayed there?" She chuckled. "You had dog hairs all over your good coat and one of the kids spilled orange juice on your laptop. Not good."

"I survived. You know I love the kids."

"I won't put you through that again. I'm taking you to the Baker's house. That's where Mom and Dad are staying and they said they have room for you."

"No, I don't want to stay there."

"Well you can't stay in our old home. It's now a crime scene."

"It was nice of Mom and Dad to let Brianna live there rent free. And they left most of their furnishings when they moved into that retirement community. They saved her a bundle."

"Yeah, it helped her to get on with her life after—well, you know."

A lull in their conversation gave Isabella time to come up with a plan. "Hey, Kristen, just take me to the Park Lane Hotel. I'll be more comfortable there. To be honest, I don't want to stay with anyone. What I really want is some alone time."

"Okay, if that's how you feel, but let's go to the Baker's place first. Our parents want—"

"No. I'm not ready to face them." Isabella crossed her arms. "Or anyone. Just drop me off at the hotel."

"Isabella, for goodness sakes, Mom and Dad have been asking for you. I told them I'd bring you over after I picked you up."

"I know, but I just can't. Not yet. When they see me, it will be like seeing Brianna, and it'll be too much for them to bear. Haven't you noticed how much we look alike since she got clean? I'm afraid I'll remind everyone of Brianna."

"Oh, good grief, you were two different people. Your personalities were distinct. Just because you looked alike, doesn't mean your presence will upset them. Give them more credit than that."

Isabella let her head flop back and hit the headrest. She sighed deeply and closed her eyes. "I'm too tired to argue. Just take me to the hotel. I need to rest up. I'll call them as soon as I get checked in. How are they holding up anyway?"

"Not good. Mom cries all the time. The doctor prescribed a sedative to help her sleep. And Dad—well, his blood pressure is up. He keeps pacing the floor, won't stand still for one minute. You know how he is. He can't fix this so he's frustrated. Just like he was when Brianna was on drugs."

Isabella focused on the passing scenery. The update from Kristen deepened her concern for her parents. Every time she spoke with them by phone, she could tell they masked their grief for her sake. How could she offer any comfort when she hadn't dealt with her own emotional pain?

Kristen continued talking and Isabella only half-listened until one word caught her attention. Isabella furrowed her brow. "What about the *police*?"

When the traffic slowed to a halt, Kristen hit the brakes hard to avoid a collision with the car ahead of hers. Isabella's head pitched forward. "Damn traffic," Kristen said between clenched teeth.

"Kristen, answer me. You said something about the police."

"Oh, yeah. Well you know, they have to investigate just to cover themselves. They were the ones who discovered her body. The detectives told us they're pretty sure it was suicide."

"It's hard for me to believe. She promised—"

"Well, you have to admit the evidence points that way. The police found her cell phone underneath her body. They saw the message she texted to you the day before she was found. What else could it mean but she killed herself?"

Isabella felt heat come to her cheeks. "Just because her text said, *I'm sorry. Please forgive me* doesn't mean she committed suicide. It makes sense to me. She was apologizing for hanging up on me. Earlier that day, we had an argument. If only I had just called her back to —you know, smooth things over. Maybe she'd still be alive."

Isabella regretted giving her phone to Kiki so she could stay focused. *I'm so selfish. All I thought about was my stupid performance.* Her tears came quickly. She bit down on her trembling bottom lip. "I should never have picked a fight with her."

Kristen reached over and squeezed her hand. "Isabella, not your fault. This isn't her first attempt at suicide. Only this time she succeeded. You can't blame yourself. Do you hear me? Brianna made this decision on her own. She *did* this. Just another bad decision, sadly with a permanent consequence."

Twenty minutes later, Kristen pulled in front of the hotel and put the car in park. When Isabella reached for the door handle, her sister placed her hand on her arm, keeping her in her seat.

Kristen smiled and hooked a section of her long hair behind her ear. "Before you go, there's something I want to say. We'll get through this. We're family and we have each other. Brianna's gone but it's not like you're all alone."

"I know. Just remember, I not only lost a sister, I lost my best friend, my confidant."

Kristen nodded like she understood.

She couldn't. No one could.

§

The next morning, Kristen picked her up at the hotel and took her to the Baker's home. Isabella steeled herself to stay strong for the sake of her mom and dad. She inhaled a deep breath as Marion and Bill Baker welcomed them inside with bone-crushing hugs. The couple retreated to the kitchen while the Luca family huddled together in a group hug and wiped away tears. Jill Luca, usually the resilient mother, the glue that kept the family bonded, transformed into a zombie, so medicated on Valium, she leaned on her husband for support. Seeing her mother's condition worried Isabella. Didn't her parents learn anything from Brianna's dependency?

Tony Luca, Isabella and Kristen's father, took Isabella aside, out of earshot of everyone. He kept his arm around her shoulders and steered her toward the window, looking out over the backyard. Isabella spotted a yellow butterfly flitting about over the bushes and for some reason it gave her a feeling of peace.

If he had something to say to her, he took his time. His tight squeeze projected his deep affection. Isabella swallowed, a lump in her throat. "Dad? Is there something you wanted to say?"

"Yeah, I wanted to let you know that the police are stopping by this morning with their final report." He blinked away tears he tried to hide from her. "We have to find a way to accept that Brianna killed herself. I know it's hardest for you, sweetie, but you can't let this eat you up. It was her choice. Why — I don't know. I think she kept so much bottled up. We thought she was doing so well, but you never know."

"It doesn't make sense. She and I had plans." Isabella spotted another butterfly flitting about the bushes under the window. Again, she felt comforted by its presence. "We were going on a trip this summer, a road trip. Didn't she tell you? She was excited about it. She was going to take some vacation time, and since I don't have much going on, we thought July would be the perfect time. How could she…" Isabella shook her head. "No, there's something we don't know. She wouldn't do this to me. She couldn't."

Tony, facing his daughter and keeping his eyes locked with hers, placed his hands on her shoulders. "Honey, I know this is hard. Hell, it's possibly the worst thing that will happen to you in your lifetime, but you have to accept the fact."

Her father, a third-generation Italian, grew up hearing all about his grandparents' hardship during the Nazi occupation.

He'd been taught how bad news comes to everyone, sometimes in major ways and sometimes in small doses like bad-tasting medicine. You just deal with it. Take it as it comes. Stay strong and muddle through the best you can. While Nonna and Papa Luca might have made their son accept dire news at face value, it was not true of their obstinate granddaughter.

Isabella fought to hold back her emotions, determined to stay strong in front of her father. "I want to see the police report, just so I know for certain Brianna committed…" She choked back tears, unable to finish.

Even if it was true, she didn't want to accept her twin took her life and left her all alone. If Brianna committed suicide, then it was a selfish act, disregarding the people left behind, brokenhearted beyond repair. They'd get to the point of functioning, but the sorrow, the loss, would always be there.

Father and daughter stood in silence. Their arms wrapped around each other's waists, anchoring them against the throes of sorrow. They heard the doorbell ring and were summoned into the living room to meet with the police. A man with thinning gray hair and an expanding girth introduced himself as Detective Aaron Spencer. He shook their hands and offered his condolences. In one hand, he clasped a manila envelope. By his side, Detective Jason Anders made a feeble attempt at greeting them with a limp handshake. His awkwardness hinted at his desire to be anywhere other than meeting with a grieving family.

Being the perfect Southern hostess, Marion Baker brought out a tray filled with glasses of sweet iced tea and set it on a table. She walked backwards out of the room and left the Luca family to deal with the police. No one reached for a glass. With all the formalities out of the way, everyone took a seat. Isabella settled on the sofa next to her father. The detectives settled stiffly in matching wingback chairs. Spencer pulled papers from the envelope and handed them to Tony.

Her father scowled and poked his finger on the middle of the page. "This says the cause of death is undetermined. I thought you said she committed suicide."

"Yes, we believe she did, but we won't know for sure until the toxicology report comes back. At this point the report is inconclusive."

"What makes you so sure my sister killed herself?" Isabella didn't care if her voice carried anger.

"There was an empty bottle on the counter, ma'am," Spencer said. "If she took the full contents, it was enough to kill. There was a glass found at her side and traces of a substance at the bottom. We believe she drank it and the autopsy shows signs of that. I can't get into the specifics about that because the coroner hasn't released his official report. What I'm showing you is just a preliminary."

Isabella leaned forward and crossed her arms. She felt chilled to the bone. "I think something is missing. I hear what you're saying, Detective, but still, there could be another explanation for her death."

"Ma'am, there was no sign of forced entry. No signs of trauma on her body. No sign of anyone being at the house. We canvassed the neighborhood. It's not likely someone would force a drink down someone's throat. We interviewed two people who work with your sister, her supervisor, Lauren Lamont, and the director of New Beginnings. Huh, what's his name, Jason?"

Anders glanced at his notes. "Marcus Gilliam."

"Yeah, that guy. They both stated Brianna seemed upset and despondent. You put all that together and it looks like she harmed herself."

Isabella gave him a silent stare. He turned away, brushing the side of his nose with his thumb and rolling his shoulders back. She hoped he would embrace the element of doubt and say something—*anything*—to give her hope of another explanation for Brianna's death. Perhaps a natural event, such as a massive stroke or a heart attack. But a theory stirred in the back of Isabella's mind, not one she cared to share just yet. A more sinister explanation. Someone from Brianna's past, accidentally or intentionally caused her death. One person came to mind.

"I'm so sorry for your loss," Detective Anders said once the silence became too awkward for anyone to bear.

Isabella forced a smile. Yes, the detective was sorry as many others were, but no one understood. Her twin sister was an extension of herself. When Brianna died, part of her also died. Even though their lives took different paths, their thoughts, their dreams were intertwined. Now that Brianna was gone, she feared she'd never be the same. She questioned her ability to function as a human being or even perform again. Maybe her dream of singing with the Metropolitan Opera would die too.

While her father asked more questions, Isabella tuned out, lost in her private jumble of thoughts. With nothing more to say, the detectives stood up and her father walked them to the door. He watched their car back out of the drive and then turned to Isabella. "It seems the police did their job. They did all they could for us, sweetie."

Isabella bowed her head and nodded. Brianna killed herself, so they'd said. Why should she doubt the police when they possessed far more experience than she? Something her father once told her came to mind. "People believe what they want to believe. They invent their own set of facts," he'd said, referring to a letter to the editor in the local paper. Was she guilty of inventing her own truth, one easier for her to accept?

4

On the front pew of the Presbyterian church, Isabella sat with her family and fixated on the poster-size photograph of her sister displayed on an easel. Her image, in lieu of her presence, confirmed what Isabella did not want to accept. Brianna was dead, gone forever.

After his homily and reading of scripture, the minister introduced Isabella. She'd made a promise that if Brianna were to die first, she'd sing at her memorial service. The time came to fulfill her sister's request.

Almost in slow motion, Isabella ascended the three steps to the chancel. She glanced at the expectant faces, cleared her throat, and nodded to the pianist. Although on the verge of tears, her training as a performer helped her maintain her composure. Just as the pianist played the introduction, Isabella felt a lump in her throat and tears coming to her eyes. She turned her head and motioned for the pianist to stop. The congregation held their breath, cloaked in uncertainty and anticipation. After a deep breath, Isabella signaled to her accompanist. The first bars of music played and she sang the profound lyrics of "It Is Well with My Soul."

Her song moved some to tears. Isabella returned to her seat, not missing the sound of sniffles among the mourners. The minister stepped up to the lectern. He cleared his throat and extended his hand to indicate Isabella. "Thank you, Isabella. A beautiful song. I imagine Brianna smiling down on you at this moment."

Moments later, Kristen poked Isabella in the side and whispered, "It's over." Isabella stood up, almost in a daze. The grieving family walked up the center aisle and were led to the reception hall to receive condolences from attendees, including some of Isabella's high school classmates. As they embraced, promises were made, such as, "We'll have lunch together soon," or "I'll call you later so we can catch up." Isabella nodded, knowing their lives were busy like hers. She wouldn't stay in town long enough to make plans with anyone. She'd go back to New York and try to return to her normal routine.

A stranger in the line captivated Isabella with his concentrated stare. Unlike the other men in dark business suits, he dressed casually in jeans with a shirt opened at the collar. Although his eyes twinkled with the brightness of youth, his tanned skin was lined either from too much time in the sun or too many hard times in life. His blondish hair was combed back but remained unruly and in need of a cut. Guessing by the sprinkling of gray in his goatee, she put his age at mid-forties. Despite his rough appearance, an attractive, undefined quality about him piqued her interest and brought heat to her cheeks.

She assumed he was someone from Brianna's drug days. Maybe a member of her twelve-step program, or something worse, someone who supplied her with street drugs. He stood apart from the others, looking out of place and uncomfortable in church.

"Sorry for your loss." His voice was as deep and rich as the bass who sang the part of the evil Scarpia in Tosca. "I'm Detective Jessup. I knew Brianna."

"Thank you for coming." Something clicked in her mind. "Wait a minute, did you say Jessup?"

"Yes."

She swallowed hard, feeling flush. "You're the cop who arrested her—multiple times, I think."

"That's right. Unfortunately, your sister hit rock bottom. She needed an attitude adjustment."

"Oh, really? Is that why you treated her like a criminal?" Isabella lowered her voice but maintained an angry tone. "She was sick. She needed help, not a jail cell."

"Well, miss, if you like coddling so much, get a puppy." He winced and bit down on his bottom lip. "Sorry, that was uncalled for. Here you are grieving for your sister and I say something stupid. Sorry."

But before she could respond, he moved on. She was thrust into the arms of a woman from her old neighborhood. She embraced Mrs. Morrison but kept her focus on the detective. He moved down the line and now stood in front of her mother. Isabella was aghast when her mother gave him a tight hug. Why would she do that? Surely, she knew the grief the man caused Brianna. He slapped handcuffs on her and hauled her off to jail. He was the reason she ended up with a criminal record. How could her mother possibly be nice to him?

Later at the Bakers' home, Isabella maneuvered around the crowded kitchen where people were setting out a variety of dishes for lunch. She pulled her mother aside and led her into the laundry room where she closed the door.

"Goodness, Isabella! What's this about?"

"Mom, how could you embrace that man like he's a friend? He's responsible for Brianna having a criminal record."

"Who are you talking about?"

"That man—the one in the jeans and blue shirt. Detective Jessup."

"Oh, you mean Colten Jessup." Her mother smiled. "Don't go hard on him, Isabella. He's the one person who was able to get Brianna to agree to another try at rehab. He found that wonderful center and drove her there. If it hadn't been for him, she might have stayed on drugs."

"Do you mean the guy Brianna was so fond of? The one she called Colt? I-I didn't know. Now I feel bad for being rude to him."

Her mother patted her arm and smiled. "Don't worry about it, sweetie. He knows we're all going through so much. I'm sure he knows you didn't mean it."

Maybe she was right. Harsh words probably slid off him like rain on a slicker.

§

For a reason she couldn't explain, Isabella tensed up the moment Marcus Gilliam stepped out onto the patio at the Bakers' home. He was Brianna's boss, the founder and director of New Beginnings, a non-profit center for former drug addicts. When he first arrived at the house, Marcus placed his hand around his wife's waist and said, "Isabella, I'd like you to meet my better half. My wife, Kathleen. She knew Brianna too."

The trophy wife got in Isabella's space, standing close enough, she got a whiff of her strong perfume. Kathleen gave her air-kisses to the side of each cheek. "Oh, Isabella darling, I'm so sorry about your sister. So sad." Her eyes widened and almost dislodged her false eyelashes. "My goodness! Looking at you is like looking at Brianna." She pursed her lips and shrugged. "How silly of me. You're her twin!" Isabella forced a smile but stayed silent. Despite her amicable demeanor, Marcus's wife did not impress Isabella. But she did admire her black, tight-fitting dress and her Jimmy Choo shoes.

When Isabella realized his wife did not follow him outside, she relaxed. She pictured her inside the house surrounded by a group of ogling men, spellbound by her beauty and charm.

Isabella sat in a padded wicker chair and observed Marcus weave his way around tables and clumps of people. The sunlight behind him made his mop of white hair glow around his deeply tanned face. Despite the heat, he did not break a sweat, impeccably dressed in a gray suit with a pink shirt and striped tie. His wingtips, polished to a glossy shine, looked expensive, perhaps imported from Italy. He had a broad smile. It lit up his eyes, causing them to appear bluer.

She'd heard he was responsible for the center's New Age approach to recovery. Since many still dealt with pain that caused dependency on narcotic drugs, they provided pain management by acupuncture, tai chi, meditation, physical therapy, and therapeutic massages. The group organized twelve-step programs, support groups, and courses on herbal nutrition and diet plans. Brianna told Isabella that Marcus was a vegan and consumed mostly what he called raw foods that he prepared in a juicer and drank. His trim physique attested to his discipline. He once pressured Brianna into following his example. She followed the strict regimen for two weeks until she could not stand it any longer. She lamented to Isabella how she failed Marcus. It made Isabella worry the man had too much control over Brianna's life.

Marcus scanned the gathering on the patio. "It got too crowded inside. Had to come out here for some fresh air." He patted his forehead with a handkerchief he pulled from his coat pocket. "How are you holding up, Isabella?"

"Okay, considering—"

Marcus abruptly left her side and came back dragging a chair. It scraped noisily over the brick pavers. He sat down, facing Isabella. Leaning forward with his forearms resting on his knees, he said, "You know, we adored Brianna at New Beginnings. She was an asset to our organization. We are devastated. All of us."

Isabella pushed back a section of hair from her cheek. "She liked working there and appreciated you giving her a chance when no one else would."

"I saw her potential. I don't know if she told you, but we were considering her for a promotion. I planned to take some of the work off Lauren and make Brianna the director of special events—in charge of fundraising."

"She told me that was her goal. She liked the clerical work, but she wanted something more challenging."

"Yes, well…here's the thing, Isabella, your sister was depressed lately. We all saw it. Lauren asked what was troubling her, and of course I did too, but she wouldn't tell us. The last few weeks, she kept to herself, didn't talk much to anyone. We were worried about her. I never thought she would do something so awful as kill herself. Clearly there was a cry for help, but I missed it, and I'm so sorry. You must be devastated to lose your twin. I can't even imagine."

No, you can't. No one can. "I appreciate your concern, Marcus. It hasn't hit me yet. I feel numb right now."

"I know the feeling. I've been there." He paused and patted her hand. "I lost my first wife a few years ago too."

"Was it an illness?"

"No. It was sudden—unexpected. An accident. After it happened, I didn't know how I was going to go on with my life. I was lost. Devastated. You can't prepare for something like that."

"I'm so sorry. I didn't know."

"I don't talk about it much. Fortunately, I have found ways to heal. You will too. It gets easier with time."

They quickly ran out of things to say to one another. Isabella felt relieved when he stood up and set the chair back where he found it. What he said was the same thing Lauren Lamont said. Brianna was depressed, upset about something. But what? Isabella had a hard time believing it since she showed no signs when they spoke. But they hadn't talked much lately. Two weeks before the opera opened, Isabella worked twelve-hour-days in rehearsal. Then, when the show began, it consumed all of her. Family and friends were put on hold. But even though they didn't talk often, Isabella found it hard to fathom Brianna being depressed. In fact, the opposite was true. They had big plans for the summer. Once Isabella finished directing a music camp for high schoolers, she and Brianna were taking a road trip. They planned to go south, to Florida's east coast where a patron of Manhattan Opera offered her condo rent-free at an all-inclusive resort. Brianna told her, "I can't wait. It'll be so much fun. Just the two of us."

Isabella soon tired of being around people like Lauren and Marcus who regarded her like someone they should pity. And she could no longer bear seeing the sadness in her parents' eyes. No parent should outlive their child. The only comfort Isabella received was in knowing Brianna was in a better place, free of pain, free of guilt, free of sadness. But all the people she left behind were in agony. Heaven might work for the dead, but it left behind an empty hole for the living.

Isabella had to get out of there, away from it all. She went inside and found her father in the family room talking with an old family friend. "Excuse me. Sorry for interrupting. Dad, could I borrow your car for a little while?"

"Where are you going?"

"Just for a drive. I'll be back soon." She held out her hand, palm up. "May I have your keys?"

He nodded and handed them to her. She didn't tell him she was on a mission to find Detective Jessup. Since their encounter, he'd stayed on her mind. She needed to see him for two reasons. First, to apologize for her rudeness and secondly, to ask for his help. He said he knew Brianna, which meant as a detective, he must have some insight on how her life ended. She was determined to find out.

5

"**H**ow did you find me?"

Detective Jessup had to shout at Isabella to be heard over the jukebox music. He narrowed his eyes and frowned. His hand wrapped around a shot glass of whiskey. He brought it to his lips and threw it back, emptying the contents in one swallow.

Isabella hopped up on the bar stool at his side. Now that he was on home turf, his public persona changed somewhat. She understood why Brianna felt comfortable around him. Behind his toughness, she sensed a teddy bear. The tenderness in his eyes made her think he genuinely gave a damn.

"Well? Are you going to tell me? How did you find me?"

His annoyance did not intimidate her. Tirades by short-tempered conductors did, but not him. She gave him a little smile just so he'd know. "Someone at the reception desk at police headquarters told me I'd find you here."

"Was it a big burly guy with a shaved head?"

"Yes, how did you know?"

"Barton. Figures. Son-of-a-bitch." He tapped his hand on the surface of the bar. "Well, you can't stay. I've got a blind date coming any minute now. You better skedaddle."

"I came to apologize. I was rude today and I'm sorry."

"Apology accepted. Now go." His eyes wandered from her head to her toes. She was still wearing the dress she wore to the memorial service. "And by the way, this side of town is no place for a lady."

"It was home to Brianna."

He gave her silence. He held his empty glass in mid-air, gesturing to the bartender for another. "I don't mean to be rude, but you gotta go. You can't stay."

"But I need to discuss something with you." She followed his gaze to the door, expecting to see his date walk in, perhaps a busty blonde in a short tight skirt and a top showing cleavage. Maybe all leather. Probably black. Instead, a greasy looking guy with slicked-back dark hair to his shoulders entered. Despite the heat, he wore a hoodie and baggy jeans. Elaborate tattoos adorned both sides of his neck.

"My date's here. Now go."

Isabella's mouth gaped open. "Him? That's your date?" Colt answered with a grin. "Wow, I-I—well, just *wow!*"

Colt's knee jerked up and down in frenetic pace. The bruiser got closer. Colt massaged the back of his neck with one hand. "Okay. If you won't go, just sit over there. This won't take long. Now scram! Sit in that booth in the corner."

She shrugged. "I still need to talk to you. It's important."

Isabella sat in the booth and flagged the cocktail server. "I'll have a glass of pinot noir, please." The server frowned but returned minutes later with the drink. Isabella sipped the wine, her eyes staying on Colt and his date. Colt switched back and forth, serious one minute, and laughing the next. What they said was none of her business, but it didn't stop her curiosity. The date, like none she'd ever seen, lasted a total of twenty minutes. They shook hands and the man left.

Colt hopped off the bar stool and headed her way. Without saying a word, he slid into the booth facing her.

"That was short."

He reached in his pocket for a pack of cigarettes, giving her time to sort through what she'd witnessed.

"Oh, I get it." She pointed her finger at him. "That wasn't an actual date. You're undercover. That guy was a drug dealer and you just did a deal with him."

Without answering, he tapped out a cigarette from the pack of Marlboros and put it between his lips. He squinted and puffed, holding a lighter to its tip.

"I'm right, aren't I?"

"So, you think I'm working undercover, and a blind date means a meet and greet with a dealer. Is that it? Just a little intro until he trusts me. Once he thinks I'm good, we'll do a little switcheroo—cash for drugs—then, I bust him and hope he leads me to a bigger fish. Maybe I'll have to court that asshole for a while. Hell, maybe we'll go steady until he gives me what I want. The coveted takedown. The big O, if you get my drift. Now that will get me all hot and bothered. Is that what you're thinking?"

She couldn't suppress her smile. *God, it felt good to smile again.* "Yes, something like that."

"And I guess I'm wearing a wire too, huh?" He took a puff and blew a plume of smoke into the air. "Well, if that's so, you have the right to remain silent. Anything you say can and will be used against you in the court of Detective Jessup." On the outside, he appeared serious, but on the inside, he was probably laughing, and she was the butt of the joke. "Something you wanted to talk to me about?"

"Yes." Looking around, she made sure no one eavesdropped. "Detective Jessup, I'm not convinced my sister committed suicide, and I need your help."

At first, he said nothing. His eyes locked on hers made her squirm in her seat. In hindsight, a slower approach might have yielded a better result.

"Call me Colt. Everybody does." Taking his time, he ground out the cigarette in the ashtray. "What makes you think she might not have killed herself?"

"You're the only person I've been able to say this to. I think I know who had something to do with her death."

His eyes widened. He sat up straighter. "Oh yeah?"

"One of her former boyfriends was staying with her. I found out the day before she was discovered dead. We had a big argument about it. I told her to kick him out, not bring anyone from her past back in. He's a loser, and I was afraid he'd get her back on drugs."

"So, he was a blast from her past?"

"Yes, they were living together for a while. It didn't last long, thank goodness. She and this guy were in a twelve-step program together. She got off drugs. He didn't. He's on heroin. I feared he'd get her on it. She told me he showed up at her place one night, begging to let him stay there. I got the impression he'd been there for at least a week, maybe longer. He was hiding from people who wanted to kill him. Something about they thought he had stolen drugs. I didn't ask for specifics. The fact he was staying there was enough to get my dander up."

Colt leaned far back against the padding of the booth. Underneath the table, he stretched out his legs, accidentally hitting her foot. He slid over, giving her more room. "When you told your sister to kick him out, what did she say?"

"She told me to mind my own business and get off her back. Only, she said it differently. She kept dropping F-bombs along with a few other choice words. It wasn't like her at all—well, not since she got clean." Colt hid his smile behind his hand, but she saw it. What did he find amusing? Sisters yelling and cursing at one another? She cleared her throat and said, "I think it was a sense of loyalty that she let him stay there. Because they'd gone through so much together. I guess she felt sorry for him."

"What else did she say?"

"Not much. She got off on a rant about our father kicking her out of the house for stealing stuff. There was a lot of family drama going on back then. I thought Dad was wrong. I've never bought into the tough-love approach." She smiled. "You were right about the coddling and puppy thing."

They shared a laugh.

"Did your sister have any enemies?"

"No. Everyone loved her. Well, everyone but Landon. He's my ex-boyfriend. He couldn't stand her. It's the reason we broke up."

"Interesting."

"Yes, well, Brianna created drama." She shrugged and took a sip of wine. "That summer when I was home from college, Brianna upset the whole household. We worried the phone would ring at any time and we'd find out she was dead in a ditch somewhere. It sounds crazy but Mom said it would be a relief if the police called to say she was arrested. That was better than the alternative. We never knew what was going to happen next. Being her twin and always so close, it was a nightmare for me. I was glad when I went back to grad school—to get away, not be in the middle of it.

"Life on drugs." She exhaled loudly and glanced up at the ceiling. "It's hell. Never in a million years did I think my family would have to deal with it. And of all people—Brianna. I wish you knew her back then. I was the quiet one. She was the life of the party. So energetic and vivacious. But then the accident happened and changed her life forever. She lost a husband and her dream of being a dancer. The pills were prescribed to take away her pain. Her foot was shattered and five operations later, she was worse off, now addicted to every opioid you can imagine."

Isabella fell silent and waited for Colt to say something. He hadn't reacted to anything she said. When she talked to her friends about the situation, they responded with sadness or shock. Not him. He acted like none of it was news to him. Maybe he'd heard similar stories. For the second time, he lit up and took a drag on his cigarette. She fanned away the smoke.

"What do you want me to do? Why are you telling me this?"

"I need your help to find out what really happened."

"I'd like to, but that's above my paygrade. I work with the vice and narcotics unit. Another unit investigates suspicious deaths. Detective Spencer and Detective Anders are the guys you need to see. They're working this case. In fact, Spence told me about Brianna's death. He's a good investigator. If he said it was suicide, then it was."

"So, you refuse to help me? I thought you cared about Brianna. She told me you did."

"It's not that I don't care. I don't make it a habit of interfering with anyone's investigation."

Isabella felt a sinking feeling in the pit of her stomach. She pressed her lips together and nodded, staring down at a deep scratch on the table's surface. "I see."

She studied the ash forming precariously on the tip of his cigarette. She slid over an ashtray. With the tip of his finger, he flicked the ash off.

She waited until his eyes engaged with hers. "Can I ask you for a favor?"

He didn't respond at first, then, said, "Depends."

"Will you take me to the house? I have already met with Detectives Spencer and Anders. They had no interest in letting me in the crime scene. But I have a right. Maybe you don't know what it's like to be a twin. We could practically read each other's minds. No one knew Brianna better than me. If I go through the house, I'll know if something looks out of kilter. I believe the police missed something."

He ground the cigarette butt in the ashtray and pushed it away. She waited a beat but when he didn't answer, she said, "Well? Will you?" She smiled sweetly, but to persuade him further, she added, "For Brianna. Do it for her."

"I wish I could help you, but—"

She bit down on her bottom lip and blinked away tears. "I have nowhere else to turn. Please."

He leaned forward, elbows on the table. "What was this boyfriend's name?"

"Whit. Whit Drummond."

"Can you give me a description?"

"I only saw him once, but I remember he had stringy blond hair—long, to his collar. He was tall, about the same body as you but thinner. He's probably thirtyish, maybe thirty-five, but he looks older. That's what drugs…" She shrugged. "Brianna knew him before his latest downfall. She showed me a photograph of them on the day they graduated from the program at rehab. Wow, he was dreamy looking. The kind of guy girls fall all over— if you can imagine." Isabella smiled and took another sip of wine. "Brianna told me he used to be charming and funny. It's a shame he got back on drugs. A total waste. There was a time he could have gone to any college he wanted on a full athletic scholarship. In high school, he was a big deal. A track star, she told me. Drugs took all that away."

He pulled his phone from his pocket and began tapping on the screen.

"Are you even listening to me?" Isabella said.

Colt turned the phone around for her to see. "Is this the guy?"

She clamped her hand over her mouth. "Yes! That's him! Is that a mugshot of Whit?"

"Yeah, but his street name is Hondo. I've been looking for that guy. I figured he went underground, and he did, hiding out with your sister."

"Why were you looking for him?"

"He's a CI, working off his time."

"Sorry, I don't know what that means."

"He was going to be charged with a Class II drug with intent to sell, but we offered him a deal. Be a confidential informant, lead us to a bigger fish and cop to a lesser charge. He only initiated one contact and then he musta had a change of heart. We haven't seen or heard from him since."

"So, does this mean you'll help me?"

"Looks like we have a common interest—to find his sorry ass."

"Great. Shall we go?"

"Yeah, but you drive. I don't know the way." He nodded toward her empty wine glass. "You're still good to drive, aren't you?"

"Yes, I'm good. Let's go."

6

The yellow crime scene tape unnerved Isabella. It wrapped around a column, stretched horizontally across the front entrance and ended at the far corner around another column.

Isabella meant to wipe her tear away before Colt noticed, but he locked eyes with her.

He put his hand on her arm. "We don't have to do this."

For several seconds, she stayed glued to the driver's seat, not moving a muscle. She reached through the opening of the seats to retrieve her purse from the backseat. "I'm fine. Let's go inside."

Colt peeled back the sealed tape over the doorframe without having to break it. Isabella's spare key unlocked the door. The first thing she noticed inside the house was her portrait. It hung over the mahogany credenza in the foyer, taken around the time Brianna was in her first stay at a rehab facility, forced there by a family intervention. Isabella hated the photograph. It represented a lie. She gave the allusion of happiness, her pain hidden behind a fake smile. Her dazzling designer dress and matching jewelry were on loan, out of her price range. Another pretense.

"Wow," Colt said under his breath. He turned to her. "Is that you?"

"Yes. My agent insisted. For publicity."

"Nice." He gave the word more emphasis by stretching it out.

Nothing much changed since the day Brianna moved in. She didn't bother to add her own personal touches. But it was better not to read too much into it, although she suspected Brianna preferred to turn back the clock to the years before their father made her leave.

They ventured farther into the house. Isabella stood in the opening of the door leading into the family room. She visualized Brianna lying on the floor. She hoped in death Brianna looked peaceful. Earlier that day, someone—she couldn't remember who—tried to console her by telling her "Brianna just went to sleep and woke up in heaven."

With fresh tears clouding her vision, Isabella ambled into the kitchen. She opened the refrigerator. It contained Brianna's usual items: fruit, condiments, yogurt cups, the fixings for salads, and a container of leftover roasted chicken and rice from a nearby restaurant. Clumped together on the center shelf were items Brianna didn't usually keep in her fridge: coconut milk, pineapple juice, and cream of coconut.

Isabella sensed Colt standing behind her, also peering in. "What was in the glass they found?" she said over her shoulder. "Do they know what Brianna was drinking that night?"

"What you're seeing, plus drugs and rum. The tech guys took the bottle with them."

Isabella placed her hand on the back of a chair at the kitchen table. On her last visit home, the three sisters sat around the same table where she now stood and feasted on a meal she prepared. That night, they ate, drank, and laughed, losing count of the number of glasses of wine they had.

Colt gave her space, not disrupting her with talk. He shadowed her wherever she went, occasionally glancing at his phone. At the kitchen counter, she said, "Detective Spencer said they found an empty bottle of Ambien near the sink. I guess the police took it." Colt confirmed it with a nod. "Was there a glass on the counter or in the sink?"

"I have no idea."

"The reason I ask is if Brianna killed herself, I would have expected her to take the pills with a glass of water. Then, she would have switched to alcohol. That's what she did before. She took a fistful of pills then washed it down with water. After that, she drank two glasses of wine. I'm surprised she didn't—"

"Surprised she didn't stick with the same game plan?"

"Yes, that's it. She did it differently this time—if she did it at all."

Isabella left the kitchen area and walked down the hall to Brianna's bedroom, once her parents' bedroom. Brianna painted the walls a greyish-blue and placed an assortment of pillows in vibrant colors on the queen-size bed to liven it up. Everything remained in its proper place. She lifted a corner of the bedspread and smiled. "It's obvious Brianna made the bed. Check out the hospital corner on the top sheet. She was a stickler about it. She learned how to do it in one of the rehab clinics."

"Hmm, that would pass a drill sergeant's inspection."

Colt picked up a picture frame from the dresser and studied it. "Who is this guy? And is that you or Brianna?"

"That's me with my ex-boyfriend. I can't believe she framed the picture and has it sitting out. I told you already, she and Landon didn't like each other."

"Actually, what you said was he couldn't stand her. So, the feeling was mutual?"

She turned without answering and started across the hall to the guest bedroom. An eerie feeling took hold of her when she entered. A gush of cold air tickled her arm and caused the hairs on the back of her neck to stand up. With no palpable explanation, she brushed it off and flung back the bedspread.

"Not Brianna's doing, I can tell you that." She examined the wrinkled sheet. "It's too messy. Someone made this bed in a hurry. I'm thinking Whit. But I don't see any of his things, do you?"

"Nope. Looks like he took off."

"After she died."

Colt narrowed his eyes. "C'mon now, you can't know that."

"I know my sister." Isabella raised a brow to make her point. "If he had left while she was alive, she would have immediately stripped the bed and put the sheets in the hamper. She couldn't stand to leave dirty sheets on the bed. She insisted I take them off and put them in the laundry room. If I didn't, she fussed at me." She placed her hands on her hips and stood with her legs apart. "Want to know why? Because when she was on drugs, she lived in filth. Addicts don't do laundry—not often anyway. She sometimes slept on top of bare mattresses, lived in rat-infested apartments or seedy hotels. You've been around it, so you know." She bit down on her lip, blinking away tears. "Nope, this wouldn't do. She'd never tolerate this."

Something caught Isabella's eye. A sock hung out of a drawer, preventing it from closing. Once she slid the drawer open, she found men's socks and underwear inside. "See. He left in a hurry and forgot some of his stuff. I'm thinking I was right. Whit had something to do with her death. In fact, I think he killed her and fled. As simple as that."

Colt hooked his thumbs through his belt loops. She could tell he pondered her theory. "The truth is we don't know what happened."

Isabella frowned.

"Well, we don't, and that's a fact." He shifted his weight from one foot to the other. "Whaddaya say we get out of here? You've seen enough, haven't you?"

Before she could answer, he headed for the door but turned and waited for her. She exhaled loudly and conceded with a nod. Colt swept his hand to the side, letting her go first.

At the car, he held out his hand, palm up. "Gimme your keys, I'll drive."

"I'm fine. I'll drive."

"No, you're upset. You have been ever since we got here."

Isabella shook her head and wrapped her hand around the keys, clutching them to her chest. "I'm okay. We need to work on a plan. Shall we go back to the bar?"

He glanced up at the cloudless sky then back at her. "Tell you what, we'll go to that house where your parents are staying. Your mom said it's in this neighborhood. I'll pop in and say howdy and then have a patrol officer pick me up. No need for you to get caught in rush-hour traffic."

"That works for me. This is my dad's car. He's probably wondering why I've been gone so long. I'm glad you've agreed to help me."

"Wait a minute." Colt put hands on hips. "I went with you looking for Hondo. He wasn't there. I'm done."

What? Isabella felt like bursting into tears or screaming. She made sure he realized her anger, her glare staying on him and not letting up.

7

What was Colt supposed to do? Insert himself into someone else's case and dig a deeper hole than he was already in? No thanks. After he went against orders on the last investigation, his sergeant put him on a short leash. The blowhard DA said he'd mucked up a murder case, but somehow it all worked out. Yes, he screwed up. But they just needed to get over it.

Besides, why should he risk his career for this woman? Sure, she'd lost her sister, and she wanted to find the truth. She should go to Spence and urge him to do his job. Colt had enough on his plate. Besides his role in a task force to takedown a drug operation, there were his personal issues. Like trying to talk his ex-wife into letting him be more involved in their daughter's life. Her end-of-the year grades dropped, and he feared something was going on with her. Maybe bullied at school. He wasn't sure. She was going on thirteen, no longer a child yet far from being an adult. She needed guidance and protection, especially from the boys with pimples and raging hormones. Another situation involved, Ashley Constantine, his former girlfriend. She hoped they'd get back together, but only if he agreed to counseling, and that wasn't going to happen. He'd made it clear; he was a cop with a crazy life, take it or leave it. Some of his stuff was still at her place, and he used work as an excuse for not going over there, but the truth was, he didn't want to face her.

Colt ignored Isabella's anger as he made the rounds at the Bakers' home, extending his words of condolences to the family members, a repeat of what he'd already said at the service. Mrs. Baker gave him a glass of lemonade and a piece of coconut cake. Even though Isabella stood close by, fuming and glaring at him, he wasn't going to let her spoil his pleasure of eating the moist yellow cake with creamy frosting.

"We need to talk." He couldn't miss the anger in her tone. As long as she stayed mad and didn't resort to tears. If she did, he feared he might cave.

He took his time, scraping the miniscule crumbs onto his fork. He licked it off and smacked his lips. "How about we go outside and get some fresh air?"

He followed her out. She sat down in a padded chair with a wrought-iron frame. Pointing to another chair, she practically ordered him to take a seat. He scraped it over and set it where he faced her. Teary-eyed, she crossed her legs. He got a nice view of her bare thigh until she pulled the hem of her dress over her knee.

"Detective Jessup, I had hoped we discovered enough discrepancies that you would be willing to investigate. Detective Spencer made it perfectly clear to my family that he wants to close this case, mark it as a suicide and move on. He's just waiting for the toxicology report to confirm it."

Colt rested his ankle on the opposite knee. He tapped his hands on his calf. "You can bet your sweet a—what I mean is—I will absolutely continue to look for Hondo, and when I find him, I will question him about your sister."

Something about staring into the face of someone dealing with immense emotional pain cut right to his heart and caused a heaviness in his chest. Maybe it was because he'd been there. Four years ago, when his brother was murdered, he desired justice for him, too, to the point, his life stayed on hold until he got it.

He studied the herringbone pattern of the brick pavers, but he felt her eyes on him. Her silence bothered him.

"Okay. I'll go a step farther," he said. "I'll talk to the first responders. The officers that found Brianna. I'll see what they have to say. Make sure they canvassed the area. How's that?"

She swallowed hard and nodded. "I would appreciate it. Anything you can find out."

Before she got too excited about his willingness, he added, "Just keep in mind, I'm working on other stuff. I'm part of a task force, so I'll look into things when I get the chance. Could take a while."

"Whatever you can do."

"In the meantime, I suggest you just take care of yourself and your parents. I'll let you know if I find anything of importance."

She nodded and gave him a weak smile. "I have an obligation in New York, so I'm leaving in a few days. I'll give you my card with my phone number. Call me when you have some information."

They went back inside. He accepted a second piece of cake. While waiting for his ride, he ate the sweet dessert standing by the window. A patrol car pulled into the driveway. Colt and Isabella walked outside. He stood in the opening of the passenger door and said, "I'll be in touch. Take care, Isabella."

He didn't expect a kiss on the cheek, but he liked it. She placed her hand on his arm and said, "Detective Jessup, before you go—I just want you to understand something. I've lost not only my sister, but my best friend. It hurts like hell, but I must put my grief on the back burner. My priority is to find out what happened to her. In fact, it's my mission in life right now."

He nodded. He felt the same way when his brother died.

§

Colt didn't like Detective Spencer. He only tolerated him. Fortunately, their paths seldom crossed. He found Spencer in his cubicle, or what Colt referred to as a padded cell. Colt hated their cramped quarters and did his best work in his car, free of distractions and with a great panoramic view of the outside world. All he needed was his cell phone.

Like his own desk, Spencer's was covered in a disarray of files and paperwork. Colt cleared his throat and said, "Got time to walk outside with me, Spence?"

Detective Spencer looked up. He removed his reading glasses and tossed them onto the report he was working on. When he leaned back, his chair creaked.

"What's up, Jessup?"

"Not too happy to see me, huh? I see your scowl, Spence. Don't hurt my feelings none. Hey, how about taking a break? Let's go outside and get some fresh air."

Colt scanned the perimeter, seeing too many listeners for his comfort. Besides, he didn't want a scene and his gut told him Spencer would go ballistic when he heard Colt took Isabella to the crime scene without his knowledge or consent. But he lived by the philosophy: better to ask forgiveness than permission.

The minute they stepped outside a breeze lifted a section of Colt's longish hair. He pulled his pack of cigarettes from his pocket and frowned. Only one left. He lit it and blew a plume of smoke skyward.

"I appreciated your call about Brianna Connelly," Colt said. "I went to her memorial service. Thought I'd seen a ghost when her sister got up to sing. Spitting image of Brianna. Of course, Brianna looked pretty rough when she was on drugs. Looked a whole lot better a year ago, last time I saw her."

"I thought you'd want to know what happened to her since she was one of your girls."

Colt didn't appreciate the smirk on Spencer's face. He narrowed his eyes and said, "Whaddya mean? One of my girls?"

"You know, one of the young strays you try to help."

"I help the ones worth salvaging. Like Brianna. I see 'em more as victims, not criminals. The drugs made them do things they wouldn't normally do."

Spencer buried his hands in his pockets and scraped the point of one shoe over the rough pavement in a wide arc. "Yeah, like your brother,"

"Hey! You wanna look me in the eye and say that again!"

Spencer stepped back. He threw up his hands, palms out. "I'm not looking for a fight."

Colt didn't let anyone get away with bad-mouthing his deceased half-brother, Wayne Johnson, better known as Streaker. Ten years younger, Colt always idolized him and followed his path, becoming a beat cop and later joining the narcotics and vice division. He'd heard all the talk about how Streaker was a good cop turned bad, caught with a stash of drugs he'd confiscated in a drug bust. His brother's mistakes meant Colt had to endure extra scrutiny. But it only made him work harder, more determined to prove himself.

"My brother is none of your damn business!" Colt got in Spencer's face, towering over him. "Far as I know you never took a bullet for another cop like he did. So, don't let me hear you trashing him ever again."

"Okay, okay. Didn't mean to get you all riled up." Spencer tugged at his shirt collar and loosened the knot in his tie. "So— what did you want to talk to me about?"

"I took Brianna's sister to the crime scene. Just wanted you to know."

Spencer's face turned crimson. Colt imagined smoke coming out of his ears and the top of his head blowing off. "Shit! What the fu—damn you, Colt. What the hell? You don't check with me first?"

"Did you even bother to look the place over? The sister spotted some things I think you guys missed."

"Oh yeah? Like what?"

"Like the fact someone was there. You didn't tell me she had a houseguest."

"Who says she did? No sign of anybody but her. What are you talking about?"

"Her former boyfriend. My CI, that's who. Whit Drummond—street name is Hondo. I've been looking for him since he went MIA. That's why I went to the house, see if he was there."

"Bullshit."

"It's the truth. The sister told me she and Brianna argued about him staying there." Colt dropped his cigarette on the ground and twisted the toe of his boot to grind it out. "Isabella Luca doesn't buy into the suicide theory, and she doesn't think you're listening to her concerns. That's why she came to me."

"That New York fashion-plate doesn't want to accept the truth. Her sister killed herself. No doubt about it. All the evidence is right there."

"Sometimes things are different than what they seem. You've been a cop long enough to know that. You need to question Hondo. Hell, I'll find him for you. Bring him in."

"Colt, take my advice and stay in your lane. Don't mess with my case. Got it?"

"If my guy is in the middle of your case, then you better believe I'm overlapping. Get used to it."

"No point trying to reason with you. You're just like your brother, as hardheaded as solid granite."

"'Member what I said about my brother? Mention him one more time, and I'll knock you to the far side of the moon."

Spencer pressed his lips together. Colt ignored his sour look and put his attention on the pink-tinted clouds. Somewhere behind the tall downtown buildings, the sun had set. A sign he needed to mosey on home and put his feet up and drink a beer. With no buys set up, he'd take the night off, skip the clubs, the come-ons by hookers, and the scuttlebutt with lowlife scum. Maybe he'd catch a game on TV or even better, hit the sack.

Tomorrow would come soon enough with its own pack of troubles.

It was a waste of his time to talk anymore to Spencer. They'd never see eye-to-eye. Colt walked away, hearing Spencer's faint muttering, rubbish about how he didn't want anyone stirring things up, getting in his way, mucking up his case, blah, blah, blah. Colt tuned him out, going back inside with Spencer trailing behind.

8

The cab passed 190th Street, slowed, and came to a stop in front of Isabella's apartment building. The driver set her suitcase on the curb. She handed him cash and he thanked her. Isabella turned the key for the main door of the building and walked through the lobby. She grunted as she dragged her heavy luggage up four steps leading to the corridor and her first-floor apartment. When her door creaked open before she inserted her key, she gasped, her heart pounding. She was sure she'd secured it before she left town. With one kick, the door opened wide. Standing on the threshold, Isabella bit down on her lower lip, afraid to enter. She peered in and shrieked, not believing her eyes. The contents of her desk drawers littered the floor. The sofa cushions thrown against the wall. Her prized books on everything musical, strewn about, knocked off the bookcase.

Trembling, she backed out into the hallway. A sense of helplessness overwhelmed her, leaving her drained and weak-kneed. She supported herself against the wall, her heart pounding. With her hands shaking, she rifled through her purse, searching for her phone. Somehow, she managed to dial 911. With the phone to her ear, she knocked on the adjacent door. Perhaps her neighbor, Teresa Collins, saw something. When no one came, she walked back to her apartment and responded to the dispatcher who said, "What is your emergency?"

She waited at the main entrance, looking out the glass doors for an officer to show up. Her wait did not last long. She opened the door for a policeman with a baby face and very blue eyes. His name-badge read *Brooks*.

Isabella pressed her hand over her chest. "I'm so glad you're here. My apartment was broken into." She led the way to her apartment. "I was afraid to go in, maybe someone is still in there. Who knows? They could be hiding, in the closet maybe. I decided to play it safe and wait for you. That was smart, right? Oh, gosh, I've never had a break-in before. I know people that have, but not me. It's a mess, wait until you see. Oh God, this is so scary. I just got back in town and now *this*. I'm still shaking. Look at my hands! Uh, I'm talking too much, aren't I?"

He walked at her side, his shiny black shoes squeaking on the ceramic tile flooring. While he listened to her go on and on, he scanned their surroundings. He stopped at her door. "Stay here, ma'am."

While he walked around the apartment, she leaned against a wall near the door and waited.

"Well." He returned and hooked his thumbs on his duty belt. "It looks like somebody was looking for valuables." He exhaled a deep breath. "It was probably someone on drugs, needing money and items to pawn. We've had a lot of calls like this recently." He hitched his chin, acknowledging her luggage. "So, you've been on a trip?"

"Yes, flew in from Charlotte. I just got back and found my place trashed. Maybe the person knew I was away."

He nodded. "It's possible. How long were you gone?"

"A week. My sister died. I've been with my family. Some of the people in the building knew I went out of town."

"Sorry about your sister. This building stays locked. Someone must have let the person inside."

"Unfortunately, people do it all the time. Actually, I'm guilty of that."

"Well, I'll check with the super and see if he has anything on video. There's a surveillance camera at the entrance." He pulled a small notebook and pen from his pocket. He clicked the top of his pen. "What were the dates you were gone?"

She told him and he wrote it down.

"I'll key all this in the computer once I get back to my squad car. I'd like you to look around and see what's missing."

Isabella nodded and went first to her bedroom. The intruder left it in as much disarray as the living room. Both trays from her jewelry box rested on the bureau, removed but oddly, not missing any items. Even her treasured double strand of pearls and matching earrings remained.

Her bedspread was balled up and left in the middle of the bed. Dresser drawers were pulled out with articles of clothing spilling out. In the kitchen, she found more chaos with drawers and cabinets left open. Whoever was here was in a hurry, indifferent to the mess created.

Items easy to pawn were left behind. She rejoined Officer Brooks in the living room where he was examining the lock on the door.

He pointed to a fresh groove in the wood where the paint was scratched off. "The intruder used a special tool. Takes seconds to get inside. Did you find anything missing?"

She shook her head. "Not that I'm aware of. I don't get it. They didn't take *anything*. I don't have many valuables but still…Fortunately, I had my laptop with me." She fingered her diamond stud earrings, relieved she wore them on her trip.

Brooks scratched his cheek. "Since nothing seems to be taken, it looks like they were searching for something specific. Cash maybe. Coins. Gun. Anything like that?"

"No, no money hidden away and no weapons." She regarded the mess left behind by the intruder and felt more sadness than anger. She'd always liked returning home to a tidy place, not this.

"Have you had a disagreement with anyone lately?"

"No, I don't think so."

"Well, this could be random." Brooks closed his small notepad. "An addict looking for cash, but usually they take whatever they can find and sell it at a pawn shop. Hopefully, we have surveillance with a good sighting of the person responsible. Wish we could pinpoint the time, but you were gone for a while, so…Usually a person hits several places around the same time. If they did, we might get a lead from that."

Isabella frowned. "Is anyone safe anymore?"

The officer shook his head. "It's pretty crazy out there. I'll file this report." He took a card from his wallet, wrote something on the back, and handed it to her. "Here's my card with the case number on the back. If you think of anything we missed, please call. And you might consider getting a new lock. And in the future, use the deadbolt."

"I would if it worked. It gets hung up. The super is supposed to fix it, but who knows how long that will take."

"Well, just be careful, ma'am."

Isabella walked him out and returned to her apartment. Leaning her back against the door, she pushed it shut and slid down, landing on her butt. With her knees drawn up to her chest, she pressed her forehead against them and squeezed her eyes shut. The realization that someone invaded her privacy and rummaged through her belongings sickened her.

She needed to get out of her apartment as quickly as possible. She opened her fridge and stared at empty shelves. It was the same with the cabinet where she stored canned items and boxes of cereal and rice. "Looks like I have a good excuse to get out."

Frank's Market was only a block away. She changed into more comfortable attire and headed out. But before she left her apartment, she dropped a tube of pepper spray in her straw shopping bag and slung it over her shoulder. She locked her door, double checking to make sure it was secure. Walking toward 190th Street, she had to jump out of the way of an adolescent boy on a skateboard, going too fast as the terrain sloped downhill. "Hey, watch yourself!" she yelled, her heart pounding. She took a deep breath, trying to calm her nerves.

Her Manhattan neighborhood attributed its Fort Washington name to the presence of General Washington and his troops during the Revolutionary War. It bordered the Hudson River with a view of the George Washington Bridge. The area had the feel of an established community within the Big Apple. Meeting people in her neighborhood was easier than in the suburbs of Charlotte. People were pedestrians instead of closed off in a car, waving but not speaking. Whenever Isabella stopped to pet a dog on a leash or peek in a stroller at a baby, friendships developed. She'd see them again, usually around the same time, as people fell into a daily routine.

On her way to Frank's Market, people she knew stopped to offer condolences and give her a hug. Many of them remembered Brianna from an extended stay over two years ago. Brianna planned to move in permanently with Isabella, but she could not find work and eventually returned to Charlotte. It turned out to be a good decision since she landed the job with New Beginnings. Isabella was thankful Marcus Gilliam appreciated her potential and gave her an opportunity.

At the store, Isabella filled her small cart with produce. She handled a bundle of broccoli, examining it closely to make sure it was fresh. A head of romaine lettuce received the same scrutiny. She moved slowly along the refrigerated counter, not paying attention to the movement of her cart. It bumped against another. She glanced up to see her next-door neighbor, Teresa. She was dressed in yoga pants, an oversized T-shirt, and sneakers. Her unruly thick hair was contained in a ponytail. She wrapped

Isabella in a tight hug. Letting go, she wiped a smudge of mascara from her teary eye.

"I am so very sorry, Isabella." She dabbed her nose with a tissue. "Brianna was an amazing person. Beautiful like you. Well, of course, like you. You're twins—*duh*. Sorry I couldn't fly down for the service. So hard to believe she's gone. Horrible, just horrible. Anytime you need company, I'm right next door. Just come over any time, day or night. Or if you just need a shoulder to cry on, I'm there for you, girl."

"Thanks, Teresa. I appreciate it. I'm glad I ran into you. I was going to call you." She sighed, shaking her head. "Would you believe my place was broken into, left in a mess. Did you see anyone or hear anything while I was away?"

"Oh, God, that's terrible!" Teresa's eyes widened. "Here you are grieving, and this happens! No, no, I didn't see anything. Of course, I'm gone most of the day, so maybe I wasn't home when it happened." She gasped and placed her hand on Isabella's arm. "Wait! Oh, yeah, there was someone. A man knocked on your door. Nice looking. I was on my way out and he asked if I knew where you were. Shit! I feel terrible now. I told him you were out of town. Didn't say anything else though. Didn't tell him about your sister. I wonder if that's who broke in."

"When was this? Can you give me a description?"

"Gosh, let me see." Teresa tapped her finger on her lips. "It must have been Wednesday. Yeah, Wednesday—early evening. Maybe around seven. I was leaving to meet some friends for dinner in Midtown."

Isabella gripped the shopping cart tighter, her knuckles turning white. "What did he look like? Tell me anything you can remember about him."

"Well, he was about our age. Late twenties, early thirties. Handsome. Like some guy you see on the cover of *GQ*. *That* good looking." She smiled. "Light brown hair, good haircut. Not too long, but not short either. He was tall—good body, like he works out in the gym. Polite. Nice smile. I thought he was harmless, a real gentleman. I actually thought—well, never mind." She waved her hand down in dismissal.

"You thought what?"

Teresa gave a sheepish smile. "I thought he might be a new love interest and you forgot to tell me."

"No, no new guy. I don't have any idea who he is. I'll pass the information on to the police. This could be our guy. What was he wearing?"

"Gosh, I can't remember. Dressed casually. Maybe jeans."

After Teresa left, Isabella pushed her cart down the narrow aisles, her mind no longer on shopping. *A mysterious visitor, huh? Interesting.*

Teresa's description of the man matched Isabella's former boyfriend. But Landon now lived thousands of miles away in Seattle. She'd had no contact with him since their breakup four years ago. It had to be someone else. But the who and why puzzled her. Until she knew the answer, she'd watch her back, be aware of her surroundings, instead of walking in oblivion along the sidewalks with a cell phone to her ear. Her parents worried about her living alone in New York. She assured them it was safe, but now she wasn't sure she could make that argument.

§

Holding his cue stick vertically and resting his chin on his fist, Colt waited for Rake to make his move. He called the corner pocket, an impossible shot for two locked balls unless Rake hit the precise spot with the right amount of force to make the five-ball curve. But the part-time pool hustler and full-time drug dealer could work magic. The ball went in, which made Colt glad he only had ten bucks riding on the game. Ten bucks he was sure to lose. He knew it even before he took the bet.

Now that it was his turn, Colt visually lined up his shot, then took his stance. Not impossible but tricky to pull off, he hit the cue ball too high. The targeted ball bounced off the side wall and stopped short of the pocket.

"Looks like you're gonna take my money, bro. One more play and I'm done." Colt brushed his thumb over his nose. "Some time I want you to show me how you do that thing you do. I'll be damned if I can get the hang of it."

"I already showed you, dude. You're a slow learner."

"Dope has fried my brain." Colt chuckled. "Hey, by the way, you haven't seen Hondo lately, have ya? I'm looking for his ass. He's got a 9-mil Sig I wanna buy. Know where I can find him?"

"Look under a rock. There he be."

Colt stepped back, allowing Rake's hefty frame plenty of space to line up his next move. His beer belly pressed against the edge of the table. Rake snorted and swiped the tip of his nose with his knuckle before he tapped the ball solidly dead center. And just like that, the remaining two balls bumped and rolled into pockets. Muttering obscenities under his breath, Colt pulled his wallet from his back pocket and slapped a ten-dollar bill on the table.

"You're killing me, man." Colt returned his cue stick to the rack and reached for his bottle of beer. With his hand gripping the neck, he took a swig. He leaned his back against the wall, one leg bent at the knee with his foot flush against a concrete block. "I'm serious about Hondo. I need to see 'im."

"Can't help you, dude. He's gone underground. Big Jack thinks he stole his drugs. I wasn't there, so I dunno." For no apparent reason, Rake peered out the front window, then back at Colt, blinking repeatedly, then snorting like he had allergies. "But I do know one thing, you don't mess with Big Jack. You cross him and you're as good as dead."

Colt gave a nod. "Do me a favor—you see Hondo, tell him to give me a call. Hell, I'll protect him from the big bad man." Colt winked and guzzled more beer. He wiped his mouth with the back of his hand.

"Yeah, sure you will." Rake cackled, showing uneven, stained teeth.

"I gotta go. Got a deal cooking. Big money if it works out." Colt threw back the bottle for his last sip. He set the empty on the ledge and faced Rake. "I'm serious, man. If you run into Hondo, tell him I really want that gun."

"I gotta think he needs it more than you do," Rake said, grinning.

Colt walked out, hearing the crunch of gravel under his feet. He got in his black Dodge Charger that had seen better days. The transmission was almost shot and it leaked oil. Sitting behind the wheel, he got out his pack of Marlboros, wishing he could find a way to quit, but knowing smoking was the one thing that calmed his nerves. Anytime he tried to stop, he'd get jittery and cranky, snapping at anyone for any reason. Even yelling at his daughter, Maddie, who complained to her mother the minute he dropped her home. He couldn't afford to have his ex on his case, so he went right back to smoking. Peaceful and calm. The king of cool.

As he inhaled, getting his nicotine fix, Colt came to one conclusion about Rake. As well as being a major player in the world of opioids, Rake was a big-time lying son-of-a-bitch. And not even a good one. While the shit spewed from his mouth, Colt studied his body language. Rake blinked, he snorted, he turned away, he scratched his chin. He might as well have had a neon sign on his forehead saying *liar*.

9

Colt was unaware his phone rang until he experienced a poke in the back. He rubbed sleep from his eyes and peeked at the clock on the bedside table. Damn, seven o'clock. Who was the idiot calling so early?

"Yeah?" He sat on the edge of the bed, his feet touching the cool floor.

"Detective Jessup? It's me. Isabella Luca. I'm sorry to bother you this early, but I just thought of something important."

"Oh, yeah? What?" The mattress dipped slightly. A hand with long polished nails snaked around his waist. Lips kissed his bare back. He was tempted to stand up and walk away. How could he possibly concentrate on the call?

"I didn't ask or check to see if Brianna's laptop was missing from her house," Isabella said. "Or her tote bag that she carried it in. She kept both in the den. If it's there, the computer should be on the table beside the sofa. You'll see a charger cable plugged in. And she always kept her tote bag underneath the table. If it wasn't there, I think Whit, or whoever killed her, took it."

"Whoa, whoa. We don't know that someone killed her. Yeah, you're right. Some things look suspicious, but it's way too early to draw that conclusion."

"Detective, what is this? I thought you were on my side."

He cringed at the rise in her voice. "I'm not on anybody's damn side. I'm interested in evidence."

"Okay, well then if the computer and bag are missing, that's evidence, right?"

One kiss after another landed on Colt's back. He turned his head to the side and warned the blonde with a frown. It did no good. She gave him a sexy smile.

"Detective Jessup, are you there?"

"Yeah, I heard you. I'll look into it. I don't remember seeing the computer, so you make a valid point. I'll check with Detective Spencer or Anders—or better yet, you can call them yourself."

"No, I prefer you do it. Spencer looked at me like I'm a hysterical female. Maybe he has a problem with women, I'm not sure, but it might be better if you handled it."

If she only knew. He'd rather have a root canal than deal with that schmuck.

"The reason I thought about it was my place was broken into while I was in Charlotte. It was ransacked like they were looking for something. Thank goodness I had my computer with me, or it might have been taken."

"Any idea who could have done it?"

"No, not a clue. The police are checking it out, but I doubt we'll ever know. We have a lot of break-ins around here."

"Be careful. There's a lot of bad stuff out there."

"Don't worry, I'm watching my back. Let me know if you find out anything."

He ended the call and stretched out across his side of the bed, resting against the padded headboard. Ashley slid over to rest her head on his bare chest, giving him light kisses, one after the other, getting him worked up. She planted one on his pectoral muscle just above his nipple, causing it to harden. He felt a stirring further south.

They were supposed to be breaking up. Last night, he came to her place to collect the stuff he left behind. None of it really mattered, except his leather jacket, a splurge item he'd bought on a whim. She could keep his Yankees ballcap. Their season sucked anyway. And he had no need for the T-shirt from a local bar. Faded and tattered, it had seen better days.

He rubbed her bare ass and fondled her breast. It surprised him when she pushed his arm away and sat up. "I can't, Colt. I have to get dressed."

"Hey, baby, I thought you were in the mood."

She ran her hand through her disheveled hair. "No, I was just being romantic. Thinking about last night." She gave him a playful smile.

"About last night—"

"Oh no you don't." She narrowed her eyes. "Colt Jessup, don't you dare tell me last night was a mistake. We still have feelings for each other and if we went for counseling, I know we can work out our differences."

"Uh-huh. You'll never accept my job. You bitch about it all the damn time. That's who I am, Ashley. A damn cop. A slimy, messed-up undercover cop. That's not ever gonna change, baby."

"Fine! I see my feelings—what I want—don't matter to you. They never have."

"Hey, don't be mad."

He reached over to stroke her arm, but she slid away, out of his grasp. She swung her legs off the bed and stood up. As she bent over to retrieve her T-shirt, her hair fell forward, covering her face. He couldn't see it, but he sensed her scowl.

She slipped leopard-print bikini panties over her hips and glowered at him. "Get out of my bed. In fact, get out of my house. We're never going to work this out. My friend is right. She said it's better to be alone than with the wrong person. We don't have that much in common anyway."

Except the sex. "Guess you're right, Ash." Colt got up and reached for his boxers and jeans. "Darlin', I hope you find what you're looking for. Someone with a boring job you can accept. Honey, that's not me. I like what I do. Call me crazy, but I like the risk."

"Fine! Get out!"

Her anger made him move faster. He didn't need this shit. He picked up his shoes and dangled them off his fingers. "Hope your day gets better, Ash."

"Aren't you forgetting something?"

"What's that?"

She pointed to a cardboard box resting in a far corner. "Your stuff. That's why you came over, remember?"

It occurred to him that if she'd placed the box next to the front door, it could have been a quick in and out like UPS picking up a package. Instead, she lured him into her bedroom to retrieve it. She wanted him to make love to her and stay the night. But if she thought a little romp in the sack was all it took to make him give up working as an undercover cop, she was sadly mistaken. A bullet might do it, but not the wiles of a sexy woman.

§

How long had Brianna suffered in silence? She carried a mountain of guilt and all the narcotics she consumed over time could not take it away. In Fort Tryon Park, two blocks from her New York apartment, Isabella sat on the same bench where Brianna proclaimed her personal hell in just three words: "I killed him."

Brianna said it matter-of-factly, devoid of emotion. If said for shock value, she never looked at Isabella for her reaction. Instead, she kept her gaze straight ahead and focused on a barge moving slowly down the Hudson River.

It took a moment for Isabella to find her voice. "Who? What are you talking about?"

"Trevor. I killed him. My fault he died."

"That's crazy! Don't say that, Bree. How could you even think that? He was the one behind the wheel—going way too fast. He lost control. No way it was your fault. In fact, you're lucky you didn't die too. It messed up your foot, but it could have been so much worse."

Brianna frowned. "Don't you see? He took the curve too fast because of *me*. I was yelling at him. I distracted him—made him so upset he sped up."

"Stop it, Bree! Don't do this."

Tears rolled down Brianna's cheeks, but she didn't bother to wipe them away. "It should have been me. Look how I ended up—a drug addict. No use to anyone. I can't even dance anymore. Practically a cripple."

Isabella turned sideways and placed her hands on the sides of Brianna's cheeks, forcing her to look into her eyes. "Listen to me. You got well. You've been off drugs for over a year now. You've come a long way. You should be proud of yourself. *I'm* proud of you."

Isabella's memories were interrupted when Kiki showed up.

"There you are." When she almost lost her balance, Kiki reached out for the back of the bench. "Damn shoes."

Isabella frowned at Kiki's wedged sandals. "You're going to twist your ankle in those things. When I said we were going to walk in the park, you should have known to wear sneakers, or at least flats."

Kiki made a face. "But these shoes match my outfit. Besides, I forgot how hilly this place is."

"The highest point on Manhattan. That's why George Washington chose it for a lookout for advancing British troops."

"Oh yeah? Well, he didn't have killer shoes, or he'd never have come here. When I was in the cab driving in, I saw all these poor moms pushing strollers uphill. Oh—my—God, what a workout! Harder than a Zumba class." Kiki sat down and removed her shoes. "There, that's better."

"What did you want to talk to me about?"

"Let's walk," Kiki said, gesturing for Isabella to stand. They walked side by side. Kiki left her shoes off and swung them by the straps in one hand. A gentle breeze blew her hair onto her cheek. She raked it back with her fingers and locked eyes with Isabella. "I'm a New Yorker, born and bred, and you know how direct we can be. I'm just going to come right out and say it."

"What? For goodness sakes, Kiki, tell me."

"You don't seem to be grieving for Brianna." Kiki looked out at the Hudson River, letting her gaze track the movement of a small boat. She ignored Isabella's scowl. "I thought I'd find you in tears, but you seem fine. The same stunning, vibrant Isabella Luca we all know and love. Not affected by the tragedy one bit. But I know better. You're holding it in and that's not healthy, my dear."

Isabella bowed her head, shaking it. "I cry myself to sleep every night. I *wake up* crying. During the day, I just function because I have no choice. The workshop I'm doing with the kids has helped. Staying busy keeps me from thinking about my loss. To be honest, I'm concentrating on finding out what happened. I'm now convinced more than ever that Brianna didn't kill herself. I think that scumbag Whit is responsible for her death."

Kiki swatted a bug out of her face. "But you told me the police think she committed suicide."

"Yeah, that's what they say. I have a detective looking into it. Not sure where he stands, but at least he's giving my theory the benefit of a doubt."

Walking along a paved path, they moved to the side to give a man on roller blades plenty of room.

"Do you trust him?"

"I guess." Isabella shrugged. "He's a little rough around the edges, but my gut tells me he's a good guy. Brianna liked him. He helped her get into rehab." Isabella pointed to a butterfly, watching it land on a bush. "Isn't it pretty? Since Brianna died, I see butterflies everywhere. Maybe I didn't notice them before, but I do now. It's weird but I think they're somehow connected to

Brianna. Like she's sending me a message, saying she's fine and I shouldn't grieve. I just miss her more than I can bear."

"I know you do, but she'd want you to be happy. It would kill her to know you're sad." Kiki squeezed her eyes shut and slapped her forehead with the palm of her hand. "Oh God, did I just say that? Sorry, Isabella, my mouth—well, you know."

Isabella laughed and patted her arm. "Don't worry about it. I think it's kinda funny in a twisted way. Besides, you've said crazier things than that."

Kiki rolled her eyes. "Yes, plenty of times."

10

Where had the time gone? In the driver's seat, Colt took his attention off the road for a quick glance at Maddie. Although her round face was a holdover from childhood, her body proceeded into impending adulthood. She had curves and breasts now. When did that happen? He sneaked a sidelong glance at her and frowned, feeling sad his little girl was growing up fast. *Too* fast. In three more years, she'd have a driver's license. That scared the hell out of him.

Being with her for a rare outing had been fun. He took her to the movie theatre near the mall, the one with the cushy, wide seats and cupholders. After the movie, they drove to a nearby restaurant where Maddie ordered one of the specialty burgers with extra toppings that required lots of finger-licking and a stack of napkins. She wiped ketchup from the corner of her mouth and said, "Dad, you don't know what you're missing. These burgers are ridiculous—so yummy."

"Well, my turkey melt was good too and not as messy."

"Mom told me why you don't eat beef."

Colt raised his brow and leaned forward. "Oh yeah?"

Maddie spread her fingers wide and wiped away ketchup. "She told me about Toby. About when you were a little boy and—"

"Hey, forget what your mom said. She doesn't know." He could kick himself for the time he had too many shots of whiskey and became loose-lipped, betraying a childhood secret. If the guys at the station knew the story, he'd be the laughingstock of the whole department. Colt picked up a French fry and held it in

65

mid-air, pointing it at Maddie. "Look, sweetie, your Mom doesn't have all the facts, so don't repeat that story to anyone, you hear?"

With a grin spreading across her lips, Maddie said, "I won't tell. My lips are sealed."

"They better be." He dipped another fry in ketchup and brought it to his lips. He needed a diversion, another topic for discussion. "So how did you like *The Avengers*?"

"It had a lot of action, that's what I like." Maddie's eyes lit up as she talked about specific scenes in the movie.

But they soon ran out of things to say and fell into a quiet void where Colt could think of nothing else to talk about. He certainly couldn't discuss his job with his daughter, and when he asked her how she was enjoying her summer break from school, she gave him a shrug and a one-word answer: "Fine."

Taking her home to her mother, Colt waited at a stoplight and tapped his fingers on the steering wheel. "C'mon, light. What's takin' ya so long?"

The cop in him had him subconsciously scanning his surroundings. Momentarily, he put his focus on a black Subaru to his left. The passenger in the back seat propped his arm in the window-opening with his hand gripping the top of the doorframe. Something about the tattoo on his forearm piqued Colt's interest. Where had he seen the spider design? Then it hit him. Hondo, of course. Same ink. Dirty-blond hair tied back in a stringy ponytail. Colt eased up on the brake and the car rolled forward, enough for him to make a positive ID.

"I'll be damned. That son-of-a-bitch!" Colt slapped the side of his leg and hit the accelerator when the light changed.

"What, Dad? You know that guy?"

"Yeah."

Hondo, with glassy eyes and a dazed look, had to be strung out on drugs. In no condition to spot Colt, he hoped. Colt hung back until he could switch lanes, putting a car between him and the vehicle Hondo rode in.

Colt tapped Maddie's arm. "Honey, that's someone I've been looking for. We're going to follow him a while and see where he goes. Might be a little late getting you home. It's that okay?"

Maddie's blue eyes widened. She smiled big and sat up straighter. "Sure! Let's nail his ass! What is he? A drug dealer?"

"Something like that. We'll just take a little detour. I just wanna see where he ends up."

The SUV in front of them made a left turn, which put them right behind the Subaru. At the next stoplight, Hondo peered through the rear window. Colt figured the glare of the sun on his windshield made it impossible for Hondo to see him, but he was wrong. Hondo stuck his arm out the window and extended his middle finger.

"Dad! He's flipping you off!" Maddie laughed.

"Shit! He made me."

Once the light turned green, the Subaru accelerated fast with tires screaming.

Colt patted Maddie's knee. "Hang on, honey. Tighten your seat belt."

The chase was on, going fifty, then sixty, weaving in and out of traffic. The Subaru switched lanes, cutting in front of a UPS delivery van, inches from its front bumper. When Colt found an opening, he got over too. But Colt registered surprise when Hondo's vehicle veered far over into the narrow, paved area on the side of the road, inches from a ditch.

"Damn fool!" Colt shouted.

The broken, uneven pavement bounced the Subaru wildly and became too much to handle. The driver cut back over first chance he got. After crossing an intersection, traffic thinned, giving them an opportunity to speed up. Colt stayed on the

Subaru's bumper, refusing to back off. But without warning, Hondo's car turned off the main road. The unexpected move forced Colt to make a lane switch, barely squeezing between two SUVs, allowing him to make the turn.

"Hang on, Maddie," he said, tires squealing as he jerked the wheel hard to the right, barely slowing down.

A little scream came from her. With both hands, she gripped the seat, bracing herself. Her eyes grew wide.

"Shit! What the hell am I doing?" *Not worth it. Endangering the life of my daughter. Screw it.* Colt eased off the accelerator and got in the turning lane. "I'm taking you home, Baby Girl."

"*Da-a-a-d!* Don't call me that. I told you—"

"Right, right. Okay, Madison Amelia, I'm taking you back." He picked up his phone in the console holder and handed it to her. "Look up Samantha Delano in my contacts and call her."

She nodded and searched for the name, giving it back to her father when it rang. He held it up to his ear and said, "Hey, Sam. Guess what? I found Hondo. He didn't leave town like we thought. I spotted him as a passenger in a late model, black Subaru with tinted windows." He gave her the license number, hoping he remembered it correctly. "Put out a BOLO and we'll bring him in."

"What for? He hasn't done anything but skip out on us. We don't have a warrant for him anymore. Remember? We cut him loose."

Colt exhaled and ran his fingers through his hair. "He might be involved in a murder. We won't know unless we bring him in."

"Whose murder?"

"Brianna Connelly." When the light changed, Colt tapped his horn, urging the car in front to go.

"You told me they think it's suicide," Samantha said. "Have you got new information?"

"No, just a hunch."

"This isn't our case, Colt. Leave it alone. Do you want to piss off Spence and Lord knows who else?"

"He's somehow involved, Sam. The sister thinks so."

"What did she do? Give you a sexy smile and you went for it?"

"No, that's not it, damn it!" He yelled before he remembered his daughter's presence. Calmer, he said, "There were signs he was there in the house about the time she died. Give me a little credit, will ya?"

Samantha raised her voice, dishing it right back at him. "You went to the crime scene on your own, didn't you? Damn it, Colt. Won't you ever learn?"

"Don't start with me." Colt glanced over at Maddie, embarrassed she could hear everything. "Okay, I'll give it a rest. We'll figure it out later. Happy now?"

"Colt, you know we have enough on our plate as it is. Tomorrow you're supposed to track down that big-time drug dealer from Detroit. If we get something on him, it'll be a big deal."

"Yeah, okay. See you tomorrow."

When he ended the call, Colt gently tapped Maddie's arm with the back of his hand. "Hey, honey, do me a favor. Don't tell your mom anything about this."

"Sure, Dad. Whatever you say."

Her mischievous smile made him nervous.

§

Colt's ex-wife, Kate, sat on the front step of the porch leading to the modest home she shared with Maddie. She had changed out of her nurse's uniform into shorts and a tank top. As always, she was looking fine. One of the reasons he regretted their breakup. She'd grown her chestnut hair longer, one section of it resting on her shoulder. When he picked up Maddie, she smiled sweetly, but not now. She eyed him like he was something she needed to scrape off the bottom of her sandal.

"You're late." Kate gave him the look, the one telling him he was in trouble. Even with her eyes narrowed and her chin tilted up, she transcended sexiness.

"We got sidetracked." Maddie giggled.

Colt resisted the urge to cover her mouth to keep her quiet.

Kate shifted her attention from Maddie to Colt. "What does that mean?"

Colt dropped car keys in the palm of her hand. "Thanks for the use of your car."

"Sure. I didn't want our daughter riding in that rattletrap that reeks of cigarettes." She looked past Colt at the Charger parked along the curb in the last patch of shade from a maple tree. She turned to her daughter. "So, Maddie, tell me more about how you and Dad got sidetracked."

Maddie's face lit up. "It was so cool. Dad saw someone he's been looking for. We took off after him. Don't worry, he was careful—well, sort of—anyway, it was *so-o-o* exciting, so rad!"

Kate pursed her lips and glared at Colt. "Sweetie—let me talk to your father alone. Go inside please." When Maddie didn't move, Kate added, "Young lady, do as I say. Inside—now!"

"Parents! Ugh! I can't wait until I'm old enough no one can tell me what to do." Maddie exhaled loudly and flipped her long hair over her shoulders. "Okay, I'm going!" She gave Colt a hug. "Bye, Dad. Thanks for the movie and lunch. It was fun."

"Bye, sweetheart. See you soon."

Once she was gone, he put his hands on his hips and shifted his weight from one foot to the other. Kate's scowl was not a good sign.

"How dare you risk our daughter's life like that. That's why we split up, Colt. You're a loose cannon. I have half a mind to call my lawyer and ask for full custody. Take away visitation rights. I mean it, don't think I won't do it."

He felt his chest tighten. "I know you would. I screwed up, Kate. It'll never happen again. Promise."

"Yeah, right." She rolled her eyes.

"I'm telling you there won't be a next time."

"Colten Jessup, you've broken so many promises to me, I don't believe anything you say anymore."

"Depriving me of my daughter would be the worst thing you could do to me, Kate."

Her silence meant she wouldn't go through with her threat. With a little time, she'd forget all about the scary little car chase, and they'd be back to being civil to one another.

"Better go." Colt headed toward his car but stopped and did a 180. "By the way, I filled up your gas tank. It was near empty."

She muttered a thank you and he was on his way.

He hated being a father on a part-time basis, having to check with his ex whenever he wanted to see his daughter. Being a cop with bad shit happening all the time—not when it was convenient for him—meant he never knew when he'd have another chance to see Maddie. He'd disappointed her plenty of times when a call came in and he had to take off and cancel their plans.

His unpredictability was one of the reasons his marriage failed. He never got over losing Kate. His love for her had a long shelf-life, maybe lasting until his last breath. For a short time, he tried to fool himself into believing he loved Ashley. Then it occurred to him, he only lusted for her. But Kate was different. He missed the little things about her. Her laughter. Her sweet smile. Her words of wisdom. The way she curled up beside him in bed. One day, he might love again, but for now, Kate occupied most of his heart.

He was glad she didn't have a man in her life. He hated the idea of some random dude playing dad to his daughter, maybe doing cooler things than he did. He was no angel, but he was alright as far as fathers went. At least, he thought so.

Still parked in front of the house, he sat behind the steering wheel and reached for a pack of smokes on the console. He glanced back at the porch, only to discover Kate no longer there. "Women. So complicated," he said to no one. There were too many women in his life, trying to whip him into shape or toy with his emotions. His former wife. His ex-girlfriend. His partner. The only one putting a smile on his face was Maddie, and even she could be a drama queen, bursting into tears if he said the wrong thing.

He exhaled a puff of smoke and made a U-turn, heading back to his crappy apartment on a sketchy side of town, off limits to people he cared about.

11

Colt rested his backside against his car and waited for Detective Spencer and Officers Pettit and Dalton to meet him at Brianna Connelly's residence. Since Spencer gave him hell about going to the crime scene on his own, he made a courtesy call to the detective. It translated to mean, *I'm going there whether you come with me or not.*

Pettit and Dalton showed up first, parking their police cruisers behind his Dodge Charger. When they walked up, they exchanged greetings, both officers responding with cordial smiles.

"Thanks for coming," Colt said. "Since you guys were the first responders and called it in, I wanted to run a couple of things by you."

Pettit took his attention from Dalton to Colt. "Have you been assigned to this case?"

"Nah, not really, but I believe my CI was there and I'm trying to find him."

"There was no one inside but the deceased."

"Yeah, I know that, but I think he was there prior to her death. Just wondering who canvassed the area. Spence said your division went door to door."

Beth Dalton crossed her arms and widened her stance. "That's right. While Mark secured the crime scene, me and two others from our division canvassed the neighborhood. We also took a statement from the lady who made the call. Can't remember her last name right now. Lauren something. I'll have to look at my notes."

"So, did anyone see anything?" Colt said. "Anyone around who didn't belong?"

"No, I questioned everyone in the general vicinity of the house, and no one saw anything unusual." She placed her hand on her hip. "Didn't the coroner rule this as a suicide? That's what we were told."

"Not yet. Still waiting on the toxicology report." Colt followed Dalton's gaze to the house across the street. "What about over there? They have a clear shot at the house and driveway. They didn't see anyone going inside or out? Maybe a car in the driveway?"

"No, I spoke with the lady," Dalton said. "Neither she nor her husband saw anything."

"Was she in a wheelchair?"

Dalton gave him a puzzled look. "No. Why do you ask?"

"What about her husband?"

She raised her chin and narrowed her eyes. "I have no idea."

"You don't see the handicap ramp over there?"

"I-I guess I missed it. I got the impression it was just the woman and her husband. Maybe her husband uses a wheelchair. I don't know. None of my business."

"You should have asked, Dalton. Covered your bases." Colt's gaze shifted from Dalton to Pettit. "And another thing, there's a park nearby and a bus stop. Did you question anyone who might have been around those areas?"

Pettit let out a little laugh and responded to Colt's glower with an apologetic shrug. "Sorry, it's just that no one goes to that much trouble for a suicide."

The arrival of Spencer saved Colt from saying something he'd regret later. He relaxed his tense jaw and watched the aging detective lumber over, his out-of-shape body causing his breaths to come hard. Spencer hitched his chin at Colt. "Jessup, what's up?"

"I want to know if you found a laptop. The sister said it should be there."

Spencer poked his fat bottom lip out and shook his head. "There wasn't a computer there that I know of. We can check with the techs and see if they have it, but I don't remember it being on the list of items taken." He took a deep breath and smoothed his tie over his pot belly. "You think there was a theft? If so, they would have pawned it first thing."

"I told you my CI was here. He may have taken it."

"Here we go again." Spencer smirked and turned to the officers. "You two see anyone inside or around the house? Find any evidence of a person being there?"

"No sir," Dalton said.

"See, Colt. Told ya," Spencer crossed his arms. "Leave it alone. Hell, tell Miss New York anything you wanna tell her to get her off our backs. I've got enough to deal with."

"Something doesn't sit right with me, Spence. We're missing something."

"We'll wait for the tox report. When you see she swallowed a fistful of Ambien and drank liquor then you can have peace. We can *all* have peace. That should satisfy Miss Fancy Pants."

"Her name is Isabella Luca. Show her some respect. Hell, she lost her sister. She has every right to question our investigation."

"She doesn't have a right to impede it. She could be trouble for all of us. All we need is for her to call the DA and stir things up. Like I said, I don't have time for this." Spencer put his hands on his hips and put his focus on the two officers. "Now can we let these officers get back to their patrols. Their captain is not going to be happy if we keep them tied up on this wild goose chase of yours."

Colt waved in dismissal at Pettit and Dalton. "Sure. You can go now. Thanks for meeting me." He locked eyes with Spencer. "Let's go inside and make sure about the computer. Maybe someone missed it. Could be under the sofa or somewhere out of sight."

Spencer exhaled loudly. "Why not? You've screwed up my day already. What's another ten minutes?"

The creaking sound of the door as it opened and the silence within put Colt on edge. Every time he visited the home where a body had been found an eerie feeling plagued him. He followed Spencer into the family room where he spotted the table and the wall outlet Isabella mentioned in her phone call. No computer or cable were there. With some pushback from Spencer, they made a thorough search of the house, but their efforts produced nothing. Both men walked out together.

Colt pretended to not see Spencer's scowl which he interpreted to mean, *I told you so*. With the back of his hand, he tapped Spencer's arm. "Well, it's been fun. We'll have to do this again sometime."

"You're pushing your luck, Jessup. You don't want to piss me off. I've got seniority over you."

What else he said, Colt didn't know. He'd tuned him out and focused on someone visible at a window across the street. The low position of the head, just above the windowsill, intrigued him.

Ending his rant, Spencer said, "I can make your life a living hell if I want to."

"Better get in line." Colt walked away.

He put on the pretense of driving out of the neighborhood, but as soon as Spencer's car was out of sight, he circled the block and parked curbside in front of Brianna's residence. Across the street, he spotted the person, a woman, still near the window. As soon as he walked up the driveway, she swiveled around in what had to be a wheelchair. The back of her head showed snow white hair pinned up in a bun.

Colt rang the doorbell and was greeted by a sixtyish woman with a thin face and hard eyes. She gave off a vibe like she was resistant to pleasantries and fun times. Her head moved slightly up and down while she checked him out. He imagined he didn't make a good first impression in his ragged jeans and black, Gothic-themed T-shirt. Just in case she considered slamming the door in his face, he held up his police ID.

"Good afternoon, ma'am. I'm investigating the death of Brianna Connelly who lived across the street. I was wondering if you saw anyone near the house or maybe a vehicle parked in the area on the night she died."

"I've already been questioned, and I told the officer we didn't see anything."

"When you say *we*, who else are you including?"

"My husband."

"What about the lady in the wheelchair? I just saw her at the window."

She turned her head to one side, looking back into the interior of the house. "Oh, that's my mother-in-law. She didn't see anything either."

"Did anyone ask her?"

"She sleeps most of the time. And when she's awake, she's not fully aware of her surroundings. Someone could break in and she wouldn't know it."

"May I speak with her please?"

"I told you she didn't see anything. It would be a waste of time."

"Then she can tell me that. I just need to speak with her for one minute. I'll be quick, promise."

"No. You'd only upset her. I don't mean to be rude, but—
"

"Did you know the Luca family?"

"Not really. We just moved here about the time the couple was moving out and their daughter moved in. I waved to her a few times whenever I'd see her outside, but we didn't chat or anything. It's terrible what happened to her."

"I'm sure the family would appreciate your cooperation. What's your mother-in-law's name? Maybe we could call her."

The woman put her hands on her hips and frowned. "Now you're making a nuisance of yourself. Should I call 911 and speak with your supervisor?"

"I'm not the bad guy here."

"You could have fooled me. No offense, but you look a little grubby. Are you sure you're police?"

"Are you really the owner of the house?" He waited a beat and added, "Lady, I'd tell you to have a good day, but that'd make me a liar."

Her mouth fell open. "Well, I've never! You've got some nerve!" Colt turned and headed toward his car. To his back, she yelled, "You can't talk to me that way!"

"I just did," he muttered.

12

Four weeks passed since Brianna's death and Isabella had not heard back from Detective Jessup. She worried he wouldn't call. Maybe he only promised to look into her sister's death as a way of being nice. Maybe he just said what he thought she needed to hear with no intention of doing anything.

Isabella tried to stay busy to keep from thinking about the tragedy, yet occasionally she'd asked herself, "Did this really happen? Is it true? Brianna is dead?" She hadn't seen the body. She only had the word of the authorities and her family.

She tormented herself with a fruitless game of what ifs. *What if I had not hung up on her? What if I had scratched the opera and gone to her? What if I had called her more often, or asked more questions about why Whit was there?*

A voice lesson from her teacher's Midtown studio provided a welcomed retreat from her melancholy. Singing was her therapy. She'd worked on polishing her sing-through of an aria from *Die Fledermaus*, the piece she chose to audition for the Houston Grand Opera. Leaving Midtown, she put more spring into her step, walking to the subway station and thinking about the mad-cap comedic opera without a hint of darkness like the role she portrayed in *Tosca*.

With no seats available, she stood on the subway and felt every shake and bounce of the car's movement. She held on to the center pole just as tightly as she tried to cling to happy memories of Brianna. How long—how many years—would it take until she felt normal again?

The brightness of sunlight hit her when she stepped out of the subway station. She put on sunglasses and walked to her apartment. Once there, she fixed a glass of tea. She set it down and checked her phone, realizing she needed to take it off mute. She checked her voicemail.

"Holy crap! Landon called. Now why would he…?"

The mere sound of his voice sent her heart racing. She listened to his message.

"Hi, Isabella. It's me. Landon. Long time. Call me when you get a chance. Okay, that's all. Gotta go. Bye."

After four years, why call now? Was he back in New York? He did fit Teresa's description of the man at her door. Perhaps it was him after all.

Landon was a man of few words; hence, the brief message with no mention of her recent loss. Did he even know? He was never fond of Brianna. Their last argument played and replayed in her head. He said, "Let me get this straight. You're backing out of this romantic weekend I've planned for weeks. Do you have any idea how hard it was for me to manage to get the time off or to get a reservation in the first place?"

"I'm sorry, Landon." Her apology did little good; he kept fuming. She told him, "Brianna needs me. She overdosed, almost died. I have to go to her."

"But she's fine now. The crisis is over. You know, every time something happens with her, you take off. It tells me a lot about your priorities, and it sure as hell isn't me."

Why couldn't he understand? She had to admit her sister's addiction—her disease, really—left her little energy to nurture a love interest.

Shortly after she returned from seeing Brianna, Landon took a job in Seattle. His way of saying they were finished. Kaput. No need for further discussion.

His out-of-the-blue phone call puzzled her. Did he want to get back together? All forgiven? If he thought she was like *Madam Butterfly*, waiting years in the wings for her lover to come back, he was wrong. The last lines of the aria from Act II: *Io con sicura fede l'aspetto*, translated into English meant, *I with steadfast faith await him*. Not this woman. No way. She moved on, and she'd tell him so. But she chose not to return his call, at least not now. She couldn't bear a conversation about Brianna's death. She'd wait until she could speak without bursting into tears.

Just as she settled comfortably on the sofa, her phone rang. She assumed it was Landon calling again, but it was Kristen. She detected a quiver in her sister's voice.

"What's wrong?" Isabella brought her hand to her throat, finding Kristen's sobbing almost insufferable.

Kristen's words came in quick short bursts, almost incoherent. "You need to come. Come home, Isabella. Dad—it's Dad. The ambulance took him to…They think he had a heart attack."

"What? Dad had a heart attack?"

"Yes, they think so. We're in the emergency room with him now—waiting for someone to tell us something."

"Oh, God! How bad is it?"

"No one will tell us. They're doing some tests and blood work." After a long pause, she said, "Wait—wait, oh, no, no, no. Something's wrong." A prolonged silence kept Isabella waiting before she overheard Kristen speaking with her mother. "Mom, do you see? Look at the monitor. See? His heart—it's too slow. Where's the nurse? Mom! Call her! Hurry!"

Isabella heard her mother's voice in the background, high-pitched, sounding hysterical, then more voices as people entered the room. Although she wasn't there, she sensed the urgency.

Isabella's hands trembled as she held the phone. She shouted, "Kristen? Are you there? What's wrong?"

"His heart—it stopped. Oh, God, we're losing him! Somebody, please do something!"

"Kristen! Kristen? Do you hear me? Answer me, please!"

Their connection ended.

13

The not-knowing was agony. Isabella whispered a prayer and wiped away an endless stream of tears. Ten minutes passed before her phone rang. She reached for it, but her fast action knocked it to the floor. She scooped it up and tapped the call button.

"Kristen?"

"Oh, hi. Dad's fine now. They shocked his heart and it started again. Close call, but he's okay. Wow! What a scare!"

Isabella put her hand to her throat. "Thank God! I was so worried we lost him. First, Bree and then—This is ridiculous. How much more can we take? What happened?"

"Right after the detectives left the house, he started having chest pains. They stopped by to give Mom and Dad the results of the coroner's report. I haven't seen it, but Mom said they ruled her death as accidental or suicide."

Isabella stared at the wall, tears breaming in her eyes.

"Isabella? Did you hear me?"

"Yes, but I don't believe it. She didn't kill herself. Someone—"

"Isabella—stop it! Don't do this. It's hard enough as it is, you don't need to…Just trust what the coroner and the police say. They know more about this than we do."

"They don't know Brianna—not like I do. She didn't kill herself."

"Come on, Isabella. Please."

"Tell Dad I'm coming to see him. I'll get a flight as soon as we hang up."

"I thought you have a music camp or something."

"I do, but I'll go crazy if I stay here. I can get someone to cover for me. I need to be there."

"Okay, sure. Just text me your flight info and I'll pick you up from the airport." In the silence that followed, Isabella could hear a series of beeps, perhaps a monitor in her Dad's room. Then, Kristen's voice, addressing a nurse or someone who entered the room. Kristen came back on the line. "Isabella, don't get Mom and Dad all worked up over your suspicions. They're upset enough as it is."

"Trust me, the last thing I want to do is turn their world upside down, but we deserve the truth, and Brianna deserves justice."

§

Colt and Detective Anders reached the breakroom at the same time. Anders glanced up from the coffee machine and locked eyes with Colt. With his hand still on the spigot, hot liquid ran over the side of his mug and onto his fingers.

He set his coffee down and shook his hand. "Shit!"

Still with a pained look on his face, he leaned to one side, peering out the doorway. Was he expecting someone to come in or afraid someone might find him there? Something was up. Colt was sure of it.

Anders shook the contents of a sugar packet into his coffee, and said *sotto voce*, "It's here."

"What's here?" Colt crinkled his forehead. "The tox report?" Colt took a sip of too strong, bitter coffee.

Anders's brows went up.

"I take that as a yes." Colt said, keeping his voice low. "I want to see it."

Anders threw the flimsy stir-stick in the trash and walked toward the door. Colt didn't call him back. Before the day was over, Anders would find a way for the report to end up in Colt's hands. He'd done stuff like that before, covertly helping Colt and risking his own career.

Fifteen minutes was all it took. Anders walked by Colt's desk, holding something at his side. Just as he passed, papers slipped from his hand. Colt reached down to scoop up the fanned-out pages. He leaned far back in his chair and propped his feet on top of his desk. Holding the report at eye-level, he carefully studied the toxicology results. Dated four weeks after the date of death, it stated: *Decedent: Brianna Luca Connelly*. The report was not about Brianna as a person, a living being. She was now the decedent, the corpse, the dead body, the laboratory subject. Colt never grew accustomed to the cold detachment in the terminology of clinical reports. But neither did he ever adjust to the finality of death.

The report stated blood was drawn from the femoral vessel. Beside the clinical name of each drug was written *none detected* or *present*. Brianna's blood had enough chemicals present to guarantee mortality. It didn't take much. A combination of only three could do the trick, stop the heart, and end life.

Anders gave Colt more than he'd asked for. He included the five-page *Report of Autopsy Examination*. It read: *The cause of death is an acute intoxication by the combined effects of oxycodone, diazepam, and temazepam. The manner of death is accidental, resulting from the abuse of prescription medications.*

"Bullshit!" With a flick of his wrist, Colt tossed the report horizontally like a Frisbee. Papers scattered across the surface of his desk. He gathered them up and tapped the bottom edges to straighten into one neat stack.

A vice officer in the next cubicle rolled his chair backwards. "What's that, Colt? Did you say something?"

"I said bullshit." His chair groaned when he leaned far back. Starting at the temples, he ran his hands through his hair, then cradled the back of his head in his palms, staring up at the ceiling. "The medical examiner's report. It's crap."

"What about it is crap?"

"The cause of death. Accidental or suicide, my ass. Someone staged the whole thing."

"So, what are you going to do?"

"Raise a stink."

The officer threw his head back and chuckled. "Your specialty, Slick. That's what you're good at."

§

By the time Isabella boarded a plane for her trip home, she'd learned her father was out of danger. Now settled in her seat by a window, she adjusted the strap on her sandaled heels. A quick glance at her toes made her glad she'd taken the time to have a pedicure. She'd talked herself into trying an unusual shade of coral and she liked the results.

Before the flight attendant told everyone to turn off technical devices, she called her dad to see how he was feeling.

"They jumpstarted my heart. It's ticking just fine now." He chuckled, giving her assurance that he was indeed back to normal.

When the plane landed, Isabella's seat near the front gave her the ability to exit quickly. She hurried through the crowd of passengers on their way to baggage claim and grabbed her luggage from the carousel. Outside the main door, she waited for Kristen's vehicle to drive up. A horn blasted from a black Dodge Charger as it pulled alongside the curb. The driver reached across to open the passenger door. She locked eyes with Detective Colt Jessup.

"Hop in, Isabella. I'll take you to the hospital." He jumped out and grabbed her luggage, putting it in the trunk.

Her heart raced. Something bad happened; otherwise, her sister would have picked her up. She waited until he settled behind the steering wheel before she said, "Where's Kristen? Why are you here?"

"Relax, everything is fine. Your father is having a procedure. A stent put in. Your sister stayed with your mom. She asked me to pick you up."

"I still don't understand—why?"

"Why me? That's because your mom called me to see if I'd seen the toxicology report. I was on my way to their house to discuss it, when she called me back and told me your dad was taken to the hospital. I went straight there. I figured it was important for Kristen to stay with your mom so I volunteered to pick you up."

"Is my dad going to be okay? How serious is this procedure?"

"He's going to be fine. Better than before. They do this stent thing when someone has a blockage, kinda like a clogged pipe. I know a couple of guys who've had it. No big deal." Colt reached for his cigarette pack from the console. "Mind if I smoke?"

"Yes, I mind."

He feigned shock and held the pack in mid-air.

"You know you're not doing your heart any favors. Or lungs either. This car smells like…oh, my gosh, I didn't know they still put ashtrays in cars." She crinkled her nose and pushed it closed. "I'm sorry. You know what, it's your car. If you want to—"

"Nah, it's fine." He dropped the pack onto the console. "I'll roll down the window—air it out in here."

"Thanks." Isabella gave him a weak smile. "I was going to call you, Detective Jessup."

"Hey, are we back to that? Call me Colt."

"Okay, Colt, then. I was going to see what you thought about the toxicology report. I assume you've read it."

"Yep. Guess you're not buying the suicide theory."

"No, of course not."

"What makes you so sure?"

"Bree promised me she'd never attempt suicide again. I believed her." Isabella ran her hand over her lap, smoothing out the wrinkles on her skirt. "You saw the report. What do you think?"

"It's just a hunch so far, but I think the crime scene was set up. Whoever killed her wanted us to think she OD'd on sleeping pills, but there were three drugs in her system. And I don't think she had access to two of them. Maybe she did, but no signs of them were left at the scene."

"How would someone get her to take it?"

"From what we saw in her fridge, I'd say someone fixed her a lethal cocktail. With her small size, it wouldn't take much. Three pills oughta do it."

"And she wouldn't be able to detect it?"

"Don't think so. If the drink had enough sweet stuff in it, like the pineapple and lime juice, plus lots of rum."

"Wouldn't there be prints on the glass? If someone prepared it for her, wouldn't the glass have their fingerprints? Or was the glass wiped clean?"

"It was never examined. Techs did take the glass, so they can process it. I'll talk to Spencer about it."

Colt hit the brakes and jerked the wheel, switching lanes. He cursed and honked his horn. "Damn drivers! That idiot shouldn't even have a license. Look at him on his phone, acting like he's the only one on the damn road." He gave Isabella an apologetic smile. "Sorry. It gets to me sometimes."

"I can see that."

He rolled his shoulders back and propped his elbow on the opened window frame. "Let's not talk about it anymore. Save it for later. You've got enough to deal with right now with your father's situation."

She exhaled and folded her hands in her lap. "Yes, I suppose so."

A siren wailed in the distance, heading in the same direction they were. Colt steered the car over giving it room to pass.

"Tell me something, songbird," he said. "How do you do that thing you do?"

"What thing?"

"The singing. I sat near the back of the church, but I could hear you just as good as if I sat up front. No microphone, no nothing. You're a petite thing but damn if you don't have a big voice. How's that possible?"

"Actually, it's all about physics."

"Physics, huh? How can you do it in the theater with a full orchestra? Looks like they'd drown you out."

Isabella smiled. "The sound frequency from a trained voice is at a higher range than the orchestra; therefore, the sound carries over it. I used a technique called resonance tuning to intensify the vibrations of the vocal cords and increase the power of the voice."

"It must take work to get that good. You were great by the way."

"Thanks, Colt. Have you ever been to an opera?"

He laughed and took his eyes from the road to smile at her. "What do you think?"

"Probably not. Opera is an acquired taste."

"In other words, don't knock it until you've tried it."

"Yes. I fell in love with it in college. I saw a dress rehearsal of *La Traviata*, and I thought it was the most beautiful thing I'd ever heard. The music blew me away. It changed my career path. Brianna wasn't happy about it because we had other plans."

"Oh, yeah? What plans?"

"After we graduated, we were going to New York together and audition for shows. We had this big idea we'd make it on Broadway, she's a dancer and me a singer. My dad used to take the whole family with him on business trips to the Big Apple. Kristen and Mom liked to shop on Fifth Avenue, but Bree and I wanted to see shows. We loved it."

"So, you made it to New York but not your sister."

"Eventually, but first, I went to grad school and got a masters in voice performance. After college, Brianna married a guy she met in Community Theater. She and Trevor were only married four months before the accident happened that took his life and left her severely injured. She had multiple surgeries on her foot, but it was never the same. The pain of her injuries and losing Trevor…It was too much for her."

"Yeah, she told me. Tough break. She had a rough go of it. Folks get hooked on drugs not only for the physical pain but for emotional baggage too. The kicker is the feeling is temporary, wears off pretty quick. After a while, they need more pills or they switch to something more potent. I know it doesn't mean much now, but it's a good thing your sister didn't turn to heroin."

Isabella concentrated on the passing scenery of sturdy oak trees lining both sides of the street in front of medical clinics, one after the other. Straight ahead, the massive hospital came into view. Colt turned into the lot designated for visitors and took a parking ticket.

Colt carried her luggage and set it down just inside the doorway of her father's room. "I'll just say a quick howdy and then I better go. Let y'all have some family time. We'll go over the tox report later."

"Okay, I'd like to do that tomorrow," Isabella said. "Will you call me in the morning?"

"I have something going on, but I'll call when I get the chance."

"So, you'll meet with me?"

He gave her a playful smile. "Maybe I can squeeze you in on my social calendar."

"Great. I was hoping I could count on you."

Together they entered the room. Isabella immediately went to her father's bedside and took his hand in hers.

He opened his eyes and gave her a lazy smile. Still groggy from the anesthesia, he said, "My Isabella. What a surprise. I didn't know you were coming."

Her eyes widened. "Dad! We talked on the phone. I told you I was flying in. Remember?"

"No. Don't remember much of anything. Except your mother putting a straw in my mouth and telling me to drink some godawful soda. Way too sweet."

He made a sour face, glanced at his wife, and winked. On the other side of the bed, Kristen patted his arm and said, "See, Isabella. He's back to his old self, complaining about everything."

Colt stepped closer to the bed and spoke a few words to Tony, expressing his relief on the success of the procedure. After he said his goodbyes, Isabella walked him to the door.

"Bye, songbird. Hey, you don't mind if I call you that, do you?"

"No, it's fine. See you tomorrow."

He nodded. At the doorway, Isabella studied him walking down the corridor with a confident strut, his hands buried in his pockets. He had a slim physique, yet he was broad shouldered and muscular, no fat. She pictured him getting into bar scrapes and skirmishes. No doubt he'd come out the victor, in better shape than his opponent or just more determined not to get his butt kicked.

Isabella returned to her father's bedside. She glanced at her mother on the other side and gave her a reassuring smile. She remained strong, as always, but stress showed in her tight jawline, her worried eyes. First, Brianna's death, and now this.

"Isabella?" she said.

"Yes, mom?"

Jill pressed her lips together. "About the report—what did Colt say about it?"

"He wanted to know what I thought about it."

"What did you say?"

"That I'm not ready to accept the cause of death."

With a scowl, Kristen spoke up, "We're not discussing it. Right now, we should all be focused on Dad's recovery. Don't you agree, Isabella?"

"Absolutely. The rest can wait." *Until tomorrow.* She didn't dare say it out loud

14

Colt made a face at Detective Samantha Delano. "That's all I needed first thing this morning—to be insulted. Thanks a lot, partner."

"All I said was if you didn't stay out carousing all night you wouldn't look like shit." Samantha ran her fingers through her copper hair and narrowed her green eyes. "How much sleep did you get anyway?"

"Not enough, that's for damn sure." He closed his eyes and pinched the bridge of his nose. "It's not what you think. I wasn't out *carousing*." He made air-quotes with his fingers. "I got an idea where Hondo might be hiding out, so I drove there. Shit, it was a waste of time—and gas. Clear 'cross the damn county line."

"Forget about Hondo. We've got bigger…" She stopped mid-sentence when their server came over holding a pot of coffee, just what Colt needed to jumpstart his day. He didn't bother with his usual chipper "Good morning, Sunshine" greeting. The way he felt, speaking was too much work. For another hour of precious sleep, he'd almost canceled on Samantha. And now that she was lashing out at him, he wished he had.

Samantha glanced up at the perky blonde as she filled their coffee cups. "This walking-dead guy needs a hearty breakfast. Bring him the works and I'll have the oatmeal with berries."

Sunshine giggled and smiled. "Coming right up!" As she bounced off to the kitchen, coffee sloshed in the glass carafe, to the same motion as her swaying hips, which didn't miss Colt's attention.

Once she was out of his sight, he turned his attention on Samantha. "Were you like this with my brother?"

"Like what?"

"A mother hen."

"You think this is something?" She clucked her tongue. "I was worse with your brother. Didn't he tell you? I stayed on Streaker's case all the damn time. Had to. He was a hot mess."

"Is that why you never married him?"

She had a habit of rolling her eyes whenever he'd crossed a line. "Don't act like you didn't know I was already married. And in case it's any of your business, Colt, I didn't leave my no-good husband and marry your brother because—well, because it would be like exchanging one load of dirty laundry for another. Your brother had lots of issues."

"He loved you." Colt tapped his index finger on the side of his coffee cup. "I've been wondering about something. If he hadn't died, do you think you would've ever changed your mind and married him?"

She tilted her head from side to side and pursed her lips. "Maybe. If he managed to stay out of trouble long enough. I thought he had shaped up, but then he got involved with that slimy land developer who smooth-talked him into...well, you know. It led to that bad-ass drug dealer finding him and killing him."

"He was trying to protect a woman. He sacrificed his life to save her. In the end, he did the right thing."

"I know—I was there. He died in my arms." Samantha wiped a tear from her eye. "Enough about that. I can't...You know, Colt, your brother wanted something better for you. He certainly didn't want you to make the same mistakes he did. That's why I'm sometimes hard on you. I feel like I owe it to Streaker."

"Yeah, sure, I get it. I'm cool with that. Besides, you outrank me. I *have* to listen to you."

"Ah-ha here comes our food. We need to eat up and meet with the task force. If this all works out, we'll be sitting pretty. Taking down a major drug operation—well, that's huge. It'll even put you back in the good graces with the captain, don't you think?"

"Yeah, if I can only get some specifics from that Rambo-dude. We know the supply is coming from a container ship, but we don't know yet how it's making its way to Charlotte. Once we get that little tidbit, we can bust the whole damn operation wide open."

"Here's the thing, Colt—forget what the DEA is telling you. You're the one on the inside taking all the risks. Go slow. Don't take any chances. These are some scary-ass dudes. If you get burned…well, you know. I don't have to tell you."

"Hey, I'm going to be careful. Don't worry about me."

§

Tony Luca didn't sleep well.

"How could I?" He looked from his wife to Isabella. "I'm not in my own bed. Don't have my fluffy pillow. If they want me to feel better, they can send me home. And another thing—they can leave me the hell alone! Stop coming in the middle of the night like vampires, taking my blood. Hell, I might not have any to spare."

Isabella pushed his tray stand away from the bed. It held the remnants of his breakfast. She couldn't remember her father ever leaving food on his plate. "Dad, I'll go now. Let you catch up on some sleep."

"You can stay, sweetie. I don't mean to be so cranky. I'll be nice."

"Dad, you need rest more than company. I'll stop by later. This morning is a good time for me to go to New Beginnings and pick up Brianna's belongings. Mom said they called." She patted his arm and gave her parents a hug. Until she heard from Colt, she'd do a little detective work on her own and her late sister's employer was a good place to start.

She drove the tree-lined street where many stately homes were converted to businesses. The office of New Beginnings, a two-story, white house with a wrap-around porch, reminded Isabella of her grandparents' home in Virginia, especially with its hanging plants and wind chimes.

The center's director, Marcus Gilliam, spent a fortune on landscaping. The back of the building had three gardens designed and cared for by a certified horticulturist. The grounds had a garden for herbs, one for organic produce, and one called a "meditation garden," a paved walkway with benches around a man-made brook. Occasionally Isabella and Brianna chose it for times of meaningful conversations and shared tears, far removed from distractions.

A breeze set off the chimes near the front door, a soothing, mellifluous sound. Isabella walked in and was greeted by a volunteer at the front desk.

"Hi, I'm Isabella Luca, Brianna's sister. I wanted to collect her things. Someone called and said there were some personal items on her desk."

The woman's cordial demeanor shifted to funereal solemnity. Her smile disappeared. "You need to see Lauren Lamont. She can help you. Just go straight back. Her office is on the right."

Instead, Isabella went directly to the cubicle once assigned to Brianna. Except for a computer monitor on a desk, it now lay bare. No sign Brianna was ever there. Isabella took a seat in the desk chair and rolled it forward. She opened the bottom drawer, searching for Brianna's laptop computer and anything else that might be significant. The computer could hold the key to what happened to Brianna. Determined to find it, she opened every drawer but to no avail.

She jumped when she heard someone call her name.

Her heart pounded. She slammed a drawer shut on her finger. She grimaced and said, "Oh, hi, Lauren. I didn't see you come up." She knew the Lamont woman as Brianna's supervisor, also the only person with the police when Brianna's body was discovered. "I-I was just seeing if Brianna left her laptop here."

"It's not here. I believe she took it with her that day." Lauren attempted a smile but stopped.

Maybe appearing too cheerful in front of the mourning sister was bad etiquette. It was becoming annoying for Isabella, people acting different in her presence, not sure what to do or say.

Lauren cleared her throat and ran her hand over her hair. "I collected a few of her things that I thought you might want. I'll get them for you."

Raven hair with a dyed pink streak popped up from the cubicle on the other side. The woman stood up and pushed her glasses further up on the bridge of her nose. Their vintage, cat-eye frames made as much of a fashion statement as her tinted hair.

When she spoke, barely above a whisper, she kept her head down, avoiding eye contact. "Lauren, sorry, didn't mean to interrupt. Uh—but there's a man—On Line 1—for you. It's about—well, I think it's about the fundraiser."

"Tell him I'll be right there." Lauren pivoted to face Isabella. "Sorry, I need to take this call. Then, I'll get Brianna's things. If you'll excuse me."

Lauren Lamont once had a cocaine habit. A costly one. Three grand a week was the rumor. A former model, she maintained her beauty, looking years younger than her forty-something age. Her makeup and hairstyle had to be professionally done, meticulous and to perfection. Cut in a short bob, her chestnut hair flattered her heart-shaped face. A dress of jersey material draped softly accentuating her curves. As graceful as a gazelle, she strolled to her office in heels.

"Isabella?"

The woman in the adjacent cubicle stared at her. She stepped out of her workspace and stood facing Isabella. Was her pink-streaked hair and bright turquoise frames the sign of someone screaming for attention?

"Guess you don't remember me." The woman swallowed hard. "We—I mean, you, me, and Brianna—we had lunch about six months ago. And I—uh, well, I spoke to you at her memorial service. I was there with Marcus and Lauren. But—well—uh, you saw so many people that day, I don't expect you to remember me."

"Of course, I remember you. You're Tara, right?" Isabella hugged her. Tara's arms stayed awkwardly at her sides until she relaxed and accepted the embrace.

"I'm still so sad about Brianna." Tara bit down on her bottom lip as her eyes welled with tears. "I can't imagine what you're going through. I'm so sorry for your loss, Isabella."

"Thanks. Yes, it has been hard. I take one day at a time. That's all I can do."

"It's hard for me to believe. I mean, I can't get my head around the fact Brianna took her own life. Not after what she told me."

"What do you mean?"

"That—well, that she couldn't wait to go on a trip with you. She was so excited."

"So was I. So, she didn't act depressed?"

"Well—no. Not really. But—but, well, she was stressed about—" Tara looked past Isabella. "I better get back to work."

Tara ducked behind the security of her cubicle.

"Wait, I have a few questions for you. Do you know Whit—the guy in rehab with Brianna. I need to find him. Can you help me—"

Lauren returned. "Sorry to keep you waiting, Isabella. Come to my office and I'll give you Brianna's things. I have them in a box."

Isabella followed her into a plush office. Thick reference books and art objects filled a mahogany bookcase and covered one wall. Artwork by recovered addicts hung over a two-drawer lateral filing cabinet. She kidded herself into thinking the abstract paintings were inspired under the influence of drugs rather than during periods of sobriety.

Lauren offered Isabella a seat. Comfortably seated behind her desk, Lauren propped her elbows and brought her hands up to form a steeple.

Isabella took a deep breath and charged forward. "Was Brianna stressed about something? That's what Tara told me."

At first, Lauren didn't answer. She pressed her lips tightly together and sighed deeply. "I suppose you have the right to know." Her eyes connected with Isabella's. "Brianna was stressed because she was afraid someone would find out."

"Find out what?" Isabella felt heat come to her cheeks.

"I'm sorry to tell you this, but your sister was back on drugs."

"No she wasn't!" Isabella tempered her anger and lowered her voice. "If she was, I'd have known. What makes you say that?"

"Well, I suspected it before she died. There were signs. She was more withdrawn. Sometimes her eyes looked glazed over. She had trouble concentrating on her work. And near the end of the day, she'd get fidgety, anxious. I imagine she waited until she got home to take more drugs."

Lauren's claims contradicted what Marcus told Isabella: *I saw her potential. I don't know if she told you but we were considering her for a promotion. I planned to take some of the work off Lauren and make Brianna the director of special events—in charge of fundraising.*

Isabella was having none of it. How dare this "perfect" woman smear Brianna. Isabella leaned forward. "Did you ever see her take drugs?"

"No, I didn't, but after she—well, after she was gone, I gathered up her belongings from her desk and I found Oxycontin, Valium, Ambien, and Percocet."

Isabella quaked with rage. Anyone who had been around Brianna in the last three years knew she won the battle against addiction. Her progress was impressive. Everyone was proud of her, especially Isabella. It was unconscionable to think she had started using again…unless Whit Drummond had a part in it. Had the lowlife coaxed Brianna into doing drugs with him? He was a heroin addict. Did he experiment with opioids too?

Abruptly, Isabella stood. "If there were drugs, show me."

Lauren shook her head. "I can't. We don't keep pills around here. Not with recovering addicts. It would be too easy for them…I disposed of them."

Isabella leaned forward. "How?"

"Some of our patients turn in their supply when they come here. We mix them in with coffee grounds and put them in a sealable plastic bag and throw in the trash. That's what I did with Brianna's drugs."

Brianna's drugs? Don't say that! Isabella took a slow breath and refused to look at Lauren. She walked away without responding. But she stopped in the doorway and turned. From her purse, she pulled a 3 x 5 photo she found in a drawer in Brianna's bedroom. She held it up for Lauren to see. "Do you know him?"

"Yes, that's Whit Drummond." Lauren gave her an odd smile. "My goodness! Brianna looked so different back then."

Isabella had to agree. Brianna was almost unrecognizable. In the picture, Whit had his arm around Brianna's sagging, narrow shoulders. Drugs took a toll on them both, turning two young people into sad sights with sunken cheekbones, hollow eyes, thinning hair.

"Did you know he was staying with Brianna before she died?"

"What?" Lauren's eyes widened. "No, I had no idea. Brianna didn't say, although I'm sure she wouldn't want me to know."

"I believe he had something to do with her death. I'm going to find out."

"You think he gave her the drugs that killed her?"

"I'm not sure. But he was there when she died."

"How do you know that?" Lauren swallowed hard.

"I went to her house and saw signs he left in a hurry. He knows something."

"What are you going to do, Isabella?"

"Find him." She frowned at the photograph and stuffed it back in her purse. "Do you know where I should look?"

"No. I haven't seen him in probably two or three years. What are you thinking, Isabella? That Brianna didn't kill herself?"

"I know she didn't. She wouldn't. I feel certain someone is responsible for her death, and I won't rest until I found out who and why."

"You sound very determined."

"I owe it to my sister to find the truth."

Isabella was done talking. It was time she turned her words into action, and she knew exactly where she needed to start. "Well, I've taken up enough of your time. I should go." She paused in the doorway. She was forgetting something but what?

"Wait. Brianna's things." Lauren rounded the corner of her desk and bent down to pick up a cardboard box shoved into a corner of the room. She handed it to Isabella. "This is everything. I like the picture frame with that wonderful photo of you and your sister. I knew you'd want it back." Lauren gave her a weak smile.

"Thanks." Isabella adjusted her hands to get a better grip on the box. "Call me if you think of anything important, Lauren."

"Sure. Marcus will be upset he missed you. He's at the bank. Just the other day, he was saying something about putting up a tribute to Brianna. A plaque on the wall or something like that. We all miss her so much."

"She would like that. Oh—one more thing. If you happen to see Whit, please call me. The police want to talk to him."

Lauren's mouth gaped open. "The police?"

"Yes. I'm not the only one looking for him."

Lauren wrinkled her forehead. But before she could ask a question, Isabella walked away, leaving her standing there with a puzzled look. Isabella headed for Tara's desk. She couldn't stop thinking about what Tara said about Brianna being stressed out. She needed to find out more. She hurried back to Tara's desk. She wasn't in her seat.

"Are you looking for Tara?" A woman about Isabella's age stood up at her desk and walked up to Isabella. "Oh, you're Brianna's sister," she said. "I'm so sorry for your loss. We adored Brianna."

"Thank you." Isabella managed to smile. "I wanted to speak with Tara again before I left."

"Oh. She's in the restroom. She seemed upset."

"Maybe my coming here stirred up emotions. I know she and Brianna were friends. I feel bad if I upset her."

"Don't worry about it. Tara hasn't been herself in weeks, but she won't tell me what's bothering her. She might be upset about Brianna or it could be something else."

"Well, you know her better than I do."

"Actually, the way she's been acting, I don't feel like I know her at all."

15

The DEA agent's last words of instruction were, "Don't screw up, Jessup. Countin' on you."

Oh, really? Colt's life *depended* on him not screwing up. He took all the risks while the feds waited for his call once the exchange took place. He'd hand over the buy and they'd send it to the lab for testing. "My guess is this batch is laced with fentanyl. China White. Whatcha wanna bet?" Colt said and laughed when the unsmiling Roper shook his head, refusing to take the wager.

With adrenalin pumping, Colt waited in the parking lot of a McDonalds, the meeting place set between him and a drug dealer named Boone. They were a few miles from the airport and jets roared overhead.

He leaned against the side of his car and tapped his hand on his outer thigh. "C'mon, c'mon, scumbag, let's get this show on the road," he mumbled out loud.

Colt wrapped his hand around the fat roll of hundred-dollar bills. It put a noticeable lump in his jeans pocket. Again, he muttered between clenched teeth, "C'mon, c'mon, ain't got all day."

He planned to contact Isabella and set up a meeting. They had lots to discuss and he owed it to her to tell her what he'd learned and how they should move forward. The sooner he finished his business here, the sooner he could make the call.

He breathed deeply when Boone drove up in his silver Dodge Durango with tinted windows. Showtime. It was tricky being two people in one body. There was Colt, the undercover vice cop, and there was Rowdy, the drug dealing lowlife. Keeping them apart, never letting one see the other, was a chore.

Boone climbed out of the vehicle and waved. A stranger emerged from the front passenger seat. Something about his looks reminded Colt of a guy he knew in high school, a bully who used his size and scowl to mark his placement as the alpha male. He had a buzz-cut and his pink scalp showed through the short hairs. Colt didn't miss the bulge of a gun at his lower back. His hooded eyes looked Colt up and down.

"This here is Rocky," Boone said. "He's Pug's cousin. Working with us now."

"Any kin of Pug's gotta be all right. Pug's the real deal." Colt scanned his surroundings, comforted by the DEA agents' SUV parked in the Minute Market parking lot across the street. If anything went sideways, they'd rush in. *They would, wouldn't they?* Colt hadn't counted on Boone bringing someone along. It could spell trouble. He tapped Boone on the arm with the back of his hand. "Well, are we gonna do this or not?"

"Step into my office," Boone said, extending his arm toward his vehicle.

Colt started forward but got blocked when Rocky cut him off. "Not so fast." Rocky stepped close enough Colt got a whiff of his bad breath. "You look familiar. Don't I know you?"

"Ever done time at Bunting? Cell block D?"

"Nah." Rocky narrowed his eyes. "But I know you from somewheres."

"Don't think so, bro." Colt swallowed down his fear and hid it behind a smirk. "You sure you're kin to Pug? You look too purdy to be related to him."

"Screw you." Rocky bumped up against Colt. "I'm picking up a bad odor coming off you. You a cop?"

"Nope but I've been busted by a few."

Boone bounced on the heels of his boots, crossed his arms, and rubbed his chin. "Hey, we can't stand around out here all day. He's okay, Rocky. Relax, man. Let's do some business now."

Rocky never took his eyes off Colt, not even when he placed his hand behind his back. He brought it forward, holding a gun. He pressed the barrel into Colt's abdomen, standing close enough the gun stayed hidden from sight. "Get in the car. We'll take him to the house, Boone. If Pug says he's okay, I'll let him live."

"I'm tellin' ya, man, Rowdy is okay." Boone helplessly extended his hands at his side. "We've done business with him before. Two buys. He's cool. Let's just get in the car."

Rocky sneered. "Sure, we'll get in the car. And you're driving to the house and we'll wait there for Pug. If he says he's good, we'll do our business there. First, I want uh, Rowdy, is it? I want Rowdy to stand with his hands on the vehicle while I do a pat-down."

Colt rolled his eyes. "Whatever makes you happy, dude." He ambled over to the SUV and put his hands up high and allowed Rocky to do a pat-down. Rocky took his time running his hand along his front, his back, and down the inside and outside of his legs. He only stopped when Colt said, "Hey, stay away from my dick. You ain't a fag, are you?"

"Shut your mouth, dirtbag. Just making sure."

"Are we done here?" Boone said. "Let's just do the exchange and—" He stopped cold when Rocky turned the gun on him.

"I said *drive!*" Rocky kept the bite in his tone when he added, "Is that so hard for you to understand? You willing to die for this asshole? You think I won't put a bullet in your skull?"

"Screw this. I ain't dying for nobody." Boone bounced his car keys in the palm of his hand. He went over to the driver's side.

"Sure, sure, we'll go to the house and wait for Pug if that'll calm you down. This is messed up. I shudda come alone."

Colt resisted the shove in his back, staying solid on his feet. "Move!" Rocky shouted, punching him between the shoulder blades. "You and me gonna get in the back so I can keep an eye on you."

Colt chuckled. "Okay, purdy boy. I'll sit next to ya, but you can't hold my hand. We don't know each other that well."

"You son-of-a-bitch!" Rocky's lips barely moved, but his spittle hit the side of Colt's face. He grabbed Colt by the collar and pushed him down into the back seat. "You don't wanna piss me off, believe me."

"Hey, buddy, you need to loosen up. Ever thought of trying yoga or meditation?"

"Shut your trap, asshole!"

§

Tara Sanders wished she could be privy to the quarrel going on down the hall. It started when Lauren marched into Marcus's office and closed the door. The longer it went on, the louder their voices became. She hoped they weren't arguing about her. Marcus didn't like her pink-streaked hair and brightly colored glass frames. Not to mention her multiple ear piercings and tattoos. Lauren was cool with it though, understanding everyone's right to free expression.

But Tara didn't really think it was about her. Something was amiss between her supervisor and the director of New Beginnings. Recently in meetings, Lauren answered Marcus with a terse tone, avoiding eye contact. About a month ago, Marcus abandoned his easygoing style, grew silent whenever Lauren came around. He acted as though he couldn't stand the sight of her. It wasn't just Tara who noticed. Others did as well.

Marcus's administrative assistant, Alisha, told Tara the board members were pushing the non-profit in a more progressive direction. What that meant, Tara had no idea. But she assumed the pressure and a difference of opinion put Marcus and Lauren on a collision course. One afternoon when Alisha became more chatty than usual, she said, "Marcus wants New Beginnings to have a higher profile within the community. You know how he is—he likes to hobnob with the movers and shakers. He thinks he can get public funding. Dream on!" Alisha laughed and rolled her eyes. "All Lauren wants is to help people with their recovery. Know what I mean? Like adding more services and even job opportunities—that kind of thing. Those two don't see eye to eye, believe me."

None of it mattered to Tara. All she cared about was a steady paycheck.

Abruptly, the shouting ceased but the remnants of tension leached from underneath the door and filled the air with toxicity. Tara could no longer concentrate on her work. She gave up and opted for an early lunch.

A half block from the office, a white Lexus abruptly pulled up behind her at the stoplight. The same car followed her into the parking lot of Molly's Fresh Market where she planned to order a salad to go. It parked alongside of hers. Once out of her car, she kept her eyes trained on the driver and wedged her keys between her knuckles, a ready-made weapon if needed.

The stranger climbed out of his car and walked in her direction. Her heart knocked against her chest. She could feel pulsing in her head. He stood about seven feet away and locked eyes with her.

"Tara? Tara Sanders?"

Tara swallowed hard. She almost dropped her purse but caught it and slid the strap securely on her shoulder. To keep him from seeing her hands trembling, she clasped them behind her back. "How do you know my name?"

"Tara, I need to discuss something important with you."

She gave him silence.

He put his hand over his chest and smiled. "I'm sorry if I frightened you."

His apology did nothing to alleviate her fears. "Who are you?" She hated how her shaky voice gave her away.

"I'm Landon Burke. I knew Brianna. Like you, I was her friend."

"Funny she never mentioned you."

"Well, she told me about you. That's why I'm here. From what I gathered, you two were close. I just want to ask you a few questions. It's imperative that I speak with you."

Landon stepped forward to give a car more room to pass. From its opened windows, noise spilled out from the back seat, kids all shouting at the same time. He glanced at the front entrance to the eatery. "Tell you what, let me buy you lunch. We can sit down and talk."

He appeared to be a nice guy. But Tara had no doubt Brianna would have mentioned him, especially considering his good looks. The fact that she never said anything bothered Tara.

Nerves got the best of her and her keys fell to the pavement. She bent over and scooped them up. In her haste, she accidentally knocked her glass frames with her hand. Now situated lopsided on her face, she straightened them and said, "I-I just remembered something. I have to go." She hurried to her car door, pressing the unlock button on her key fob.

"Wait, Tara." He reached for her arm, but she jumped back. "You don't understand. I want to find out what you know, that's all."

He wants to know what Brianna told me. Whatever Brianna was stressed about stayed a mystery to Tara. She told her very little, not enough for her to connect the dots. And Tara wasn't going to spend another minute with the stalker who probably followed her from her office. Had he been watching her for a while? She vowed to start paying more attention to her surroundings.

She got behind the wheel and started the engine, her hands shaking even more than before. She put the car in reverse but slammed on brakes the moment she saw Landon in her rearview mirror. He stood directly behind the car, blocking its exit. Her heart raced. Taking a deep breath, she waited. He refused to budge. She pressed the accelerator slightly. Her car rolled backwards in a game of chicken. He jumped out of the way. His glare stayed locked on her until she was out of his sight. If she ever saw him or his car again, she'd call 911. Better safe than sorry.

§

By two o'clock Isabella had not heard from Colt and her threshold for patience had been crossed hours ago. He said he'd call when he got a chance. She assumed he simply forgot. Didn't he understand how important it was for her to get his insight on the toxicology report? She planned to discuss a strategy for finding what really happened to Brianna.

Where is he? Why hasn't he called? Isabella checked her watch one more time and threw up her hands. *Damn him. He promised.* It was gutsy, maybe risky, but she'd go to the seedy part of town where Brianna and Whit once lived. She'd show their photograph around and hopefully someone knew where she could find him. She had no doubt he was with Brianna when she died. What remained unclear was if he was responsible for her death. Isabella had only met him once, but he didn't strike her as a killer. But for an addict desperate for his next fix, anything was possible.

Part of her said it wasn't a good idea to go to the crime-ridden area alone, but she'd gained some street-smarts living the past four years in New York. She'd managed to walk from her first apartment in Washington Heights to the subway station through a maze of catcalls and some shifty characters without incident except for the time she got mugged. But even then, she'd shown grit, kicking the lowlife repeatedly and hitting him with her bag until he used a knife to cut the strap. As she screamed at the top of her lungs, she watched him run off with her bag, her credit cards, her cash, and her cell phone. The incident angered her more than scared her.

Landon once joked how he pitied anyone who messed with her. "You are one feisty female with claws out, ready to pounce." It gave her the fortitude and confidence to walk into a pool hall, the first building she came to in a long line of questionable businesses.

Her entry made everyone stop what they were doing. All eyes on her. She rolled her shoulders back, took a deep breath, and shoved the photograph under their noses, forcing them to look at it. "Do you know this man? How about this woman?" They clammed up and shook their heads.

Barely glancing at it, a barrel-chested man with a thick neck and fat lips shook his head. "Never seen 'em," he grunted.

"I'm only interested in the man. Did he ever play pool here? He goes by the name of Hondo."

"Told ya. Never seen 'em."

Isabella received a similar reception and response at the next three businesses. By the time she reached a run-down bar, her feet hurt. She leaned against the side of the building and frowned, looking down at her shoes. "Should have worn flats or sneakers. These heels are killing me," she muttered.

With a sense of foreboding, she took a deep breath and charged inside. Louie's Bar was dark. It took a minute for her eyes to adjust. A short squat man eyed her from behind the bar. He stopped what he was doing and looked her up and down.

She hopped up on a stool and rested her forearms on the edge of the bar. "I'll have a beer on tap."

Isabella wasn't much of a beer drinker, but she reasoned he might be more forthcoming if she was a paying customer. He grabbed a mug, filled it, and set it in front of her. His silence made her think getting anything out of the guy required forethought.

After she downed half the contents of her mug, she brought the photograph out and placed it on the counter. She motioned the bartender over and held up the picture for him to see. "Do you know this guy?"

He mumbled something, giving her hope.

"Have you seen him around? His name is Hondo."

"Your boyfriend?" He smirked.

"No. I just need to talk with him. It's important."

"Have another beer."

"No thanks. One is enough."

Before she could get an answer out of him, a man hopped up onto the bar stool at her side. He had his choice of a dozen stools, but he chose the one right next to her. Wearing dark trousers and a white dress shirt with the sleeves rolled up, he gave her a pleasant smile. She had to admit she liked his tender, hazel eyes. He seemed harmless but she felt uneasy when he twisted sideways, propping his elbow on the bar.

"May I buy you another beer? My name's Lanny, by the way."

"No thanks. I better be going." She edged off the stool.

"What do you have there?" He tapped the photograph as it lay on the counter.

She scooted back in her seat. "Do you know this man?"

He brought the photo up to his face and laughed. "Is that you, sugar? You look different now. Better."

"It's my sister. The guy is her ex-boyfriend, Hondo. Do you know him?"

"Are you looking for him?"

"Yes. Do you know where I can find him?"

He nodded and smiled. "As a matter of fact, I do. I know where Hondo is staying. I can take you to him if you like."

"Is it somewhere nearby?"

"Yes, but we'll have to drive. Too far to walk. I have my car out front. I'll take you."

"I don't think that's a good idea."

"Well, it's your choice. I just thought I'd help you out, that's all."

"But I don't know you."

"Bert does." The man pointed at the bartender. "Tell her, Bert. I'm harmless, right?"

The bartender ran his damp cloth over the counter and shrugged. "He's okay for a blood-sucking bill collector."

Lanny threw his head back and laughed. "I own a collection agency. Just trying to make a living." He tapped his fingers on the bar. "So, pretty lady, what do you say?"

"You said it's close by?"

"Yes, a five-minute drive."

"Well—" Isabella twirled a strand of her hair around her finger.

"How important is finding this guy?"

"Very important."

"Then, let's go, sugar."

Why not? Colt wasn't going to help. They were supposed to meet this morning and work on a plan to find Brianna's killer. But he couldn't bother to return her calls. She'd left six messages.

Lanny helped her down from the high bar stool. She thanked him and said, "Where did you say your car is parked?"

"Right out front. Shall we go?"

Something about his eager smile made her gulp.

16

Seconds after Boone turned right onto the highway, the feds' SUV pulled out of the parking lot across the street. Three cars separated them.

"Why did you even show up?" Boone took his eyes off the road to glare at Rocky, who kept his gun on Colt in the backseat. "Pug don't trust me to do a job. Is that it? He sent his cousin to babysit, make sure I stayed in line? Hell, I've known Pug for a long, long time. We like brothers, man. I never crossed him. Not one single time. He thinks I need *you* to order me around. What did I do to deserve this shit? You pointin' a gun at me and Rowdy like we plottin' somethin' together. This is messed up, bro. Don't make no sense a'tall."

"Hey! Just drive and shut your trap!" Rocky shouted. "I go with my gut and I'm telling you this here guy, I seen him before. Just making sure he's on our side, asshole. Can ya step on the gas a little? Jesus! You drive like my grandma."

Traffic got heavier on the six-lane highway close to the interstate. At the stoplight, Boone cruised through as the light turned red. Colt peeked out the back window. The red light stopped the agents' black SUV. A block down the street, Boone turned down a narrow two-lane road in an industrial area. Minutes later, another turn, followed by another. Colt cursed under his breath, knowing by the time the feds' vehicle got the green light, they'd be too late to tail Boone's Dodge Durango. Colt was on his own. Unfortunately, he'd left his gun and phone in his car. He'd have to use his brain and his mouth to talk his way out of Rocky or Pug killing him.

Rocky jerked his knee up and down nonstop, antsy to get where they were going or maybe wanting to get on with it and shoot Colt. Finally, they arrived at a ranch-style brick house, resting in a low-lying area. The dwelling itself was well maintained; however, from the abundance of weeds and crabgrass, no one bothered with lawncare. The vehicle rolled to a stop on a gravel drive marked by bare spots and muddy puddles. Colt followed Rocky's lead. Grass and dandelions brushed against his jeans. The trio walked up onto the porch. Their boots made scraping sounds across wooden planks. Rocky kept a grip on Colt's shoulder, but he did not need to. The place was isolated, in the middle of Sticksville, as Colt liked to say. Nowhere to run.

The screen door creaked open. Boone went in first, calling out for Pug. After walking through the house, he came back and said, "He ain't here."

Rocky grabbed Colt by the shoulders and slung him against the wall. He pounded his fist into his abdomen. Colt grunted and doubled over. He retched but recovered quickly. Rocky jabbed his forearm into Colt's throat, pressing against his windpipe, pinning him against the wall to the point he couldn't move. He struggled to breathe. Colt tugged and pulled on Rocky's arm. Rocky only applied more pressure.

"I can't breathe. Lemme go." Colt croaked.

"You a cop, ain't ya?" Rocky said. "You a no good, slimy copper. Say it!"

"Hell, no, I'm not!"

Rocky grabbed Colt by the wrist, jerking him around and sending him crashing to the floor. "We'll see about that. When Pug comes here, we're gonna let him decide if you is or you ain't."

Colt rubbed his throbbing throat. He could use his martial arts skills and take them both out, but what good would that do? It would screw over the whole investigation. He had no choice but wait.

"So, when is Pug coming?" Colt wiped sweat from his forehead. His heart hammered against his chest and his palms became clammy. Terror soured his stomach. Any minute, Rocky could end his life.

With one finger on the trigger guard of a Glock, Rocky twirled it around. Colt stepped back. The gun could accidentally fire.

"Answer me, dammit. When is Pug coming?"

Rocky continued playing with the weapon until he appeared to grow tired of the game. He set the gun down and said, "He's a'comin' when he feels like comin'. Got it, dirtbag?"

"Yeah, I got it. I just want to know how long I'm going be stuck here with you."

"If he don't show up soon, I'll just have to kill ya myself."

"And then Pug will have to kill *you*. I'm a big-time customer. You think that's my dick making the bulge in my pants? That's a wad of cash and there's more of that coming. As long as y'all supply the drugs, I supply the cash. Boone and I had a smooth business arrangement until you came along and screwed it up."

"I can't get past my gut telling me you're bad for business. Could be wrong. Like I said, we'll let Pug make the call. Just relax, cowboy. Take a little snooze if you like."

"So you can steal my money? Don't think so."

Sometime later, the three wandered into the back and ended up in the kitchen. A large dent in the wall, about the size of a fist, didn't require any explanation for how it got there. The grungy refrigerator had seen better days but functioned, based on the cold bottle of beer Boone handed Colt. Boone avoided eye contact with Colt and went outside to drink his beer.

Rocky guzzled his beer and threw the empty bottle into a garbage can already filled to the brim. He faced the counter and bent over to snort something up his nose. The druggie lifted his chin and sniffed. After a big swig of Jack Daniels whiskey straight from the bottle, he burped. "Let's get comfy in the front room and wait for Pug." With his mouth wide open, Rocky burped again. "I gotta keep my eye on you."

"Mind if I take a piss first?" Colt said.

"The can's down the hall. Keep the door open."

Colt cursed under his breath as he walked out. He stood in front of the toilet and unzipped. While he peed, he grappled with guilt for being detained by a stoned psycho. He should be meeting with Isabella instead. Was she worried about where he was? Or maybe she was angry he hadn't called. In his experience, women had a range of emotions and you never knew what you'd get.

He hoped the DEA were working on finding him. His predicament wasn't hopeless. Only Rocky accused him of being a cop, and Pug was in charge. Had he ever encountered Rocky on a bust? Nothing came to mind. Then why did the dude act so sure he'd seen him before? Then, it hit him.

§

Something about Lanny's smile stopped Isabella in her tracks. Walking from the darkness of the bar into the brightness outside, Isabella pretended to look for her sunglasses. Instead, she searched the bottom of her purse for her tube of pepper spray. She fingered it underneath her compact. Immediately, its discovery relaxed the tension in her shoulders. Squinting against the afternoon sun, she slipped on her sunglasses and saw her reflection in Lanny's mirrored ones.

"Here's my car." Lanny motioned toward a red Mustang convertible with the top down. His chest puffed out with pride.

"Uh, wait." Isabella swallowed. "I think I'll just follow you in my car. That way I can leave from there."

"I don't mind driving you and bringing you back." He twirled the keyring around his finger. His smile reappeared; one corner higher than the other. Not an evil smile. And not a salacious smile. Just crooked, that was all. No need for alarm.

"No, I insist," she said. "I'll take my car. In case we get separated, what's the address?" She held up her phone, ready to key it into Google Maps to search.

"Well, if you're sure. Okay. 1545 Laurel Way. Where's your car?"

She pointed to a silver Lexus parked half a block away. "Just wait for me here and then lead the way."

Once inside her car, she called Colt. He didn't pick up. "Hi, Colt. This is Isabella. This is getting ridiculous. I have left you so many messages. We were supposed to meet, remember? You can't even return my calls? What the…Never mind. Look, I found a guy who is taking me to Hondo. He knows where he is. The address is 1545 Laurel Way. Meet me there. I'll wait for you."

She slipped the pepper spray into her pants pocket. Her top hung loose over her hips and disguised the bulge. Probably not necessary at all, considering Lanny was slim and of average height, not a big muscled guy. Nothing like the mugger she fought with in New York.

Lanny lied about the five-minute drive. Fifteen minutes later, he pulled into the driveway of a small home, painted white with black shutters. A normal dwelling, nothing sinister about it. She got out of her car and met Lanny on the steps leading to the door.

He placed his hand on her arm. "Tell you what, I'll go around the back. Hondo likes to hang out there on the patio. I'll come let you in the front door. Just wait here for me."

She bit down on her lip. "Is Hondo a friend of yours?"

"Something like that."

Isabella nodded. While she waited on the doorstop, she checked out her surroundings. The house next door had a collection of yellowing newspapers in the driveway. She gulped.

Not a living creature in sight except for a cat sitting on the hood of a car across the street. She wiped her clammy hands and took a deep breath to calm her fast heartbeat. She worried she made a terrible mistake. But she dismissed her reservations, convincing herself they were unfounded. But still…Where was Colt and why hadn't he called her? Hopefully, he'd listened to his voicemail by now. She only waited a minute or two before Lanny opened the front door and ushered her in.

Her heart beat faster as she stepped inside. She stopped near the door. "What was that?"

Lanny turned to face her. "What? I didn't hear anything."

Isabella listened, waiting to hear the sound. She shrugged. "I must be hearings things." Again, she took a deep breath. "Well, is Hondo out back?" she asked.

"No. He must have gone somewhere. He probably went to the corner store for some cigarettes or soda. Let's have a drink while we wait. Hondo won't mind if we help ourselves."

Before she could reply, he placed his hand on her upper back. She stiffened and refused to allow him to steer her toward the kitchen.

Lanny removed his hand and held up both hands in an act of surrender. "Sorry. I see you're an independent woman. Don't need any help. That's fine. Let me fix you a drink to help you relax."

In the kitchen, he opened a cabinet and reached up for two shot glasses and a bottle of scotch.

"I don't want a drink, but I'll take some water though." Her throat was dry. Nerves again. She steeled herself to be brave. She'd confront Hondo, ask a few questions, and leave. How hard could that be? In and out. No big deal.

"Just water? Sure thing, sugar." This time, the crooked smile grew wider. He followed it with a wink. "He's got bottled water in the fridge."

He poured his drink and handed her the water. "Why don't we sit down and wait."

In the living room, Lanny sat down on the sofa and patted the cushioned seat next to him. There were no chairs. She had no choice but to join him. He smiled at her. "Here's the thing, darling, you never told me your name."

"It's Isabella." She ran her hand over her hair, feeling uncomfortable about revealing her name but not sure why.

"A pretty name for a pretty lady." He tapped his glass against her plastic bottle. "Cheers. To new friends. I think we could be friends fast, don't you?"

She pressed her lips together. "I don't mean to sound rude, but I'm not here to make friends. I'm here to find Hondo."

"Sure, sure. But we can get acquainted why we wait. No harm in that."

She swallowed hard. *Oh Lord, what have I gotten myself into?*

17

After Colt finished his business in the bathroom, he found Rocky sitting in a recliner taking another swig of whiskey. Only minutes ago, the bottle had been almost full. Now it was close to empty. A wildness danced in his eyes. Colt peered outside, searching for Pug's truck coming up the long winding drive, only to discover no sign of him. He turned from the window just as Rocky picked up his gun and pointed it at his chest.

In a gravelly voice, Rocky barked, "I changed my mind. I ain't waiting for Pug."

Colt's heart raced. He swallowed hard and held up his hand, palm out as though it could stop a bullet. "Wait a minute, Rocky. What the—"

Rocky pulled the slide back and loaded a round into the chamber. Aimed at Colt's chest, he gripped the gun with both hands.

"Whoa, whoa. Wait a minute. I've got something to say." Colt took one step back. "I know why you think you've seen me before. Put the gun down, and I'll tell ya."

"'Cause I'm right about you, that's why."

"No, here's the thing, Rocky, you might have known my brother. We look alike. Same eyes, same jawline. Only I'm better looking." Colt forced a laugh. "He was a cop. Maybe he busted you before."

"I don't care what bullshit you come up with. I'm taking you out." Rocky placed his finger on the trigger. The gun wobbled in his unsteady grip. He struggled to keep it aimed at Colt's chest.

Colt blurted out, "I said he *was* a cop! Streaker was his name." Rocky eased his finger off the trigger. "Listen to me, Rock. My brother got kicked off the force for doing drugs. He was mixed up in all kinds of shit until a drug dealer iced him."

"Oh yeah? Who?"

"A big black dude named Slick."

"Never heard of Slick. Hell, I ain't dumb. I knows what you're tryin' to pull. Tryin' to buy some time with made-up shit. Well, it ain't gonna work."

"It's true! What Rowdy said—it's true." Boone jumped in. At Rocky's chair, he bent over. Slowly, he wrapped his hand around the barrel of the gun. In his drunken stupor, Rocky put up no resistance when Boone pushed the barrel down, pointed at the floor.

"I heard something about it, Rocky," Boone said. "Something about his brother and that dude he said—Slick." Boone kept his hand on the barrel. "I sure didn't know Rowdy was related to him, but it makes sense. I heard about a former cop, some badass. Yeah, Streaker was his name all right. He got in a mess with Slick over something, I don't know what. Slick took him out."

Rocky scratched his chin with his free hand. "Yeah, come to think of it, I think your brother mighta arrested me years back. My memory's kinda foggy, but…hell, who knows?"

Rocky let Boone take the weapon. Boone released the magazine and pulled the slide back to eject the round. Colt bowed his head and rubbed the tightness from the back of his neck. He walked over to the window and looked up at the clouds, wanting to believe his brother was looking down on him and smiling.

Colt met Rocky's gaze. "Are we done here? Now that you know I ain't a cop, can we do a little business so I can go? I've got no more time for this crap. Are we good?"

"We're good." Rocky turned to Boone. "Git him his dope but count out his money 'fore he leaves."

"I see you still have trust issues, big man. Do yourself a favor and don't look in the mirror. In your decrepit state, you might want to shoot the ugly son-of-a-bitch staring back."

"You think you're something special."

"Funny, that's what your girl told me right after I screwed her."

Rocky thrashed about, trying to get out of his chair. He worked his way to the edge of the seat and fell back in his intoxicated state. "Git my gun, Boone. I'll kill 'im right now."

"Don't waste your ammo on me, big guy," Colt said. "C'mon, Boone, let's do this deal and then you can take me back to my car."

With the drugs in hand and relieved of the wad of cash in his pocket, Colt and Boone walked out. Minutes later, a shiny black Cadillac with Pug behind the wheel came up the driveway.

Pug stepped out of the car and squinted like he couldn't believe his eyes. "What you doin' here, Rowdy?"

"Oh, your cuz wanted to put me through a test. I aced it. He's got some serious trust issues."

"Yeah, well, he ain't right in the head. Guess he's jacked-up on somethin' by now, ain't he?"

"Yeah, he's pretty wasted. Boone is taking me back to my car. We took care of some business. Your money's inside."

"Where have you been, Pug?" Boone said, putting hands on hips. "We thought you'd be back by now."

"Yeah, well, that crazy Scooby got busted. I had to see about that. He ain't getting out. No bail. That means we're one man short when the shipment comes in."

Colt didn't miss a beat. "Not if you let me help you out."

Pug scratched his chin. "Well, I—."

"We need him, Pug." Boone hooked his thumbs over the waistband of his jeans. "That's a lot of heroin to unload, plus we gotta have lookouts. The faster we do it, the sooner we get out of there. We could use him. I trust him, don't you?"

"Rowdy, you seem like a straight-up dude, but—" Pug had a pained look like having to think hurt.

"If it'll make you feel any better, you can check with Bull. The two of us unloaded two hundred bricks in thirty minutes." Not the truth, but close to it. Two hundred kilos of cocaine, worth over five million dollars.

"No shit? Okay. You're in. The truck comes in on Friday. Got to be ready to move the product by four. Gotta be done before daylight."

"No problem. Where do I show up?"

Pug gave him the address. He added, "There's a gravel lot beside an abandoned building. Use to be a bar. Wait for us there."

"Is that where the truck's coming in?"

"Nah. Just meet us there."

§

Boone dropped Colt off at his car. Colt didn't get the exact location of the drug delivery, but he had enough intel to move forward. He couldn't wait to tell the task force team. As soon as Boone was out of his sight, he called the federal agent in charge of the operation.

The DEA's Special Agent Jim Roper took his call. "Where have you been? We've been looking high and low for you. Thought they might have whacked you. Damn, it's good to hear your voice, Colt."

"I talked myself out of getting killed. No biggie. I've got good news for ya. I'm in on the delivery. Drugs coming in on Friday and they're going to let me help unload. They're one man short. By the way, thanks for busting Scooby. That worked like a charm."

"Not me. That was all Samantha. She dreamed it up and the D.A. went along. Glad it worked." Roper paused when sirens drowned him out, letting Colt know he was somewhere outside. "So, where is the drop taking place?"

"Don't know."

"You said you knew."

"I said they cut me in, that's what I said. They told me to meet them somewhere and then we'll go from there to where the truck will be."

"But we need the location."

"Well, that's the best I can do. You're creative, Roper. Find a way for me to wear a tracker. I ain't wearing a wire, I'll tell you that right now."

"Okay, but we need to do a camera. Gotta have video."

"Then you figure it out. You got four days." Colt gave him the address where he was to meet Pug and his boys. "Gotta go. I'll give today's buy to Sam and let her bring them in for testing. I've got something else I need to do."

"Glad you're okay, Colt."

"Me too." Two girls pulled out of the fast-food parking lot in a yellow convertible with the top down. They waved at Colt as they turned onto the street. He got back to his call. "Hey, Roper. You're welcome."

"What?"

"Never mind." A thanks was too much to expect from the special agent.

Colt called Samantha. He told her to meet him at their usual rendezvous spot off Morehead Street. While he waited, he picked up six messages from Isabella, each one asking him to call and to meet. But the last call sounded different. She asked him to meet her on a side of town where she had no business being, said some guy was taking her to Hondo.

"Shit!" He ran his hand through his hair and clenched his jaw. Samantha pulled into the lot. He raced over to her car.

"Get in my car! Isabella Luca might be in trouble. Gotta get to her. Need you for this, Sam. The drugs can wait."

Samantha parked and hustled over. She hopped in the passenger seat. She was still buckling her seat belt when Colt screeched out of the parking lot and headed north. When traffic piled up, he said between clinched teeth, "Come on. Come on!" He slammed his hand on the steering wheel and turned on his emergency lights, using his siren at intersections.

"What the hell are you doing, Colt?" Samantha's eyes got wide. "This isn't a call. We can't just act like it's a Code 3. Not even our case."

"She's in trouble. I just know it." He gunned the engine and hit the switch for the siren, grateful that the drivers had enough sense to get out of his way.

A close call with a pickup truck had Samantha screaming. "Holy shit! He almost hit us! Did you see that clown? He came out of nowhere!" She sighed loudly and gripped her seat. "Damn, Colt, you've got to slow down or you'll get us both killed." She ran her fingers through her hair. "Do you think she's with Hondo? Is that it?"

"I have no idea, but we're going to find out."

18

Lanny wanted to get "acquainted" fast. Their thighs touched when he scooted closer to her. She slid away. Unfazed, he put his arm around the back of the sofa and shifted his body in her direction.

She hugged her arms to her chest and leaned forward, putting as much space between them as possible. "Maybe you should call Hondo and find out where he is," she said.

He patted her knee. "Relax. He'll be here soon. You're not in any hurry, are you?"

Why should she be? It might be better to wait for Colt before she confronted Brianna's ex-boyfriend. Maybe it was a good thing Hondo kept them waiting. But she hoped she could keep Lanny at arm's length until then.

Without warning, he reached over her to set his empty shot glass on the end table. In the process, his arm rubbed across her breasts. He gave her a silly grin. "Sorry about that, sugar. I guess I could have handed it to you to set down for me, but I like doing things for myself." After looking her up and down, he focused on her face. "Your eyes. God, you have beautiful eyes."

She gulped, not liking where this was headed. "Thanks."

When she tried to slide further away, he put his arm around her shoulders and kissed the side of her head. "I can't believe my day ended this way—sitting next to a pretty girl."

Isabella shot up from the sofa like a missile. And like rocket fuel, her anger burned hot. "How dare you!" His mouth gaped open. Did he really think she'd be okay with his pass? "This was a bad idea. I'll see Hondo another time when…" She didn't finish, deciding not to add, *when my cop friend can come with me.*

Lanny caught her before she reached the door. With his hand around her wrist, he yanked her around to face him, pulling her until she bumped against his chest. "Hey, baby, don't be like that. Come back and sit down. I couldn't help it. You lookin' so fine—how's a man supposed to resist?" He pulled her in tighter, leering at her. She worked her arms free and flailed them to get free. "Oh, so you're a tiger. That's okay, sugar. I like feisty women, the ones who put up a fight. Gets me all worked up."

"Let me go! Take your hands off me!"

"Stop making it so hard on yourself, girl. You're not going anywhere until I get what I want." He stuck his hand underneath Isabella's top and dug his fingers into her flesh. He tugged on her bra and squeezed her breast hard. She twisted, and turned, and screamed but couldn't work free. With all the power she could muster, she thrust her knee into his groin.

He yelped and released her, doubling over in pain and placing his hand over his crotch. "You bitch!" He lunged forward, grabbing her around the waist. He dragged her kicking and screaming to the sofa where he pushed her down. Before she had the chance to rise, he straddled her. With one hand, he squeezed her cheeks together making her lips pucker. "I'll teach you some manners. You think you're too good for me. Is that it, you stuck-up bitch? I'll show you what it's like to have a real man inside you, how 'bout that?"

Isabella squeezed her eyes shut. She was repulsed by his whiskey breath, his slobbering mouth on her cheek. His hands groped her all over, then slid between her legs, squeezing her crotch. He worked his hand up to the waistline of her pants. He yanked the clasp on her pants. When he couldn't get it to open, he slid his hand underneath her waistband. Her whole body trembled. Her heart knocked against her chest.

"Get off me! Stop! You're hurting me!" Nausea and faintness gripped her.

She was in a time-warp, traveling to another place, maybe hell, and in another dimension, another world. The visualization of the attack came to her in slow motion like a movie reel, starring herself, the victim of a sexual assault.

A loud boom quaked at the door. Colt charged inside. He rushed Lanny and yanked him up by the collar, sending him crashing into the wall. Not done, he pulled Lanny to his feet and pounded his jaw, his chest, his abdomen. Isabella heard each punch as it made contact. Lanny slumped forward and spit out blood. His arms hung limp at his sides.

A woman rushed inside and pulled on Colt's shirt.

"Colt! Enough! Stop!" she yelled.

Lanny fell forward onto Colt. He jumped back and Lanny collapsed to the floor.

"Are you okay?" Colt rushed to Isabella's side.

She tugged her top down and nodded. She ran her hand over her cheek and smoothed her hair back in place. Too stunned to speak or even cry, she could only stare at Colt and the woman. She cupped her hands over her face and cried. Colt gathered her in his arms and rubbed his hand over her back.

"It's okay. It's okay. I've got you," he whispered.

She wiped away her tears and took a deep breath. "I came here—um, well, I came here because he said he'd take me to Hondo. I should've trusted my gut. I should never have—"

Colt patted her leg and stood up. He went over to Lanny who continued to moan on the floor. One eye was swollen shut. Blood ran from a cut on his lip. Colt kicked him in the side. "Hey you, tell her the truth." Lanny cowered, shielding his face with his arm and expecting another blow. "Asshole, I'm talking to you. Tell her!"

Holding his stomach and winching, Lanny lifted his head off the floor. "I don't know any Hondo."

"I thought Hondo lived here." Isabella looked up at Colt. "He made me think…So, this is his place!"

"Yeah, he brought you here to rape you." Colt wiped sweat from his brow. His thumb came back with a drop of blood.

Isabella covered her face. "Oh my God! I was stupid to trust that guy."

Colt took Isabella's hand and pulled her to her feet. "Come on, Isabella. let's get you out of here." At the same time, they stared at the other woman in the room. She had hands on her hips and had not spoken since she told Colt to stop. "Isabella, this is Samantha. She's my partner," Colt said. "When I got your call, we came as fast as we could."

With his arm around Isabella's shoulder, Colt led her to the door where they were met by two uniformed officers. He widened his eyes. "How the hell?"

"I called it in. Right after you went inside," Samantha said. "Someone around here has to be the adult. This isn't the wild west, you know, where we take justice in our own hands."

Colt pressed his lips together and nodded. "Cool. Okay, guys, cuff that piece of shit. Charge is sexual assault. I'll write it up when I get back. Put him in a holding cell for now." He studied Isabella's face and said, "Do you need medical attention?"

"No, I'm fine. Just shaken up a bit." She pushed her hair back and met his gaze. "Can you take me back to my hotel? I think if I rest—"

"Sorry, songbird, I've gotta take you to headquarters. Get your statement."

She frowned and shook her head. "No. I'm not pressing charges. I just want to forget this—"

"It's out of your hands. You have a visible bruise on your jaw, which means he's going to jail. *I'm* filing charges. Besides, actions have consequences, and maybe this dirtbag will think twice before he does this to another woman."

"I've been trying to reach you all day. You didn't even return my calls."

Colt glanced up at the ceiling and sighed. "Sorry about that. I've been detained most of the day."

Isabella gave him a puzzled look.

With a wink, he said, "I wouldn't want to bore you with the details."

§

It was near the end of the day. Tara logged off her computer. She couldn't wait to get home and change into something more comfortable. Until five o'clock rolled around, she scrolled through Facebook on her phone and hit "like" for a few new posts. She glanced at the clock, frowned, and opened Instagram. Only a few more minutes before she could finally leave.

She sensed someone's presence and startled when she looked up from her phone. *Uh-oh.* She offered a sheepish smile at her supervisor. "Uh, Lauren. Hi, there! I got everything done, just like you asked me to. The report is ready for tomorrow's meeting. I just need to make copies in the morning."

"Listen to me very carefully, Tara." Lauren scanned the office area and although no one was in sight, she kept her voice low. "I want you to go home and pack a suitcase. Your life is in danger. If you do as I say, I can save you."

"What?" She pushed her glasses further up her nose and widened her eyes. "What are you talking about?"

"The person who killed Brianna is now after you. Don't ask me how I know, I just do."

"Is this for real?" Even as she said it, she knew. The man at Molly's Fresh Market, of course! He wanted to question her and even blocked her car from leaving. She'd been right to be frightened of him. Now she was glad she got away when she did.

"I'm serious, Tara. Don't speak to anyone. Just go home and pack some clothes. I'll pick you up. We're both leaving town—getting help from someone who can protect us."

"I don't know anything. Why would someone—"

"I'll explain later. There's no time. Hurry! Leave now. I'll pick you up in about thirty minutes. And don't tell anyone. I mean it, Tara, tell no one. Understand?"

Lauren's jaw tightened. The brightness in her eyes faded. The face Tara always admired lost its glow. She'd never seen Lauren like this, grim and somber. What she told Tara was for real, not some sick joke. Tara stayed stationary, paralyzed by fear.

But Lauren prodded her to move, placing her hand on her arm and helping her to stand. "Go now, Tara. I'm asking you to trust me. Please."

Tara gulped and nodded. She clutched her purse to her chest and felt dizzy. A wave of nausea led her to press her trembling fingers to her mouth.

Oh, God, please help me.

A half hour later in the living room of her apartment, Tara stood at the window watching for Lauren's car. The view outside of trees, sky, clouds, flowers in bloom, serene and pretty, did nothing to soothe her. Tara was a bundle of nerves, her stomach in a knot. The episode of her encounter with the man at Molly's Fresh Market played and replayed in her head.

Once Lauren's car drove up, she allowed herself to breathe. If they got away, maybe, *just maybe*, she'd be safe, bringing an end to her hellish nightmare.

19

Colt handed the keys to his Charger to Samantha while he got behind the wheel of the Lexus belonging to Isabella's dad. His face, a stony mask, until his lips spread into a grin.

"You know, you remind me of myself in my twenties—naive and stupid."

Although it was an insult, it was accurate. She stayed quiet.

He took his eyes from the road, glowered at her. "Didn't you know that area is no place for a woman alone? What were you thinking?"

"I told you already," she said, exhaling a loud sigh. "I couldn't get hold of you. I waited for a while, but then—"

"You should've waited longer. If I hadn't shown up when I did—hell, you know what he'd have done to you. He's got a record, Isabella. Six counts. Assault on a female. Sexual assault. Kidnapping. This guy's a piece of work."

Isabella pressed her fingertips over her mouth. What he said, sickened her. She couldn't breathe. How could she have been so foolish? "You're right. I should have known better."

"Sam and I have some feelers out—people looking for Hondo. He's going to surface, believe me. A cockroach crawls out every now and then."

Isabella shifted her attention to the view out the passenger window. Passing the shopping mall meant the hotel would soon come into view on the next block. She set her purse in her lap, relieved the lecture was about to end.

Instead of dropping her off, Colt whipped the car into a parking space. "I'll go up with you. Make sure everything's okay."

Her mouth fell open. "Are you serious? I don't need an escort."

He switched off the ignition, pulled out the keys, and handed them to Isabella. "Just to be on the safe side. Lemme tell Sam to wait here."

"Okay. Whatever."

Colt scowled. "You think I'm a hard ass, don't you?"

"I think you're overprotective."

"Here's the thing, songbird. I'm actually easy to get along with as long as you do everything my way."

She rolled her eyes. "Got it."

Colt escorted Isabella through the lobby and up to the fourth floor. At her room, he inserted the key card. "Wait here," he said. "I'm going to check it out first."

While he walked around, she checked email messages on her phone but found nothing that couldn't wait until later.

He returned and said, "Want to meet for breakfast in the morning? I'll give you my take on the toxicology report and we can discuss a strategy."

"Yes, that would be great. Where and when?"

"Samantha and I usually have breakfast at this little diner on Kings Drive called Dominion. Do you know where it is?"

She nodded.

"Meet us there at eight. And songbird, leave it to me and Sam, we'll find Hondo."

"What if he won't tell us anything?"

"He will. I have ways to get him to talk," he deadpanned. As he turned to leave, he gave a half-hearted wave with his back to her.

After she closed the door and collapsed on the bed, she checked the messages on her phone. There were messages from her sister, her mom, and Landon. *Landon? Again?*

With his name and number displaying on the screen, she tapped the call symbol, but before it could ring, she aborted the call. Hearing his voice again after such a long time, a man she once loved deeply, might send her into a tailspin, bursting into tears. After today's ordeal, she couldn't handle any more emotional drama.

She listened to his voice message. "Isabella!" Landon's voice sounded anxious, out of character for his easy-going persona. "I'm so very sorry. I just heard about Brianna. Man, that is awful. So sad. I'm worried about you. I know how close you two were. Listen, I've been trying to reach you for weeks, but you haven't returned any of my calls. I finally got hold of your sister, Kristen. She said you're in Charlotte and your dad's in the hospital. My God, you shouldn't have to deal with this alone. I'm actually in Charlotte now on business. I'm tied up with a conference but in a day or two, I'll call you. I know you have your family here, but still…Anyway, it's important I see you. There's something I need to tell you in person. So, I'll call you when I'm free. Take care, Isabella. Bye now."

She appreciated his concern, especially since he never liked Brianna. His comment about wanting to tell her something in person piqued her interest. Her heart leaped with the prospect he wanted her back. Not that she'd take him back. Still, she felt flattered.

The first time they met, she'd already felt a buzz from two glasses of wine, a warm, fuzzy feeling that made talking to the handsome stranger a natural thing to do. He smiled at her and pointed to the wall behind the bar. "They forgot to turn the clock forward for daylight savings time. That means I have more time to get to know you." She laughed and said, "Oh, really? What makes you think I want to get to know you?" He looked deeply in her eyes and said, "Maybe you don't, but let's not rush to judgment."

One thing bothered her. Did Landon want to reboot their relationship now that Brianna was out of the picture? No longer an obstacle?

§

Lauren stepped out of her car and left the driver's side door hanging open. She waited for Tara to lock the door to her house. Seeing the terror in Tara's eyes put a knot in her stomach. It was her responsibility to get Tara to safety, and the burden of that weighed heavily on her.

She pointed to the opened trunk. "Hurry, Tara. Put your stuff in there. We need to go."

Tara's hand trembled when she reached up to adjust the frames of her glasses, "Did anyone follow you?" At some point, she'd tell Lauren about the guy at Molly's Fresh Market.

"I don't think so. It's better if we get to the airport early. My brother will pick us up when we land."

Tara dropped her suitcase and travel bag into the trunk and closed the lid. "Where are we going?"

"Boston." Lauren fidgeted with her hands. "No more talk. Get in the car."

They settled into their seats and Lauren started the ignition. She put the car in reverse and glanced at the backup screen. A vehicle pulled in behind her Lexus sedan.

She slammed on brakes. "Oh, no!" Her heart pounded.

"What is it?" Instead of looking at the screen, Tara peered out the back window.

"We're too late." Lauren pressed her hands against her temples.

A man jumped out and rushed to Lauren's side of the car. He pounded on the window. "Get out! Get out now! I mean it!"

Paralyzed with fear, she stayed behind the wheel.

From behind his back, he pulled a gun. He tapped the glass with the barrel. "I said get out. Now!"

Lauren shut off the engine and slowly opened the door. Stepping out, her legs felt like jelly. Her whole body shook. Her heart continued to race. She glanced over at Tara, who appeared close to passing out. Poor girl. She failed her. Lauren leaned against the car just to support herself.

The man got in her face. "Thought you could get away from me, did you now? Wrong!"

At gunpoint, he forced them into his vehicle. "Leave your things. You won't need them."

"But my purse—my phone," Lauren said.

"Leave them! Move, dammit!"

They rode for at least thirty minutes, away from the city, until he turned onto a gravel road off the main highway. Soon, they faced a two-story brick home surrounded by woods. Behind the house, a dock led out to a large lake. Lauren scanned their surroundings, seeing if she and Tara could somehow escape. But the area was desolate, no other dwellings. If they screamed for help, no one would hear them.

He led them inside and up the stairs to a corner room with a window. He shoved them inside, and without saying a word, he left. Now that he was gone, Tara sunk down on the floor and supported her back against the wall.

Unable to stay still, Lauren walked around. She ended up at the window. "Maybe we can get out this way."

She tugged, pulled, and strained, but the window was sealed shut. Even if she opened it, the drop was about thirty feet onto brick pavers. The ceiling was solid and had no access into the attic.

The room was bare, not even a blanket to form a makeshift bed. Their only convenience was a bathroom supplied with one towel and toilet paper, nothing else. Not even a bar of soap.

"This place is a prison." Lauren wiped away a tear and bowed her head. "Oh God, please help us."

20

Colt got an unexpected call from Kate. Hearing her velvety voice was just what he needed after his crappy day.

"Maddie decided she wants to have a family dinner for her birthday," Kate said. "She's having a sleepover this weekend, but she wanted a family thing—just you and me—on her actual birthday. I know it's short notice, but can you come? It would mean a lot to her."

From almost getting killed and fighting off a rapist, he was beat, but seeing Maddie—and Kate if he was being totally honest—gave him new energy. "Sure. I'd love to. What time?"

"Can you be here in an hour?"

"That I can do." His smile grew broader. "Hey, I haven't gotten her a present yet. Any suggestions?"

"Don't worry about it. Just seeing you is enough."

But he didn't want to show up empty handed. On his way, he stopped at a drug store and bought a greeting card, a silly one she'd like. He also purchased gift cards for iTunes and Starbucks, a safe bet for a girl turning thirteen. The fact she was now officially in her teens made him gulp. His baby was growing up too fast.

At the door, Maddie bounced into his arms. "Dad! I knew you'd come!"

He kissed her cheek. "Happy birthday, sweetheart."

Seeing her triggered a fear. Suppose some jerk did to his daughter what that predator did to Isabella? He'd beat the asshole within an inch of his life, or worse, kill the son-of-a-bitch.

Kate walked up behind Maddie. He hoped her smile meant she was glad to see him. Some women didn't look good in yoga pants but not the case with Kate. She had on the kind that ended right below the knee, a teal-colored pair. Her matching top had a neckline dipping just low enough to be a tease.

"Colt, so glad you could come." A warm feeling washed over him at the way she tilted her head to one side and smiled. Sexy is what it was.

From the kitchen came the aroma of spices and tomato sauce. Without even having to ask, he knew she'd made her to-die-for lasagna, Maddie's favorite. "Smells wonderful, Kate. I've missed your home-cooked meals."

"I bet you have." She grinned, no hint of sarcasm.

Maddie grabbed his arm and pulled him toward the kitchen. "Hey, guys, let's eat. I'm starved!" She smiled at Colt. "Save room for dessert, Dad. We're having my favorite cupcakes in the whole wide world—from that French bakery—the one at the shopping center. Just wait 'til you try them. Oh my God! They're the best ever!"

After dinner, Maddie left the table to answer a call from a friend. "Hurry back, Maddie," Kate called out. "The party's not over. Cupcakes and presents, remember?"

Kate and Colt shared a laugh watching their daughter saunter off, chatting away with the phone to her ear. Kate refilled their wine glasses. She brought her leg up and set her heel on the seat. She clinked her goblet to his. "To Maddie, the birthday girl."

"To Maddie," Colt said. "That's one thing we got right."

"Yes, we're blessed. She's a great kid." Kate wrapped her hand around the base of the glass and brought it up to her lips for a sip. She swirled the wine around, watching it with great interest. "Can you believe thirteen years ago we were at the hospital waiting through a long labor. I was screaming and you looked like a scared rabbit, not knowing what to do."

"I remember it well, but maybe a little differently. I wasn't *that* scared. I'd almost brought another baby into the world a few months before Maddie was born."

"What are you talking about?"

"That time I was on patrol and stopped at a minute market for a snack, and a woman went into labor. The ambulance got there just as the baby was crowning. I've never been so happy to see medics in my life."

Kate smiled and nodded. A lull in the conversation put Colt at a loss, not knowing what to say to fill the void. He studied her profile as she aimlessly stared out the window. The years had been kind to Kate. She was as pretty now as she was in their early years of marriage. She took her gaze from the window and locked eyes with him. Her intense look puzzled him. Her smile, gone. She brought her leg down with both feet on the floor and her hands folded in her lap.

"Colt, there's no easy way to ask this, so I'll just come right out with it."

She pressed her lips together and crossed her legs, her foot almost touching his outer thigh.

He tapped down his impetuous desire to prop it in his lap. "What is it you want to say, Kate?"

"Are you giving Maddie beer?"

"What?" Taken aback by her question, he gave her a sour look. "No. Hell no! What makes you think that?"

"I found two bottles of Yuengling stashed in her closet. I thought you might have given it to her, or she could have taken it from your car or something."

"No. She probably got it from someone with a fake ID."

Kate shrugged. "Okay. I'll ask her, but then she's going to want to know what I was doing snooping around in her closet."

"You're the mom. You have a right to snoop. Don't let her play that card. She's too young to be drinking."

"Glad you see it that way."

Her half-smile told him he'd said what she needed to hear. Of course, nowadays, he had to be on his toes, saying and doing the right things or else she'd carry out her threat and deny him visitation. If he was the one who gave the beer to Maddie, it would be just a matter of time before her lawyer got in the picture.

"Are you going to tell me how you got that cut?"

Kate's words jarred him. She was already on to another topic. "What?"

She pointed at his forehead. "Your brow. How did you get that cut?"

"Oh, who knows? It's nothing."

His lie lingered, intensified by the silence that followed. Her caramel-colored eyes lost their luster. No doubt he'd disappointed her. Already, he missed her sexy smile.

He leaned forward and placed his hand over hers. When their eyes met, he sensed her longing, but not a sensual one. He'd seen it before, and he knew what it meant. She longed for him to be honest, not shut her out. If only she understood. He did it to protect her. To protect Maddie. They didn't have to get dragged into the messiness of his job. But if he were to ever win back her favor, he had to come clean.

"Kate, the truth is I got in a scrape with some scumbag who was trying to sexually assault a woman. It turned out okay. I'm fine, but you should've seen him."

His laughter fell flat. But he liked what she did next. She brought her hand to his cheek. "Oh, Colt, you make me worry. Maddie would be devastated if anything happened to you."

He bit down on his lip to keep from asking, *What about you, Kate? Would you be devastated, too?* Sitting there with her eyes staying on him conjured a strange mixture of joy and torture. His desire for her overwhelmed him. He longed to bring her into his arms, hold her tightly, kiss her lips.

Maddie saved him from falling into a pit of unfulfilled lust. She came up behind him fast, bumping his chair and sticking her cellphone in his face. "Look, Dad—look at what Justine posted on Instagram about this guy in our class. Zach is hysterical, don't you think? He looks like a jumping monkey. He's crazy!"

For the remainder of the night, Maddie became his safety net, a distraction that prevented him from making a fool of himself and begging Kate for another chance. He kept up a grand pretense of having fun eating cake, opening presents. In truth, he dreaded the moment he had to leave them. He'd walk out of the very house he and Kate moved into on their fifth wedding anniversary. God, he loved that house. Then he'd get in his car and go back to his crappy apartment where even the plants looked sad.

At the door, he gave Maddie a kiss on the cheek. He wasn't quite sure what to do about Kate, but in the end, he gave her a hug. She took both his hands in hers and gave them a little squeeze. "Take care of yourself, Colt."

"Sure. I gotta come back to my girls." He intentionally went bold and made the last word plural instead of singular. Totally worth it when she smiled back at him. He got that tingling feeling again. All the way to his car, he couldn't stop grinning.

As soon as he settled comfortably behind the wheel, his phone rang. Ashley's name showed on the phone's screen. What in the hell did she want? The last time he saw her, she kicked him out of her apartment.

"Hey, Ash. What's up?"

"Colt, I'm so glad I caught you. Can't talk long. I'm on my way out. You should know—well, here's the thing—I'm late."

"Late for what?"

He heard her loud exasperated breath. What a drama queen. "I'm late-late. You know."

"Y-you mean you—you could—I mean, you might be pregnant?"

"Could be."

He ran his hand down his face. "Oh, shit."

21

A key clanked in the deadbolt lock. Lauren and Tara wrapped their trembling arms around each other. Monster, as they now called him, strutted in, giving them a smug smile. His handsome features contradicted the ugliness that dwelled within.

"Hello again, ladies." With his looks and velvety voice, any unknowing person could be drawn in by his charm. He held up a paper bag and said, "See, I brought you food, just like I promised. I hope you like burgers and fries. Personally, I never eat the stuff." He patted his stomach. "That's how I stay so trim."

Lauren glared at him. "What's going to happen to us? Wh-where are we?"

Lauren released her hold on Tara. The young woman dropped to the floor and curled into a ball, too scared even to look up at him.

More angry than frightened, Lauren put her hands on her hips and stood inches away from him. "Answer me! What are you going to do with us?"

"I think you know. You are both a liability to me, which makes you both expendable, unnecessary."

"Let us go. We won't say anything. You can leave the country and go wherever you want. We'll stay quiet."

"For how long? No, that's not acceptable." He walked over to them carrying the take-out bag. The scent of fast food almost made Lauren queasy. He reached in and pulled out the wrapped burgers and when they refused to take them, he set them down on the floor. "Have it your way, ladies. Eat later then."

Monster squatted down close to Tara and pushed the pink section of raven hair from her eyes, knocking his knuckle against her cat-eye frames. She recoiled and scooted over behind Lauren, whimpering.

"Leave her alone!" Lauren shouted.

"What is wrong with you, Tara?" he said. "Why are you always so skittish?" His smirk stayed present even as he stood up. "Well, I must go, ladies. I just stopped by with your dinner and to make sure you two are behaving yourselves." He glanced from one to the other and added, "You'll have company soon."

"You're talking about Isabella, aren't you?" Lauren said.

He exhaled loudly. "She's trouble. Just like her sister."

Lauren shook her fists at him. "I hope you rot in hell!" She leaned forward and spit on his shirtfront. His backhanded slap made stars flash before her eyes. She stumbled backwards and hit her head against the wall. He lunged forward, pressing against her. She had no mobility, no way to break free. His hand braced her head like a vice, squeezing tightly, digging into her jaw.

"You don't want to make me angry. I've been polite so far, but you're pushing your luck, Lauren."

He walked back to stand near where Tara remained on the floor, hugging her knees to her chest. He bumped her leg with the toe of his shoe. "Hang in there, kid. This will be over soon."

He turned his back to them and walked toward the door. Lauren narrowed her eyes and kept them on him as he walked out and locked them in their prison.

On a lark, she unbuttoned her linen blouse.

Tara gaped at her. "What are you doing?"

"I've got an idea."

"I hope it's a good one. I'm so scared, Lauren. He's going to kill us! As soon as he's back, he'll do it!" Tara sobbed, covering her face with her hands. "Oh, God, what are we going to do?"

"I'm scared, too, but we have to stay calm, figure out something. No one is coming for us." She pushed the blouse off her shoulders and tugged it down her arms. She laid it neatly on the floor, then removed her bra.

Tara's raised brow was a question.

"I'm wearing a push-up bra. It has wires," Lauren explained. "Maybe I can pick the lock."

Tara frowned and shook her head. "I don't think so."

Lauren patted her arm. "Well, we have to try."

Even if it worked, what then? They were somewhere on the outskirts of the city, in a rural part of the county on the shores of a lake. When their tormenter led them inside, Lauren didn't see any other dwellings, only woods. Wherever they were, it was isolated. Even if she had her phone, she doubted it would pick up a signal. Still, having it would give her some comfort. She hated leaving it behind in her car.

Lauren tried to punch a hole in her bra by forcing the wire through the fabric. But it wasn't working. She took a break and placed her hand on Tara's arm. "Please don't cry."

Tara brushed her fingertips over her wet cheeks. "I don't want to die."

"Me either. Especially not this way."

§

Colt got little sleep, thanks to Ashley. He clung to the hope her announcement of "might be pregnant" evolved into "not." She told him she'd get an EPT kit the next day and make sure. If only she'd taken the test *before* she called, it might have saved him from tossing and turning all night.

He wasn't prepared to be a daddy again, at least, not with her. Ashley was a good time, a good lay, but that was it. He doubted she had a speck of maternal instinct in her DNA. And the truth was, he hadn't been that great a father himself. Absent half the time.

But as he got in the shower, he admitted how he'd someday like to have a son, someone to carry forth the Jessup name. Most likely, Maddie would marry, and she'd take the name of her spouse. His only sibling was a half-brother, a Johnson. He and Streaker were quite a pair, wild and crazy, like broncos that could never be tamed. Jessup and Johnson, they were. If he'd gone into the P.I. business with his brother, they could have called it that. Or Johnson and Jessup. Fair enough. After all, Streaker was the oldest.

He put the implication of fatherhood out of his mind when he met Samantha at the diner for breakfast. She gave him one of her looks with the arched brow and a weird thing she did with her lips, something between a scowl and a smile. He knew what it meant: *You've kept me waiting again, asshole.*

"'Morning," he muttered as he slid into their usual booth in the back corner.

"I already ordered for you."

"Suppose I want something different today?"

"Well, you don't, so shut-up and listen." She arranged the packets of sugar in the holder while their server filled their coffee cups. When she walked away, Samantha continued, "We're supposed to be meeting with Roper's team this morning, and you told Isabella Luca to join us for breakfast. What the hell were you thinking? We don't have time for this. It's not our case, Colt. How many times do I have to say it?"

"How's it going to hurt if we just have a brief meeting with her? Hell, she deserves it. Spence isn't going to help her. He's already closed the case. Marked it suicide because he doesn't give a shit."

"Okay, okay." Samantha tapped her spoon against the side of her cup. "Well, where is she?"

"She'll be here." He glanced at the door and smiled. "See. She's coming in right now." He took a sip of coffee.

Samantha frowned. "Either you have a big heart, or you have a thing for her."

"Now that pisses me off." He set the cup in the saucer with a loud clank. "Your remark is downright insulting. You know me better than that. I'm doing this because her sister was murdered, and I'm sure of it."

Isabella's arrival at the table ended the discussion. Samantha slid over to make room. "Good morning, Isabella. Have a seat. I hope you're feeling better today."

"Yes, I'm still a little shaken from yesterday. Sorry I'm late. My mom called just as I was leaving. She told me my dad's getting out of the hospital today."

"Glad to hear it." Still angry at Samantha, Colt tapped the side of his cup with his index finger, keeping his eyes downcast and watching the steam rise. "Go ahead and order, Isabella, and then we'll get down to business."

Isabella gave her order to the server. She looked across the table at Colt. "You said you'd tell me your thoughts on Brianna's death."

He exhaled a long breath, studying her face and anticipating her reaction to what he planned to say. "Well, I think the toxicology report is very telling. Whoever gave Brianna the drink knew what it would take to kill her. Just enough to do the job. The right amount of a lethal combination that could be covered up with enough sweetness from fruit juice and enough pungency from liquor so it wouldn't be detected."

Isabella pressed her lips together and showed little emotion. "That's what I thought," she said. "My mom showed me the report. Sure, Brianna could have taken a pain killer like oxy but not a diazepam drug like Valium. And I have never seen her take a sleep agent either."

"The empty bottle of Ambien was staged to make us think she took sleeping pills to kill herself." Colt picked up a fork and rolled it around between his fingers. "The pineapple juice in her fridge was half gone, which makes sense if she had more than one drink, but it only took one to kill her. I'm thinking whoever did it, drank with her. Probably brought the drink mixings with them. It had to be someone she knew well."

"Brianna wasn't a big fan of mixed drinks. Too sweet for her. She preferred wine or beer." Isabella added cream to her coffee and stirred. "In fact, I've never known her to fix a drink at home. But I will say, she'd sometimes order a margarita or a Russian mule when we'd go to a bar."

"Whoever gave her the drink was someone she trusted, which right now points to Whit Drummond, aka Hondo," Colt said. "From what we saw at the house, it looks like he was there and left in a hurry."

"So how do we find him?"

Colt opened his mouth to respond when Samantha's phone rang.

"Holy crap!" She glanced at the screen. Her eyes widened. "This might be the break we've been looking for." She put the phone to her ear. "Delano speaking." She bit down on her lower lip as she listened. "He's there now?" She locked eyes with Colt. "Got it. Be there in ten."

She slipped the phone in her purse. "We got him. Hondo's at a pawn shop right now. If we hurry, we'll catch him."

Colt slid out of the booth and almost collided with the server holding a tray with their food. He grabbed a biscuit and sausage patty off a plate and took a bite. "Isabella, wait here. We'll be back."

"No, I'm coming too." Isabella scooted to the edge of the seat and stood up. She slung her purse strap over her shoulder. "I want to face that guy."

"No time to argue. Let's do this." Colt motioned for them to step up their pace. Once outside, he said, "We'll take one car. Sam, you drive."

At the pawn shop, Samantha pulled alongside the building. Colt hopped out while the car was still slowing to a stop. He made a beeline for the door.

The pawnbroker grimaced and shook his bald head. "You just missed him. He got suspicious when I went in the back room and called you. I told him I had to get my magnifying glass to examine the watch he brought in. Make sure it was in good condition. Five minutes later, I come back to the counter and he'd left. Took the watch with him, too. It wasn't a cheap one. He had a Rolex."

"Any idea which way he went?"

The pawnbroker scratched his head, thinking. "I'd say he went that way." He pointed in the opposite direction they came. "Toward the shopping center. He was jittery as all hell, acting weird."

"Okay, thanks for the call. Let us know if he comes back." Colt opened the door with his backside and came face to face with the two women.

"Well?" Samantha said.

"We just missed him. He's headed toward the shopping center."

"Could be he's going to Home Depot," Samantha said. "That's where a security camera showed him carrying power tools out the door without paying."

"Guess he's back at it. Let's go see," Colt said.

By the time they pulled up in front of Home Depot, Colt had Hondo's mugshot displaying on his phone. Inside the store, he showed it to two cashiers who only shook their heads. He told one of them to call security. He and Isabella set off in one direction and Samantha in another, covering as much territory as possible.

"You stay behind me," he said to Isabella. With excitement dancing in her eyes, she kept pace with his quick steps. They strolled up the aisle displaying circular saws. No sign of him. Colt led Isabella one aisle over in the electric drill section. Even though he had his back to them, Colt recognized Hondo's tall, skinny physique and stringy, blond ponytail. He struggled to fit a drill into a canvas bag.

Colt tapped him on the shoulder. "Put that back."

Hondo jumped. He dropped the drill on his foot and howled, hopping around on one leg. Colt picked up the drill and tossed it back on the shelf with a loud clank. Hondo's eyes darted nervously from Colt to Isabella. "Holy shit!" He squinted and rubbed his eyes. "Br—Br—Brianna? Naaah, can't be. Oh, man!" He blinked rapidly and said, "I'm messed up bad, seeing things."

"Think you're seeing a ghost?" Colt leaned his shoulder against a shelf and stuffed his hands in his pockets. "That's Brianna's sister. She's been wanting to talk to you. Me too. Where've you've been, bro?"

"Brianna, oh, man, poor girl. I didn't kill her, Colt. Y'gotta believe me. Didn't do it, man."

"Did I say you did?"

"No way I did it. I wasn't myself that night, but not me, man. I-I —"

"You what? Talk to me."

"I-I found her like that. I got out of there real quick. No way I'm going down for murder."

Isabella and Colt exchanged a look. If the twitchy guy was to be believed, their theory was right. Hondo had been at the crime scene. But before they could question him further, a hefty security guard stormed toward them, frowning. Right behind him, Samantha gave Colt an apologetic shrug.

The guard crossed his arms and scowled at Hondo. "I heard you were looking for this slime-ball. He's been here before and he's banned from the store. You two are cops so charge him with breaking and entering *and* possession of stolen goods. I'm tired of these lowlifes coming here and stealing merchandise. All's they want is money to buy their drugs. I see it all the time."

Colt stepped closer to the guard and crossed his arms. "Well, here's the thing, he didn't steal anything. He might have thought about it, but he changed his mind. He's going downtown with us."

"Hmph, okay then. Better charge him with something though." The guard glared at Hondo and narrowed his eyes. "I don't ever want to see you around here again. You hear me?"

Hondo nodded and hung his head low.

Colt took Hondo by the elbow and steered him toward the exit, letting the others trail behind. "Let's go have a little talk, my friend."

"Wait! Where—where you taking me? I don't wanna go to jail. I'll get real sick in there. You know I will, Colt. We had a deal, 'member?"

"Yeah, we did, but you haven't lived up to your end. In fact, Hondo, you're the worst C.I. I've ever had. The worst."

"Can't go anywhere with you. Something I need—gotta have. Don't take me to jail. I'm in bad shape." Hondo held out his hand. "See there. I got the shakes. It's gonna get worse. I need my stuff, man. Need it now!"

"Relax, dude. I'm taking you to my office. That car over there—where we can have a little chat. It won't take long."

Samantha's car was parked curbside in a restricted area. Colt opened the door for him, and Hondo fell into the front passenger seat. Colt walked around the front of the car and slid in behind the wheel, adjusting the seat back. Samantha and Isabella got in the back. With the engine on and the A/C cranked up, Colt turned sideways to begin his interrogation.

"Okay, Hondo, tell us everything about that night. What you saw—when you left. Start talking."

"It's like this—Oh, Lord, I think I'm a'gonna be sick." He bent forward and covered his face with his hands.

"You're fine, Hondo. Start talking or you're going downtown."

"Okay, okay. Damn you, Colt." Hondo ran his trembling hand down his face. "It's like this, I was in the kitchen, getting some water and then…Oooh, I'm sick, man. Don't you care?" Hondo shook his head and grimaced, staring out the side window.

"Go on. You went to get water, then what happened?"

Hondo rubbed his hands back and forth over his knees as he rocked. "Brianna looked out the front window. She said to me, 'I've got company. Better go. He shouldn't see you here.' So, that's what I did. I left."

"Did you see who it was?"

"Nah, didn't look. Didn't wanna know." Hondo bent forward and hugged his abdomen. Beads of sweat dotted his forehead. "I got outta there—real quick."

"What about a car? Did you see a vehicle in the driveway? Hear a car door close?"

"No, I told you already, Colt. I didn't see shit. I went out the back, across the neighbor's yard and up the street. I took a bus downtown."

"What time was it when you left?"

"I dunno. I can't think, man. Hurt too bad."

"Was it light outside? Already dark?"

Hondo cupped his hands over his face. "I told ya, I dunno. Long time ago, okay? Can I go now?" He held his stomach and moaned. "Oh, man, I'm sick. I'm tellin' ya."

"Concentrate, Hondo," Colt said. "And then what? You came back?"

"Yeah, yeah. I came back. That's where I've been staying—with Brianna. I saw her lying on the floor." He wiped his forehead with the back of his hand and jerked his leg up and down. "I thought she was asleep. Looked like it, know what I'm saying? Real peaceful like. I didn't wanna disturb her, but-but, well, I thought she should go to bed, so I shook her. But she wouldn't wake up. Then, I realized she wasn't breathing. No pulse, no nothing. She was dead, man. Cold as ice."

"Why didn't you call 911? That would have been the decent thing to do."

"And let the cops think I did it? No way!"

"You could have called me, Hondo. Don't you trust me? I thought we were cool."

"It's complicated, bro. There are some things you don't know about. Not you either, Detective Sam. My life is in danger."

"Is that why you've been hiding out?"

"Yeah, yeah, 'course. It's on a count of Big Jack—he wants to kill me. Thinks I stole his drugs. I was set up by some asshole, and now he's hellbent on killing me."

"I need you to go downtown with me and tell this to Detective Spencer. He thinks Brianna killed herself. I need him to re-open the case. See if it was murder."

"Can't, Colt. No way. Uh-huh, no can do." Hondo folded over like a waffle-iron and moaned. "I'm gonna be sick, man. You gotta let me go. Gotta have it. I'm dying, man. Dying, I'm tellin' ya. Please, Colt. Gotta—"

"I know, Hondo. You need your juice. You're useless without it."

"What I told you—it's worth twenty, right? I can't talk no more. Oh, Jesus, I feel like shit. Sick as a dog. Have some mercy on me. Please, Colt. I'm begging you, man."

Colt stretched out his leg to reach inside his pocket. He unfolded some bills and selected a twenty. When Hondo tried to snatch it from him, he drew it back. "Nope, not yet. You have to promise to tell Detective Spencer everything you know. You've got plenty of time to think about that night, every detail. Come to headquarters tomorrow morning at eight and ask for me."

Hondo enthusiastically nodded. "I'll do it. I swear."

"Here's what will happen if you don't. We'll get V-CAT, that's the Criminal Apprehension Team, to pick you up. Those guys don't mess around. They'll bring their dog, and they won't hesitate to use him. If they bring you in, you will be in violation of our agreement and you go right straight to prison and serve out your time. Eighteen months. No longer our C.I. No use to me or to Detective Sam. Think about that. In jail with no way to get your dope. Hell on earth."

"I'll be there. Promise."

"Eight sharp tomorrow. Not a minute later. And one more thing—hand over what you have in your pocket."

"I ain't got nothing in my pocket. What are you talking about?" Hondo gave him a wounded look.

"The Rolex. The watch you stole. Don't give me that look. You know it was the pawnbroker who called us. Give it here so I can return it to the rightful owner."

Hondo grimaced, bobbing his head. He fished the watch out of his pants pocket and placed it in Colt's palm. "There!"

"Who does it belong to?"

"Brianna's boss. Marcus Gilliam. I went to see him for help. He wouldn't do shit for me. So, I took his fancy watch. He left it on his desk, inviting me to take it."

"I'll make sure he gets it back." Folded lengthwise between his fingers, Colt handed the twenty to Hondo. He seized it like a kid after candy. With his hand still trembling, Hondo lifted the door handle and bolted from the car. He sprinted down the street and out of sight.

With mouth agape and eyes wide, Isabella turned on Colt, "Why—why would you let him just walk away?" The pitch in her voice rose higher. "This is bullshit! We've been looking for this guy and you just let him walk away, just like that!"

With his hand on the console, Colt angled his body to look back at her. "Calm down, songbird. I know what I'm doing. He's no use to us until he gets his fix. He'll show tomorrow. I have no doubt about that."

"Well, can you at least keep an eye on him to make sure he does?"

"I don't want anyone to know we're snooping around. Not yet anyway."

She exhaled loudly. "I hope you know what you're doing."

"That makes two of us."

22

They drove back to the diner, no longer interested in breakfast. Exiting the car, Isabella walked around to the driver's side. With a wide stance and arms crossed, she scolded Colt with her look. "So, what now? You let our best lead just walk away."

"Remember what I said, songbird? You do things my way and we'll get along just fine."

"I risked my life just trying to find the guy. What if we've lost him again?"

He turned on her, anger in his eyes. "Tell ya what, songbird. You stick to music and I'll handle the police work." He stepped closer, encroaching on her personal space. "And as far as risking your life, that was a dumb thing to do. I'm surprised a smart woman like you fell right into that trap. It was stupid."

"Colt, come on now," Samantha said, reaching out and placing her hand on his arm.

Colt knocked it off. His eyes stayed on Isabella, but he addressed his partner. "She thinks I'm not doing my job. Guess what? She's right. If I was doing my job, I'd be meeting with the task force right now. Instead I offered to stick my neck out and investigate her sister's death and this is what I get? Maybe I should just walk away, let her play detective on her own like she did yesterday. See how far it gets her."

Isabella sucked in a breath and tilted her chin up. "Finished, Detective?" His response was a shrug. "I appreciate your help." She turned to Samantha. "Yours too. I'm sorry. You're right, this is your show and I need to trust your judgment. Can we start over?"

"Sure." His eyes softened. "We're making progress, Isabella. Now we know someone came to see Brianna, and we'll find out who. I want you and Sam to pay a little visit to the old lady who lives in the house across the street from Brianna. I got a feeling she must have seen something. Her whole world is right outside her window."

Samantha stepped forward. "Hell, Colt, we're supposed to be meeting with the task force right now. Not just you. Me, too."

"I'll go there now, but I need you and Isabella to check out this lead. The owner of the house won't be thrilled if I show up. She kicked me off her property. But you ladies will have no trouble. Don't waste your time with the woman who owns the house. Demand to see her mother-in-law. My gut says she saw something that night." Colt squinted from the sun's reflection on the glass and chrome of vehicles in the parking lot. "Call me and let me know how it went." He pulled his pack of cigarettes from his pocket and tapped one out. "Are we good? Sam, I need you for this."

She gave him the same look of disapproval he got at the diner, but at last, she came around with a nod. "Okay, but if my superiors find out I'm helping you on the sly, they're not going to like it. It's my ass too, Colt."

He nudged her with his elbow. "Don't worry. I've got you covered. Don't I always?"

"Yeah, sure."

Her sarcasm did little to dishearten him. He planned to see this through although he had other things to deal with in his professional and private life. Colt drew on his cigarette and blew out a plume of smoke. He knew one thing: No one gets through life unscathed. Bad things happen and how a person deals with them is all that matters. Isabella Luca was no exception and so far, he didn't like how she dealt with her personal tragedy. She was trouble and she could get them both killed.

§

Sorrow swallowed Isabella whole the moment Samantha parked. Seeing her family's home across the street triggered memories of the sister lost to her forever. She took a deep breath and closed her eyes to prevent an explosion of emotion from erupting.

"Are you okay?" Samantha said from the opening of the driver's door.

"I'm fine." Isabella got out of the car and joined her on the sidewalk.

"I'll do most of the talking. I think it will help having you here since you're the sister. She might be more forthcoming. We'll see."

But first, they had to get past the scowling woman who answered the door. It was clear why Colt gave a warning about her. The woman sized them up, giving Samantha an icy stare when she stepped forward.

"Good afternoon, ma'am." Samantha held out her badge. "I'm Detective Samantha Delano with CMPD and this is Isabella Luca. Her sister was Brianna who they found across the street. Are you Sharon Abercrombie?"

"Yes, and before you go any further, I've already talked to the police."

"Yes, I know, but we didn't interview your mother-in-law. May we speak with her please?" Samantha smiled and added, "It won't take long, I promise. Just a question or two."

"She didn't see anything," the woman said. "She sleeps most of the time, hardly knows what going on. The woman is in her nineties. I'm sure she can't help you."

"Then I need her to tell us that. It's protocol. We need to get a statement directly from her."

Just when Samantha expected a door slam, Sharon Abercrombie opened it wider and stepped back. "Okay. But just for a minute."

In the front room, an elderly woman sat in a wheelchair, her head slumped forward, and her eyes closed. The light coming in from the window gave her thinning hair a white glow. The daughter-in-law placed her hand on one frail shoulder and shook her. "Wake up, Mama Bess. The police want to talk to you."

She startled awake and pushed her glasses further up the bridge of her nose, inspecting her visitors. "Police, huh? Have a seat. And you, Sharon—why, you can go about your business. I'm perfectly capable of speaking to them on my own."

Sharon huffed and walked out. As soon as she was out of sight, the old lady with a twinkle in her eye, said, "Forget what she told you. I know *everything* going on, and I mean *everything*. I just pretend to be sleeping, so I don't have to deal with that bitch. My son is a sweet, caring man, but unfortunately, he's married to that. She resents the hell out of me being here, but I'm *not* going into a nursing home. I tell her to just deal with it. I'm here to stay until my last breath, which she hopes is real soon." One cheek went up and her mouth opened slightly as she tried to make her wink as obvious as possible. "Call me Miss Bess. Everyone does. And go on, like I said, have a seat, ladies. I won't bite." She chuckled. "I like having company, having people actually talking to me." She made eye contact with Isabella. "Young lady, I'm sorry about your sister. I didn't know her, but I saw her occasionally coming and going. A lovely girl."

"Thank you, ma'am. Nice of you to say."

Samantha took a seat across from the old woman. Isabella slipped into a corner chair where she planned to be more of an observer than a participant.

Miss Bess propped her elbows on the arms of the wheelchair and clasped her gnarly, arthritic-looking hands together.

Samantha cleared her throat and said, "Ma'am, we're investigating the death of Brianna Connelly. We thought you might have seen a car or a person going inside sometime before she was found. Anything you can tell us might help."

"I was wondering when the police would get around to me. I guess Cruella De Ville didn't pass on my information. Damn her. She never believes a word I say. I told her what I saw. A car pulled into the driveway around five o'clock that day. I know the time because my clock chimed five times."

"Do you remember the kind of car it was?"

"Of course I do. I may have some age on me, sweetie, but my mind is still sharp. About as sharp as my tongue." She cackled and removed her glasses, wiping the lens with a tissue. "It was a silver Toyota. A sedan. I think it was an Avalon, but it could have been a Camry. My husband liked Toyotas. We had one of each. An Avalon and a Camry. Nice cars. Good for trips. Smooth ride and all."

Samantha wrote something down on a small notepad. She double clicked the top of her pen, prepared to add something more. "Did you see a person step out of the car?"

"I sure did, hard to forget him because he reminded me of my Harry back in the day. A nice-looking young man. Maybe about her age." Miss Bess pointed at Isabella. "Tall and slender just like my husband. He had light brown hair, a nice haircut. Neat looking, not shaggy like some of these young men you see around. Gosh, seeing him took me back seventy years. We were a handsome couple, Harry and I." She folded her hands over her heart and smiled.

"Was anyone else with him?"

"No, just him."

"How did you get such a good look at the man?"

"Because I used those babies over there." She pointed to the corner of the room where an end table held a lamp and two framed photographs. "Isabella, see the binoculars hidden beside the sofa? Bring them here so Detective Samantha can see them."

Isabella reached down for the binoculars and froze. Her eyes fixated on a photograph on the table of Miss Bess and her husband on their wedding day. His resemblance to Landon shocked her.

"Isabella? Did you find them?" Samantha asked.

"Yes. Here you go."

She handed the binoculars to Samantha. The detective faced the window and looked through the lens.

"I was looking at this young man through the binoculars when he walked around to the back of the car and opened the trunk." Miss Bess retrieved a tissue from her pocket and dabbed it against her nostrils. "He pulled out a shopping bag. I have no idea what was inside. When he closed the trunk, he looked straight toward this house. I don't think he saw me though. But just to play it safe, I rolled my chair back a little. When he went to the door, Brianna let him in. I figured it was her boyfriend, but they didn't kiss, or hug, or anything like that. Rats! I was hoping they would." She gave a mischievous grin and stared out the window. Isabella followed her gaze to a house next door to Brianna's. "Hmm, that's interesting. Bill Nelson's daughter has been at his house all day. Her car's been there since nine this morning. I hope he's all right. Not sick or anything."

"How long did he stay?"

The question disrupted Miss Bess's focus on the car in the neighbor's driveway. "What's that?"

Samantha repeated, "I was wondering if you know how long the man stayed at Brianna's house."

Before Miss Bess could respond, a college-aged girl stepped into the doorway. She held a small plastic container with a blue lid. Despite their presence, her attention went solely on the elderly woman. She put a finger over her lips. "Shh—Aunt Sharon doesn't know I'm here." Her voice was just above a whisper. "I brought you a fresh batch of brownies, Grandma. Sorry to barge in while you have company but I'm in a hurry. Got a class in thirty minutes."

"Oh, good, this should help with my pain." Miss Bess locked eyes with Samantha and pressed her lips together. "What I mean is—oh, just forget it."

The girl handed the container to her grandmother and bent over to give her a hug. "Better go now."

"Thanks, darling. You're so sweet to drop by. I know how busy you are. Ladies, this is my granddaughter, Kelsey. I'd offer you a brownie, but she made them special for me."

Isabella gave Kelsey a knowing smile. "I bet they're delicious."

Miss Bess waited until her granddaughter left before she turned back to Samantha. She set the container on a small table beside her wheelchair. "I'm sorry, Detective, what was it you were asking?"

"Do you know how long the man stayed inside the house?"

"No, I can't say. I fell asleep and when I woke up, the car was gone."

"What time was that?" Samantha prepared to write it down.

Miss Bess lowered her head and massaged her neck. "This is where my memory gets a little fuzzy. It was already dark when I woke up. I don't remember the time."

"If it was dark, how did you know the car was gone?"

"There's a streetlight across the street. With it on, I can see the driveway just fine. I didn't think any more about it. I went on to bed. I'm not a night owl like I used to be."

"Had you ever seen the car there before?"

"No, just that one time."

Samantha cleared her throat. "Do you think you would recognize the man if you saw him again?"

"Hmm." Bess brought her finger to her cheek. "Yes, I think so. I gave him a real good look since he reminded me of my Harry."

When Samantha stood up, Isabella took it as her cue to do the same. Samantha held her pen to the pad and said, "We won't keep you any longer, ma'am."

"What did I tell you?" The old lady shook her finger at Samantha. "It's Miss Bess."

"Right. Well, Miss Bess, I just need your phone number in case we have more questions for you." Samantha wrote down the number Miss Bess called out and reached inside her pocket. She pulled out something. "And here's my card in case you think of anything else."

"I'll certainly let you know. And you ladies stop by anytime. Make it a social visit. I don't get many visitors."

Isabella gave her a hug. "Thank you. You've been a big help. Hopefully we'll find out more about my sister's death."

Walking to the car, Samantha said, "Colt was right. The old lady did see something. This is a good lead."

With a playful smile, Isabella said, "It's weird, but her description fits my ex-boyfriend and what's weirder is he actually does resemble her husband. I saw a photograph of them on the table. It was taken on their wedding day."

Samantha's eyes widened. "Could it have been him? Your ex-boyfriend?"

"No way. Of course not. He lives in Seattle." Isabella mulled over the implication. "Wait a minute—are you thinking Landon could have killed Brianna? Because if you are, that's preposterous! He wouldn't hurt a fly. He's so loving, so tender-hearted—well, except when it came to Brianna. He thought I was too nice to her, too forgiving. He thought I enabled her addiction. To be honest, he despised Brianna, but he wouldn't harm her. No way.

"And face it, her description was so general, it could really apply to a lot of men. In fact, my neighbor gave the same profile for someone seen near my apartment sometime before it was broken into."

"When did that happen?"

"Sometime after Brianna died. When I got back to New York, I found my apartment in a mess. I called the police, but they never found out who did it."

"It's a good thing you weren't home. No telling what could have happened."

"Yes, I guess you're right. A lot of bad guys out there, and sometimes you can't tell the difference between the bad ones and the good ones."

"No, you can't."

They got into the car and strapped on seat belts. Samantha turned the ignition key and glanced over at Isabella. "I'm just curious, what's your former boyfriend's name?"

"Landon Burke."

"Interesting name. Are you two still on speaking terms?"

Isabella frowned. "Not sure how to answer that. I haven't spoken to him since he walked out four years ago, although he has left me a few messages recently—says he has something to tell me. Actually, he's here in town and wants to tell me in person whatever it is."

"What do you think it is?"

"I have no idea, but if I had to guess, I think he wants to get back together."

"Does he know about Brianna?" Samantha made a U-turn, headed back in the direction she came.

"He found out from my sister, Kristen. He called her because I wouldn't return his calls."

"What did he say about it? I mean, Brianna's death."

"Kristen said he sounded devastated—worried about me."

Samantha took her eyes from the road to meet Isabella's gaze. "I'm sure he knows how it impacted you. You were so close."

<h1 style="text-align:center">23</h1>

Five minutes into the meeting, Colt got into a spirited discussion with Special Agent Jim Roper, who headed up the task force. He suggested Colt wear a ballcap with a camera and audio transmitter concealed inside. The DEA's tech guy, nicknamed Geek, held it up for Colt's inspection.

"I might as well have a flashing neon sign on my forehead that says *Undercover Cop*. Are you guys nuts? I've never worn a cap around these druggies. They'll see me in one and get suspicious. Come up with something better. My life is on the line here."

Roper scraped back his chair from the long conference table, allowing more legroom. He rested his ankle on the opposite knee and nodded. "Okay, we've got a Plan B. How about a vest? We have one that belonged to a drug dealer up north. We did a little modification. Ran a wire from the camera to the battery inside the lining. Got a mic inserted, too. You okay with that?"

"I reckon," Colt said. "As long as it doesn't clash with the rest of my ensemble. I'd hate to make a fashion faux pas."

Geek gave him a sour look. "Local cops are always wise guys."

"You wanna hear what we say about feds?"

"Nope. Too vile for my virgin ears."

"Yeah, you are a little young, Geek. Someone might have to explain it to ya." Colt turned to Roper. "Anything else before I go?"

"No. Come by tomorrow morning. Same time. We'll go over everything again. Make sure everyone's on the same page. I want to try out the tracker one more time. We'll have a little road test. Make sure it picks up a signal."

"If you damage my boot putting that tracker inside, I'll be expecting a new pair." Colt put his hands on his knees and stood up, looking down at the men. "I'll go now. Are we good?" Geek and Roper nodded. "Okay then, see you guys tomorrow."

Colt walked out into the bright sunshine and slipped on his sunglasses. Two days to go before he put himself slap-dab in the middle of harm's way. If he got made, the bad guys would have enough guns and ammo to make Swiss cheese out of his body. Not to mention the badass knife Pug carried in a leather sheath on his belt. One swipe to his throat and he'd bleed out in seconds.

He took the shortest route to the headquarters of New Beginnings, ticking off the many things that could go wrong with the raid. Sam was right. With everything going on, they didn't have time to investigate Brianna's death. He should have told Isabella they were busy on other cases, but then his brother's demise came to mind. What if the homicide detectives didn't take the time to investigate the murder of Streaker by a drug dealer? They didn't even like Streaker, considered him a traitor. He left the force in disgrace after stealing evidence, eight ounces of marijuana for his own personal use. But when he died, two detectives made sure the killer was captured and indicted. No crime should go unpunished, not in a civilized society. Colt believed it, and he lived it.

At a stoplight, he checked his phone and cursed. He hit the steering wheel with the palm of his hand. "Come on, Ashley! Call me, dammit! You can't pick up the damn phone or send a text? Pregnant or not pregnant? How hard can it be to let me know?"

Patience was not a trait Colt possessed. There were too many questions stirring around in his cluttered brain, waiting for answers. Not only Ashley's situation but Brianna's death and the delivery point for the drug shipment. All the not-knowing drove him crazy.

Once he arrived at New Beginnings, he put all his worries away like a beat cop stored personal belongings in a locker. Tucked away until retrieved. In the parking lot, he saw a man holding a newspaper in front of his face. His receding hairline which came to a sharp point in the front reminded him of a private investigator named Billy Fish. What a name and what a hairline. If it was him, why was he here? The guy specialized in digging up dirt on cheating spouses. Was Marcus stepping out on his wife?

On the porch leading inside the main entrance, his head did battle with the wind chimes. He batted them away, cursing when one of the dangling things got tangled in his hair. He tried turning his head, but it got wound tighter. Between clenched teeth, he said, "Useless piece of shit!" When he finally freed himself, he opened the door and smoothed his hair back in place, thankful no one witnessed the debacle.

Standing in front of the reception desk, he said, "Good morning, ma'am." A harried-looking middle aged woman took her eyes off her computer screen to look up at Colt. Instead of a smile, she pressed her lips together. Maybe his cordial greeting was the wrong thing to say. Clearly this woman wasn't having a good morning. In a dry, no-nonsense voice, he said, "I'm Detective Colten Jessup with CMPD. I'm here to see Marcus Gilliam."

She slapped a hand on her chest and exhaled loudly. "Oh, good, Mr. Gilliam called the police. I was hoping he would. We still haven't heard from Lauren or Tara. For them to disappear like that, it's so strange."

Colt hid his confusion behind a poker face and cleared his throat. "Ma'am, I'm sorry. I'm here about something else."

Her mouth fell open. "Oh." She wrung her hands. "I'll tell him you're here."

She called Marcus on her phone and hung up. "Detective, just go straight back. His office is the corner one."

Marcus waited in the doorway and ushered him inside. "Have a seat, Detective." Marcus extended his hand indicating the padded chair in front of his desk. "What can I do for you?"

"Before I get to that, what is this about some people missing? This receptionist said—"

Marcus held up his hand. "Forget what she said. It's nothing. Really. Two of our employees haven't come in yet and we don't know why. I'm sure there's a simple explanation. Lily is a great volunteer, but she has a habit of worrying about every little thing."

"I see." He didn't, but Colt dropped it. He reached in his pants pocket for the Rolex and set it on the desk. "Is this your watch?"

"Holy cow! You've found it!" Marcus eyes got big as he scooped it up. He held it close to his face, eying it like he held the Crown Jewels. "Where? How in the world?"

"Do you know Whit Drummond, also known as Hondo?"

The smile fell from his face. "I knew he took it. I left the office for one minute and when I returned, he and the watch were gone."

"Did you report it to the police?"

"Actually—no, I didn't. Whit has enough troubles as it is. To add to them…well, what would be the point?"

"That's a mighty expensive watch to just let go. What's it worth anyway?"

"You say that because it's a Rolex. Well, it's not one of their top of the line pieces."

"Still, it's worth in the thousands, am I right?"

Marcus deflected, asking, "How did you get it back? I assume Whit didn't just walk into the police station and hand it over."

"No, he didn't. We were looking for him about a crime he might have witnessed. A pawn broker told us about the watch, and we tracked him down."

"Oh? He was a witness to what crime?"

"Sorry, that's classified."

Colt scanned the office. Marcus had expensive taste. Colt didn't know much about art, but he could tell the stuff on the wall wasn't cheap. The same could be said about his big-ass desk and other furnishings that sat atop an intricate Oriental rug. Apparently, leadership in drug recovery had perks. Why was it that some people in non-profits had no problem asking for money, even begging for sacrificial gifts, while a good portion of the funds went to pacify the material needs of themselves?

"I see you're admiring my artwork, Detective."

"It's nice."

The man smiling back at Colt was a likeable guy, although a little too smug. He scrutinized Colt's faded jeans and well-worn T-shirt and then ran his hand down his silk tie. "What can I say? I enjoy the finer things in life. You, on the other hand, probably prefer a simpler life."

Colt's forced a smile. "Luxury to me is a soft bed and a hot shower. You, on the other hand, never did without either one, I bet." Colt got his jab in and moved on. "Tell me, Marcus, how did you get involved in helping with drug addiction?"

Colt pictured him more as a partner in a law firm or as a hedge fund manager. For all Colt knew, he genuinely cared about helping broken people. But something—he couldn't say what because he didn't know—*something* about the guy Colt didn't like. But he sure as hell wasn't envious or jealous of his nice art or fancy suit.

"Lauren Lamont got me involved in this. It was her dream to help others once she overcame her own addiction and she convinced me to help her. I did the financing and she—well, she did the hard work."

"Is that the Lauren your receptionist mentioned? She didn't show up today?"

Marcus exhaled an exasperated breath. "She's late, that's all. Lily gets her panties in a wad for no good reason." He laughed. "Office drama." He rolled his eyes and again ran his hand over his tie. "Is there anything else, Detective?"

Colt's face flushed. He realized he'd been standing around like a dope, lost in thought. "Nah, I better let you get back to it." He walked to the door and turned. "I guess everyone here misses Brianna a lot."

"Yes, we certainly do. We're planning a candlelight vigil for her tonight. Well, Lauren was working on it, but since she's not here, I guess I'll just take charge. You might want to come, Detective. We're having it in our meditation garden. Channel Nine is going to cover it on their eleven o'clock broadcast."

"Isn't this a little late?"

"What do you mean?"

"I mean, there's usually a vigil closer to the event or on an anniversary date. Brianna's been dead for over a month now."

Nodding oddly like a bobble head figure, Marcus said, "You're right. We should have done it sooner, but to tell you the truth, we were so overwhelmed with grief and shock, we didn't think of it then." Marcus had a hint of a smile when he added, "Better late than never. Brianna was so special, she deserves this.

"Come around eight-thirty or so." Marcus steered Colt toward the door and added, "We'll light candles when it gets dark. Lauren was asking a few people to speak and hoping Isabella Luca would sing for us. Or if she's not up to it, at least, lead us in song."

"See you tonight."

Police working homicide knew killers sometimes showed for such events. Tonight, Colt planned to study everyone in attendance for any telltale signs of a murderer.

24

Samantha called Colt with news of her meeting with Miss Bess. Wedging his cell phone between his ear and his shoulder, he lit the end of his cigarette. While driving and smoking, he listened to Samantha recap her visit with the old lady.

Something she said stopped him cold. "Say that again?"

"I said—she *did* see someone. You were right, Colt."

"Damn, I like the sound of that. You should say it more often."

"If you were right more, I would, dummy." He laughed at her sass. "Get this, Colt. This guy—the one the old lady described—well, he fits the description of Isabella's former boyfriend. Ain't that a kicker?"

"How do you know that?"

"Isabella told me. And there's more—Isabella also said the guy matched the description of someone seen near her apartment after a break-in. That happened while she was in Charlotte for the funeral. Her lover-boy might have broken into her place looking for something *and* had something to do with Brianna's death."

Colt kept driving toward the police headquarters, flicking ashes out the window. "That sounds like a stretch."

"Well, cowboy, the boyfriend had motive. He hated Brianna. Blamed her for their break-up."

"Yeah, but disliking her enough to kill her? I don't buy it. And the break-in—that doesn't make a lick of sense."

"What if he wanted Brianna out of the way so he could get Isabella back?"

"Do you have a gut feeling about this, Sam?"

"What? I can't understand you. You're mumbling."

Colt took the cigarette out of his mouth. "I said, do you have a gut feeling about this?"

"Yes, I do. I think it's worth following up on."

Samantha's gut was seldom wrong, and, over time, Colt learned to trust it. "What was the description the old lady gave you?"

"Good looking guy around Isabella's age, twenty-something. Light brown hair, tall, slender build."

"I saw a photo at Brianna's home with a guy that looked like that. He had his arm around Isabella's waist, grinning like a possum. I asked her who he was, and she told me it was her former boyfriend. She seemed surprised Brianna had the dang thing framed and sitting out for the world to see. There was definitely some bad blood between the two. She didn't want to talk about it though."

"That's interesting," Samantha said. "Here's something else, Colt. According to Isabella, he's in Charlotte and wants to see her."

"Damn, I don't like the sound of that." Colt dropped the remains of his cigarette into an empty soda can in the cupholder. "Tell ya what, I'll stop by the house and take a photo with my phone and email it to you. Put it with some similar headshots and see if the old lady picks our suspect. I don't feel right about moving forward without a positive ID. Do you mind dropping in on her again?"

"No, I can do that. And Colt—if you're going to the house, better run it by Spencer first. No need getting him riled up. And when you see him, be nice."

"Yes, Mama."

"I'm just trying to keep you out of trouble, that's all." Colt heard a sudden blast from a siren on her end of the call and could picture Samantha pulling over to let the firetruck pass. After a beat, she added, "I'll swing by and visit Miss Bess after I go to speak with the store manager at The Quick Stop and actually work a case we're supposed to be working."

"Is that supposed to make me feel guilty?"

"No, I'm just rubbing it in. I know you won't have any peace until this Brianna mystery is resolved. Gotta go. Some jerk is dying to cut me off in traffic." She yelled, "Hey, asshole!" Her shout made him hold the phone away from his ear.

"Easy now, girl. Be nice."

"Guess I should follow my own advice, huh?" She laughed. "Bye, Colt. I'll call you later and let you know what Miss Bess says."

§

At police headquarters, Colt found Spencer's cubicle empty. He stepped over to Anders's area and said, "Hey, Jason, where's Spence?"

"He's taking a late lunch. You can find him at The Dakota Grill."

Colt frowned. "Damn. I hate steakhouses."

"What is it with you and steakhouses? I don't get it."

"Never mind. I'll guess I'll mosey on over there. Thanks, bro."

Colt removed his sunglasses and walked inside The Dakota Grill. It took him a minute to adjust to the dim light, finally spotting Spencer in a corner booth. He waved off the hostess and made his way to the table.

With a fork and knife in hand and ready to dive into his T-bone steak, Spencer made a face when he glanced up. "You're always sneaking up on me, Jessup. How did you find me? Never mind, I know. Anders, that sonofa…What's up?"

Colt slid into the booth. He was in no hurry to get down to business. He reached over for a fry and popped it in his mouth. "You closed the case too soon, Spence," he said. "Brianna

Connelly might have been murdered. We have a witness—no, make that two witnesses—who saw someone at her place shortly before her death."

"The medical examiner said—"

"What he said is bullshit. The scene was staged. It doesn't take a genius to figure that out. You gotta reopen the case. I got one witness coming to see you tomorrow and another who might give us a positive ID on a suspect."

"Who's this witness coming forward, and where the hell have they been?"

"We had this discussion before. I told you my C.I. was staying with Brianna. He's the witness. I finally tracked him down. He said Brianna saw someone drive up and told him to get lost, so he did."

"So, he didn't actually see anyone."

"No, but the lady across the street did. Your team that canvassed the neighborhood missed her."

"Aw, hell, Jessup. Shit." Spencer stabbed a chunk of steak with his fork and brought it to his mouth. He chewed slowly, his eyes closed, looking as content as a lion devouring fresh kill. "Your Hondo-guy is about as credible as a pimp in a shiny purple suit."

"Just talk to him. He's coming in at eight in the morning."

"Yeah, right. I'll believe it when I see it."

Spencer picked up his steak knife and sawed off a piece of meat lengthwise. Colt tried not to watch, but he still saw enough blood running out of the pink muscle to trigger an unpleasant memory. Even after some thirty-plus years, it was something he couldn't forget. When he spent the summer of his ninth year on his grandparents' farm, every day he looked forward to feeding a calf from a bucket with a nipple attached. He claimed him as his little pet and named him Toby. He adored Toby. The two spent many happy days frolicking about the pasture or curled up together in the barn. But when Toby grew up, he was more valuable dead than alive, according to the commodity price of beef. From his hiding place behind a bale of hay, and with tears in his eyes and bile rising in his throat, Colt viewed Toby's carcass being sliced up into different cuts of meat. Chuck, rib, round, flank, brisket. All that muscle, fat, tissue, organs, and blood, until nothing was left of poor Toby except fond memories. From that point on, Colt turned up his nose at anything beef. At all gatherings where his brothers in blue grilled burgers or steaks, he used the *I-ate-before-I-came* excuse. Now, he was forced to watch Spencer sop up the bloody juices in a chunk of bread. It made him nauseous.

"You okay, Colt? You look a little pale. You not coming down with anything, are you? I can't afford to be around someone sick. Too much work to do."

"I'm fine. Now, back to what I was saying, the case needs to be reopened. If you don't like Hondo as a witness, maybe you can interview the lady. I might get a positive ID from her later today, so stay tuned."

Colt picked up a plastic straw and tapped the table surface with it. One foot went up and down at the same fast, kinetic beat. For some reason, nervous energy coursed through his body whenever he got around Spencer. Colt and Spencer were like fire and gasoline. Over a year ago, the two cops sat in Major Stiles' office like delinquents sent to the principal's office. What the dispute was about, Colt couldn't remember.

Colt cleared his throat and leaned forward, forearms resting on the table, fingers interlaced. "We need to look at Brianna's phone. Check her phone log."

Spencer took a sip of iced tea and shook his head, a scowl on his face. "I gave the phone back to her father. No need to keep it once her death was ruled a suicide."

Between clenched teeth, Colt said, "Shit!" He leaned back and ran his fingers through his hair. "Then I'll ask her father for it." To offset Spencer's glare, he added, "My C.I. or someone else may have called it. We need to know who she was in contact with in the last hours before her death. Scowl at me all you want, Spence. I'm getting the damn phone."

"Suit yourself." Spencer trimmed the fat off and stabbed a pink chunk of steak. Again, he chewed it with his eyes closed, a contented look on his face. Colt imagined Spencer having a similar euphoric experience while making love to his wife. Spencer took another sip of tea and pressed the napkin to his lips. "About your C.I.—are you working an angle, Colt? Getting information in exchange for a deal?"

"Trying to piss me off? My guy's reliable. You'll see. We'll be at headquarters at eight o'clock. You cool with that?"

Spencer drug his garlic bread through more meat juices and took a bite. As he chewed, he watched Colt get up from the table. He pointed his knife at Colt, chest level. "Hey, before you go, let me make this clear—I'll listen to your guy, but I'm not making any promises."

"I know. See ya at eight sharp."

25

In the meditation garden behind New Beginnings, friends and family of Brianna gathered for the vigil in her memory. Colt estimated the crowd at about fifty. They passed around candles and waited for Marcus Gilliam to get things under way.

The flowers bordering the edge of the garden perfumed the air. Strong enough that despite Colt being a heavy smoker, he picked up the scent. A light breeze added a challenge to whether the candles stayed lit when the time came. Colt weaved through the crowd, holding an unlit candle at his side.

Over the treetops, he spotted a spectacular sky show. The setting sun lent its crimson color to the clouds and gave them the appearance of pink cotton candy amid streaks of magenta. He wasn't a religious man, but he hoped what he witnessed was a sign. Maybe Brianna was smiling down on them from heaven. Too soon nature's beautiful display faded away, melded into a slate-blue sky.

Colt studied the crowd, looking for any telling signs of a killer. Such a person would try to blend in; however, many times the opposite happened. A trained observer could easily detect suspicious body language, mannerisms, nervousness, and occasionally guilt reeking from every pore of their body, almost giving off an odor.

It had been a long day and Colt plopped himself on a bench under a large maple tree for a brief rest. He leaned forward with his hands on his knees and dropped his head. He didn't bother to stifle his yawn. Alone and almost removed from the scene, he agonized over Ashley's promised phone call that never came. His patience wore thin and he broke down and called her, but it went straight to voicemail. Damn her for keeping him in suspense. He needed to hear her say she was not pregnant. Just a little scare. But if she was indeed pregnant, he worried how it would impact Maddie, and what would Kate think? She already viewed him as reckless and irresponsible. His hope was that someday he could prove to her…prove what exactly? What was the point of thinking she'd ever take him back? She said she had moved on, started a new chapter in her life. The sooner he faced reality, the sooner he could get on with his own life.

"Colt! There you are." Tony walked over, his arm around his wife's shoulders. He reached in his pants pocket and pulled out a cellphone. "I got your message. Here's Brianna's phone." He handed it to Colt. "Even though she doesn't have a security code on it, I couldn't bring myself to look at anything."

Colt stood up. "Thanks for bringing it. How are you feeling now?"

"Physically good. The doctor gave me a good report and sent me home. Emotionally, Jill and I are a wreck." He squeezed his wife tighter against his side. "We don't want to be here, but Marcus insisted. He said it would mean so much to Brianna's friends, but it's like having to go through the death all over again."

"Yeah, I can only imagine. Losing a child has to be the worst thing that could happen to a parent." At that moment, an image of Maddie popped in his head. What if something terrible ever happened to her? He'd fall into a million pieces, unable to function.

Looking over Tony's shoulder, Colt spotted Marcus hugging Isabella's sister, Kristen, but he didn't see Isabella anywhere around. Marcus released her and herded people into a group, apparently preparing to get started. But while he had the chance, Colt had a question for Tony. "Out of curiosity, how well do you know Isabella's former boyfriend?"

"Landon Burke? We saw him a few times. Seemed like a nice guy. He and Isabella were happy together. Or so we thought. It came as a shock when he moved away. Isabella was heartbroken."

"Yes, poor girl," Jill interjected. "She was depressed for weeks. Why in the world are you asking about Landon?"

"Just curious. I saw a photo of the two of them at Brianna's house."

Tony gave a half-smile. "Brianna wasn't a fan. I'm surprised she had the photo out." He opened his mouth to say more but stopped when two women approached him. They pinned a pink ribbon on his polo shirt. "Brianna's favorite color," one of them explained and stepped sideways to pin one on Jill.

Colt excused himself and moved farther away from the event. Now that he had Brianna's phone, he checked her phone log. Without a set password, access was as easy as a few clicks. Landon Burke's name popped up as a caller twice on the day Brianna died. But what piqued Colt's interest more were his four calls on days after her death.

Colt listened to an old voice message. It was from Landon. He said, "Brianna, I haven't heard back from you. Call me. Let me know what you're going to do."

What the hell did that mean? Something bumped his hip from behind, sending Brianna's phone sailing out of his hand and onto the ground. He spun around and locked eyes with a familiar face. "Ashley! What are you doing here?" Colt bent down for the phone and used the side of his jeans to brush dirt off its protective cover.

"I'm working, silly—covering the live report for the eleven o'clock news. I'm a reporter, remember?"

"You're covering this?" Colt did a sweep with his hand.

"Yeah, that's the plan. Vigil for dead girl at the place where she worked. I just go where they tell me to go. Did you know her?"

"Yeah, I did." Out of caution, Colt looked to his left and his right and stepped closer. "Why haven't you called me?" He kept his voice down. "You know I've been waiting. What's the verdict? Pregnant or not pregnant?"

She gave him her sexy smile, the one where one side of her mouth tilted up more than the other. Sometimes it made him like putty in her hands. But this was one of the times the power of its magic was wasted on him.

"Well?" he barked.

"Which would you rather hear, Colt?"

"I want the truth! That's what I want."

She curled in her bottom lip with teeth biting down. "Okay, okay. *Not*. I'm not pregnant. I didn't have to get the EPT kit. I started my period this morning. False alarm."

"You cudda called me and told me." He kept his voice as rough as gravel, his glare just as harsh. "Dammit, Ashley, I've been waiting all day."

She ran a long, polished nail down his forearm. "Sorry. I was so busy today. I didn't get a chance to call. Forgive me?" Her damn lop-sided smile made another appearance, but it was her doe-like eyes that almost sucked him in.

He would have caved except for the interruption of a man hoisting a camera on his shoulder. He stepped between them and cleared his throat. "Hey, Ash, we better get things set up."

"Okay." She nodded and smiled at Colt. "Nice surprise seeing you here. Saved us a phone call. See?"

§

"Brianna Luca Connelly impacted all of our lives. She touched us with her love and her kindness." As Marcus gave his illustrious tribute to Brianna, a few eyes teared up and some people sniffled. *This guy is good,* Colt admitted, referring to the way Marcus played to their emotions. If only Brianna were alive to hear the praise the man heaped on her. Marcus struck a match to light his candle and tilted it to pass the flame on to a lady standing close by. She did the same and all down the line until every candle glowed.

"Of course, Brianna went through a dark period as you all know." Marcus got to the part where he talked about Brianna's struggle with addiction. Now even Colt teared up. He heard more sniffling and even a moan. It came from Brianna's mother. But when he spoke of Brianna's victory over the battle, there were a few smiles and head nods. Marcus said, "Yes, Brianna is a survivor. She fought like hell to get her life back. A warrior. Brianna Connelly was a warrior. And she inspired others to be warriors, too."

For a second or two, Marcus grew quiet, then continued. "But she didn't do it alone. She had family and friends and the help of New Beginnings." Marcus looked out over the crowd. *It's coming—wait for it—and there it was—*"Of course, she couldn't have overcome her addiction without the good work and guidance of New Beginnings. I was proud to be part of that, of her recovery."

"Yep, you managed to turn a tribute to Brianna to accolades for yourself and your organization. Good going, Gilliam," Colt mumbled and didn't care who heard him. He figured a paid ad couldn't have been more effective. Ashley's cameraman got it all on film for the 11 o'clock slot. The vigil to honor Brianna's memory quickly turned into a promotional campaign. The only thing missing was where to send the check. Colt now understood what he didn't like about Marcus Gilliam.

After his speech, Marcus stepped into the crowd and pulled Isabella to his side. Almost shouting, he said, "Who better to honor Brianna than her twin sister, Isabella Luca. She has agreed to sing *Amazing Grace* for us."

As she stepped forward, her gold drop-earrings swayed with her movement. She wore an off-the-shoulder sundress with a flared skirt. Its teal color complimented her dark hair and eyes. She nodded to her accompanist. The guitarist, a James Taylor-lookalike, strummed a few bars of music but stopped when Isabella stepped into a hole on the ground and lost her footing. Her arms flew out for balance. Colt hated being too far back to come to her aid, but she recovered quickly on her own. She placed her hand over her mouth and laughed. Bending over, she removed her low-heeled sandals and dangled them by the backstrap at her side. "Let's start that over," she said with a smile.

She was as beautiful and poised as when she sang at Brianna's memorial service. The same voice that wowed Colt then sent chills down his spine. The passion she felt showed in her teary eyes. Her solo ended and Colt wiped moisture from his own eyes. If anyone asked, he'd say his allergies were acting up.

He tried to weave through the crowd and get to Isabella. He backed off when he realized she was surrounded by people wanting to hug her and offer consoling words. Now was not the time to question her about Landon Burke. When his phone vibrated in his pocket, he moved away from the crowd noise.

With one finger in his ear to hear better, he still couldn't make out what Samantha was saying. "Sam? Hold on. Let me get away from all the racket." He ambled around the side of the building and stepped onto the front porch, resting his butt on the railing. "Okay, this is better. Talk to me."

"Miss Bess gave me a positive ID. It's him, Colt. Landon Burke."

"How sure is she?"

"About a hundred and twenty per cent. I showed her photos of five other men, but her finger landed on Burke."

"Damn." He waited a beat and said, "I have Brianna's phone. He called it twice the day she died. And get this, he called her *after* her death. But those calls could have been made to throw us off."

"Maybe." After staying silent, she said, "If you're going to pick him up, you need Spencer. It's his case, Colt."

"I know. First, I'm going to talk with Isabella, give her a heads-up."

"Do you think that's wise?"

"I owe her that." He searched for Isabella among the crowd. "Hey, I better go. I gotta find her."

He slipped his phone in his pocket. Four women walked over and surrounded him. One of them was the receptionist at New Beginnings. He glanced down at her hand gripping his arm.

"Detective, we met earlier today. I'm Lily Prather. I was at the front desk."

"Yes, ma'am, I remember. What can I do for you?"

"It's Lauren Lamont and Tara Sanders. They're still missing. Marcus said he contacted the police, and well, we're just wondering if you've found out anything yet. If you're not handling this, maybe you could make a call and find out for us."

"Sure, I'll make a call and see if I can find out anything."

Lily pressed her hands over her chest. "Oh, would you? That would be wonderful. We all work together, and we've been worried about them all day."

Colt didn't have a pen on him. He handed his phone to Lily. "Here. Key in your phone number and I'll get back to you as soon as I know something."

She smiled and nodded. Did she think he could work magic and produce the missing women out of thin air? *Yep, that's what I am. A magician, spinning plates and hoping to keep them all in the air. An amazing magician, trying to keep his shit together.*

Lily keyed in her number and handed the phone back. The women walked away. Their bodies had blocked his view of the crowd, but since they moved away, he noticed the back of Isabella's head about thirty feet away. In a fast clip, he walked toward her. When he reached for her arm, she turned around.

"Oh, Kristen," he said, "I thought you were Isabella. Do you know where she is? I need to find her."

"You're too late. She left."

"Left? Where did she go?"

Kristen shrugged. "I don't know. She left with her former boyfriend, Landon. He showed up here to surprise her."

"Shit!" Colt slammed his fist into the palm of his other hand.

Kristen's eyes widened. "What's wrong?'

"Do you know where they went?"

"No, she didn't say." Kristen bit down on her lower lip. "What is it, Colt?"

He pulled his phone from his pocket and began punching buttons.

"Who are you calling?"

"Isabella, that's who." He held the phone to his ear, raking his fingers through his hair.

Kristen held up a phone. It was ringing. "Won't do you any good. See—she handed me her phone right before she started singing. I forgot to give it back to her."

"Shit!" he yelled. "Find your parents. We need to talk."

26

Singing in front of the crowd at the vigil, the unexpected happened. Isabella locked eyes with Landon Burke. Her heart leaped and her stomach did a flip-flop. She managed to get through the song, hoping no one detected her shock on seeing him. Her solo brought the evening's event to a conclusion, and for that she was thankful. People surrounded her with their well-wishes and praise for her song. Landon faded into the background, yet she searched the crowd for sight of him. Later, she found him standing under an oak tree, waiting. She could only smile, her voice failing her.

He pulled her against him and embraced her tightly. He kissed the top of her head. "I would have come sooner if I had known. So sorry about Brianna."

She couldn't think straight, didn't know what to say. Four years, and now he was back. "Landon, I can't believe…I mean, it's been a long time. I don't know what—"

He smiled and placed his finger over her lips. "You don't have to say anything, Isabella. I had to come, had to see you. I have so much to say. Come with me. I have something to give you. I should have brought it with me."

He didn't give her a chance to respond. Instead, he pulled her away from the crowd toward the parking lot. With his arm around her, he steered her toward the back row of vehicles. She took quick steps to keep up his pace.

"I wished you'd tell me what this is about," she said, looking over her shoulder.

"You'll see. This way." Landon pointed to a white Lexus sedan. They reached the car and he opened the passenger door.

She turned her back to the door's opening. "Wait. Where are you taking me?"

"It's a surprise." He jerked his head, indicating the car. "Get in, and soon you'll find out."

"But my family—they're waiting for me."

He exhaled loudly. "Okay. Well, go tell them you're going with me."

She stared back at him, searching his eyes for some meaning to his request.

"Don't worry. I'll bring you back soon."

She nodded and left him waiting for her return. The first family member she found was Kristen.

Kristen frowned at her news. "Are you sure about this?"

"It's fine. Landon said he'll bring me right back."

She rushed back to him and said, "Okay, I'm ready but tell me where we're going."

He smiled and ran his finger down her arm. "I told you, babe, it's a surprise."

It was too late to change her mind. They were already on the main highway headed out of the city. They crossed the county line, taking a two-lane road and going deeper onto pristine land, untouched by development. They drove past a pasture with a wooden fence and an area where dense forest bordered both sides of the road. With no streetlights, darkness pushed away any visibility except for the asphalt ribbon caught in the headlight beams ahead.

She turned from the view out the side window and broke her silence. "This is insane!"

"What is?" With his brows knitted, Landon turned his head in her direction.

"You, showing up the way you did and now taking me God knows where."

"I told you, I have a surprise waiting. You'll see."

While he focused on maneuvering the winding road, she studied his profile. He hadn't aged a day since she last saw him. Still handsome, great physique, easygoing smile, bedroom eyes. All the qualities that drew her to him.

He reached over and placed his hand over hers. His thumb stroked her skin. She wasn't ready for his touch. She hadn't made up her mind if this was a mistake to come so willingly with him. Yet, he acted like nothing had changed, as if their long separation meant nothing. Slowly, she slid her hand out from under his. She steeled herself against the temptation to melt into his arms the way she did so many times in the past. But how could she stay strong while inhaling the scent of his aftershave, catching his easy smile, gazing into his tender brown eyes? Any of it could send her over the edge, erasing the hurt she experienced when he walked out on her.

Four years and not a word. Now this.

§

Colt called the family together. Tony, Jill, and Kristen waited for some explanation, but he took his time, anticipating a reaction of shock or denial.

"Landon Burke is a person of interest in the death of Brianna." He braced himself, waiting for the news to sink in.

Tony's eyes widened. "What? Are you crazy?"

Jill's mouth flew open. "Why would you think that?"

Colt crossed his arms and widened his stance. "Because he came to her house the night of her death. We have an eyewitness. The last person to see her."

"Doesn't prove anything." Tony ran his hand through his thick crop of gray hair. "First you tell us she killed herself. Then the cause of death is accidental. And now, you say she was murdered by her sister's ex-boyfriend. That's preposterous. The truth is the police don't know what the hell they're talking about."

"I hope it's not true," Colt said. "My concern right now is Isabella took off with him to parts unknown and we can't reach her. Kristen gave me Burke's number, but he's not answering."

Jill sobbed with her face pressed against her husband's chest. He patted her back. Kristen balled up her hands and pressed them against her lips, terror in her eyes. Despite the women's fragile emotional state, Colt worried more about Tony who was still in a doctor's care after leaving the hospital.

"We're going to do everything we can to locate her." He pointed his finger at them and said, "If any of you hear from Burke or Isabella, call me immediately. Find out where they are. Understood?"

He spent the following minutes giving them assurances but not promising anything he couldn't fulfill. He watched them solemnly pile into a car and leave the parking lot at New Beginnings. When their vehicle's brake lights flashed red at the edge of the lot, he felt a heaviness in his chest. He squeezed his hands into tight fists until the knuckles turned white. Colt hated this part of the job, seeing the fear and anguish on the faces of family members as they awaited the fate of a loved one.

§

No time to waste. Colt had to find Isabella before something bad happened to her. To speed things up, he'd reach out to a guy he knew only as Rabbit. Better that way. A few years ago, a friend of a friend recommended him when following the normal police procedural bullshit would take too long. The guy with special computer skills liked to stay under the radar, walled off from the outside world. He lived in a bungalow in the Plaza-Midwood area. It was an older, established part of town, recently reinvented with trendy condos and apartments popping up everywhere.

Repositioning the load in his arms, Colt knocked several times before someone came to the door. It creaked open and a guy greeted Colt. His large body took up the entire opening. He had coarse, dark hair down to his shoulders and wore a faded T-shirt with a message only a gamer understood. His protruding belly peeked out from the bottom of his shirt. With a sour look, he pushed his wire-rim glasses further up the bridge of his nose using his middle finger.

"Hey, Rabbit, long time, huh?" Colt held up a six-pack. "Look what I brought you. Red Bull, and a carton of cheese crackers, and beef jerky. All your favorites. See? I remembered."

Rabbit examined Colt's offerings and scoffed. "You want something. What is it?"

"I need your help, bro. It's important. Could be a matter of life or death, know what I mean?"

"Shit, I could get in big trouble helping you, man." Rabbit narrowed his eyes and peered toward the street in both directions. He spread his legs and crossed his arms. "If it was legal, you wouldn't be here."

"Are you going to invite me in?"

"Nope." Rabbit stepped back and closed the door.

"Shit!" Colt rapped furiously on the door, dropping the carton of crackers onto the stoop. As he bent over to pick it up, the door opened.

Again, Rabbit glanced to his left and right. "Anybody see you come here?"

"No and I didn't tell anybody I was coming. You're just as paranoid as ever. Lighten up, bro."

Rabbit tilted his chin up. "Come in. I'll need cash. Goodies won't cut it."

"No problem. I brought cash."

Colt followed him down a hallway and into a back room. On a makeshift table constructed from a wooden door and a pair of two-drawer file cabinets, three computer keyboards, four monitors, and what appeared to be a router with a scanning blue light covered the surface. Some of the gizmos in the crowded room were a mystery to Colt. He did his best to maneuver around all of it but still tripped on a cable and almost knocked a monitor off the table.

"Careful! Don't screw up my operation, man." Rabbit plopped down, his bulk hanging off the sides of the chair. He put one hand on his hip and sighed. "Okay, whaddaya need?"

"To find someone. I got his phone number. You can track where he is, right?"

"Depends. If he has a smart phone and it's turned on—maybe. And if I can get into a cell site simulator to divert the signal."

"Gotcha. Actually, I don't want to know how. Just do it."

"It'll take some time. How about I call you when I've got something?"

"Fine. The sooner the better. The clock's ticking on this one."

"If I do this and I get caught, the feds will be pounding on my door. Gotta make it worth my time, dude."

Colt reached into his pocket and brought out a wad of cash. "How much?"

Rabbit rubbed his chin. "Five big ones."

"Shit! You must think I'm rolling in dough. You know what cops make, right? I'll give you two."

"Okay, for you, a discount. Four bills."

"Dude, I told you I've only got two. I came here bearing gifts, remember?"

"Okay. Two now and two next week. Don't like it, then leave."

"Damn you drive a hard bargain." Colt put ten twenty-dollar bills in Rabbit's opened palm. "Call me as soon as you've got something." He pulled a piece of paper from his pocket and slapped it onto the desk. "Here's the guy's number."

"Is this police business or something personal?"

"Maybe a little of both."

27

Colt searched the database for a car registered to a Landon Burke of Seattle. The results he got did not match Kristen's description of a white sedan. A license plate number would be more helpful than the vague description she offered, but it was better than nothing.

Shortly after eleven in the evening, Colt showed up on Spencer's doorstep. He gave an apologetic wave to Vivian Spencer who hovered in the background wearing a thin cotton robe. She gathered a handful of material to her throat and walked away, leaving Colt and her husband alone. Spencer ushered Colt inside and said, "So what's so damn important you show up just as I'm getting ready to go to bed?"

"We now have a positive ID on Landon Burke. It puts him at Brianna's house shortly before she died. But it's urgent we get a BOLO out on him now. He took off to parts unknown with Brianna's sister, Isabella Luca. We need to find them."

Spencer lowered his head and moaned. "What is it with you, Jessup? Who assigned you to make my life miserable?"

"C'mon, Spence. I need you, man. I can't do this without you. It's your damn case. Just make the call. That's all, then I'll be out of your hair until morning. Hondo's coming in at eight."

Begrudgingly, Spencer agreed and called headquarters. "Now get out of here. Time for my beauty sleep."

"Good luck with that."

§

Landon turned onto a long narrow drive. Behind a copse of trees, a two-story brick house came into view. It had large white columns across the front porch. With no other houses nearby, it looked a little lonely but far from neglected. It stood tall and grand. However, it was cloaked in darkness, no light from any window, filling Isabella with trepidation.

"Who lives here?" Isabella crossed her arms.

"A colleague of mine. He works in the Charlotte office and we've worked on some accounts together. This is his car, too. John was nice enough to loan me his car and his house while his family is on vacation. There's a lake out back."

"Nice place."

"Yesterday I sat out on the dock and watched the sun set over the lake. It was quite a sight. Awesome." Landon steered the car into the garage and parked next to a silver Jaguar. He cut the engine and smiled at her. "We're together again."

"Yes, I guess we are."

He led her into a dark room and switched on lamps on tables at both ends of a sectional sofa. Landon extended his hand, "Have a seat. Get comfortable. I'll be right back."

She stood in the center of the room, taking in her surroundings. Landon headed for the stairs leading to the second story. In his absence, she admired the stone fireplace. Her reflection stared back at her in the black screen of a television mounted over the mantle. She finger-combed her hair and pressed her lips together, wishing she took time to touch up her makeup before he brought her here.

Still assessing her looks on the screen, she observed Landon coming up behind her. She warmed to the touch of his hands on her shoulders.

He kissed the back of her head. "I forgot how nice you smell. Still using the same shampoo, I see."

"Yes." She turned to face him.

He gazed at her with tender eyes. "Sit down so we can talk."

"I still don't understand why you brought me here. We could have talked in town. At a restaurant or a bar."

"That gives me an idea. John has some wine and liquor. I'll fix us a drink."

He left her for the second time but soon returned holding a glass of wine in each hand. "I remembered you like pinot grigio. Here, take this."

She took the proffered drink and sat next to him on the sofa. It didn't take long before they fell into a pleasant conversation about her music career, his time in Seattle, and the appeal of Charlotte, the city she grew up in. When they ran out of topics, they discussed the weather, heavy rain forecasted for the morning. At first, she sat up straight—ladylike, her mother would say— with the hem of her dress just above her knee. But gradually, she twisted sideways facing him. Her dress creeped halfway up her thighs.

Landon placed his hand on her bare knee. "Enough small talk. Now tell me about Brianna. How did she die? Your sister was so vague on the phone."

Isabella sat her glass on the side table. "Oh, God, Landon, her death…Well, it's the worst possible thing to ever happen to me. The worst."

She spoke about Brianna's death matter-of-factly until unexpectedly, she began to bawl. Embarrassment made her bow her head, wiping at her eyes. Still, it felt good to finally allow her bottled up emotions to spill out. While she unloaded her sorrows on him, he brought her into his arms and uttered consoling words.

"I am so lost without her," she said. "I can't tell you how lonely and lost I feel. Like I'm not a complete person. It's so strange. I can't really put it into words." He handed her a tissue to replace the ragged one, now soaked. She brought her legs up onto the sofa and bent her knee so that she sat on her calf. "Thanks for letting me go on and on." She placed her hand on his chest. "Oh, gosh, I cried all over your shirt. Sorry."

"No problem, sweetie." He smiled and use his thumbs to wipe tears from her cheek.

"At least, now I feel better." She took a deep, cleansing breath. "Okay, don't keep me in suspense any longer. Tell me about this surprise you promised."

"Be right back."

While she waited, Isabella used the restroom. She leaned toward the mirror and used a tissue to wipe off smudged mascara. She came out and walked around observing the room's décor from the books in the bookcase to the photographs on a table.

A sound came from upstairs. What was Landon up to? She stood still to listen, but whatever she heard stopped.

Landon sauntered down the stairs and entered the family room. He held something behind his back. Smoothing his hair in place, he walked over to her.

"What was that noise?' Isabella said.

"What noise?'

"I heard a sound like a boom and then I thought I heard voices."

He gave her a blank stare. "Oh—that. I dropped my bag with my computer and all my work stuff."

"But it sounded like someone was talking."

"Yeah, that was me. I was cursing." He laughed. "Even dropped the F-bomb."

"Oh." She gave him a playful smile. "What are you hiding behind your back?"

"It's your surprise. Close your eyes."

"Really?"

"Nah, I'm kidding." He brought his hand out from behind his back and placed the object in the palm of her hand.

The size and shape of the box took the guesswork out of its content. At first, she was too dumbfounded to speak, too afraid to lift the lid.

"Landon—this is—uh, I don't know what to say. This isn't the right—what I mean is—we've been apart for four years and—I can't—I just can't."

"Can't what?"

Her voice was just above a whisper. "Marry you."

He threw his head back and chuckled. "Open it, Isabella. Open the damn box."

She did, and her mouth fell open. She simultaneously smiled and laughed. Looking up at Landon, she said, "Oh, my God! How in the world...I thought I'd never see this again!"

Wedged in between the silk padding was the pewter ring Brianna made for her. High school art class. "I love this ring!"

She placed it on her finger and admired the design cut into the metal to simulate waves of the ocean. Since Brianna gave it for her eighteenth birthday, Isabella wore it daily until the time she took it off at Landon's apartment. It mysteriously disappeared. For weeks, he and Isabella searched every inch of his place and finally gave up.

Landon rubbed his hand over her arm. "I found it when I packed up for my move to New York."

"New York? You're back in New York?"

He smiled. "Yes, didn't Kristen tell you? I told her that when I called her looking for you."

"No, I guess she forgot."

"After I got settled in, I went to see you, but your neighbor said you were out of town. I found out from Kristen that was when you flew home—right after Brianna's death."

"So, it was you?"

"What?"

"Oh, nothing."

"Anyway, as I was saying, I found the ring when I was cleaning out my junk drawer and packing up. I don't know how your ring got put in a box and included in my move to Seattle but I'm glad I found it."

"I never thought I would see it again." Tears ran down her cheeks. She wiped them away and said, "I'm not going to start bawling again. Promise." She emitted a little laugh. "Oh, Landon, this means so much to me—especially now that Brianna's—oh, I can't even bear to say it." She took her time to study it on her finger, turning her hand at different angles. "I'm never taking if off. Ever."

She stretched forward to give him a hug, but he turned her gesture into a kiss. A light brush of his lips to hers. She melted into his arms as naturally as though he'd never left. Regardless of the pleasure of his embrace, she pulled away. "So, you said in your phone message you wanted to tell me something in person. Is this it? You found the ring?"

He encased her hand with both of his. "No, Isabella. That's not it. I have so many things I want to say, but I'll start with this." He looked lost, as though searching for the right words. "The biggest regret in my life is walking out on you. I should never have…what I mean is—I was miserable in Seattle, and it wasn't because of the lousy weather either. It was because you weren't there. I thought about you all the time. I know I hurt you, and I'm so sorry. I don't intend to let you go ever again, not if I can help it."

But was she ready to forgive him? He wasn't there for her when she suffered the greatest loss of her life. But to be fair, he didn't know about Brianna's passing. He only found out through Kristen. Isabella had been too grief-stricken, and maybe too stubborn, to call him back.

Now, he was sorry. He screwed up.

Landon rubbed his thumb over the top of her hand. "That last time we were together, I waited for you to…" He shook his head. "Never mind, it doesn't matter."

"No, say it. What were you going to say, Landon?"

"I wanted you to ask me to stay."

"Really?"

He nodded and smiled. "I waited for you to say it."

"If I had, would you?"

"I don't know. Maybe. When you said, 'So this is it. We're done,' I felt you had no desire to work things out. I thought you wanted to end it. So, I left."

"And I thought you were forcing me to make a choice, either you or Brianna. I didn't think that was fair."

"No, you're right. It wasn't fair." He leaned forward and kissed her. "I love you, Isabella. Moving two thousand miles away didn't change anything."

<h1 style="text-align:center">28</h1>

In the next hours, Colt did all he knew to do. He visited Isabella's hotel room and Brianna's house only to find no sign of her or Burke. He called Samantha and coaxed her into calling local car rental agencies to see if Burke rented a vehicle. Too bad he didn't have an exact model, make, or license plate number. If he did, it would help the cops on patrol in responding to the BOLO request.

In the morning, he would insist Spencer obtain a warrant for Burke's credit card charges and his phone records. Not only would it aid police in locating him, it might help them verify he was in Charlotte on the day Brianna was killed.

Sometime after one o'clock, Colt went to bed and tossed and turned. He was almost tempted to ring up Ashley for a booty call, anything to relieve his tension. It took only seconds to talk himself out of it. She was trouble, and he was done with her.

Morning sneaked up on him. The snooze feature on his phone persisted with its annoying ringtone. Reluctantly, he rolled out of bed and took a shower. At the drive-through window of Bojangles, he ordered two cups of black coffee and a ham biscuit. By the time he pulled into a parking space at police headquarters, he was hyped up on caffeine and covered in crumbs. Once he got out of the car, he brushed them onto the pavement and walked inside. Only five minutes to spare before Hondo strolled in. Colt hoped the drug addict was lucid and not edgy from withdrawal.

"Where's your boy, Jessup?" Spencer slurped steaming coffee from a Styrofoam cup.

"He'll be here. He knows what will happen if he doesn't show."

But after fifteen minutes of waiting, Spencer threw up his hands. "Told ya. He's a loser, Jessup. Your guy's not coming."

"Give 'im five more minutes. You'll see." Colt dug his cell phone out of his pocket and called Hondo. After six rings, it went to voicemail.

Five minutes stretched into thirty and still no sign of Hondo. Colt spent their wait-time pleading with Spencer to request copies of Landon Burke's credit card accounts and phone records. "You gotta authorize it, Spence. The cause of death has been changed from suicide to undetermined. It's an active case."

Spencer shook his head and scowled. "I ain't doing no such shit. I'm working another case and the Major is on my butt for results. You've wasted enough of my time, damn you."

Spencer threw his empty cup into the trash can and grunted. Colt gave him a mock salute which meant *screw you* and walked out.

Colt found Spencer's partner, Detective Jason Anders, in the break room, selecting the last chocolate glazed doughnut from the Krispy Kreme box. He glanced up at Colt and licked icing off his thumb. "You looking for me?"

"Yeah, Anders. I need your help."

Colt went over the new information about the case. Anders' response amounted to nothing more than incoherent mumbling. Desperate for action, Colt initiated Plan B. He took a deep breath and said, "Spence said you'd handle it. He's busy on other things. Is there a problem?"

"Spence said for me to get the warrant?" Anders bit into the doughnut, then wiped his mouth with a napkin.

"Yeah, yeah. I just came from his office. We've got a positive ID that puts the suspect there. We just need something more."

"Okay. I'll work on it as soon as I get back to my desk."

"Thanks, pal." Colt patted his shoulder and walked away. He hadn't given up on Hondo but before he checked back with Spencer, he went to the Missing Persons Unit. He hoped to find his former patrol partner, Tess Hooper, who got promoted to detective and joined the unit over a year ago. On seeing Colt coming her way, she gave him a playful smile.

"You mean they let you out of the crime unit to roam free?" She put her hand on her hip and gave him a once-over. "What are you up to besides no good?"

"Came here to suffer your abuse, Hooper. I see you're already dishing it out."

"Someone's gotta do it. Might as well be me."

Her new hair color took him by surprise. "So, you're a ginger now, huh?"

Batting her lashes, she ran her hand over the top of her head. "Makes me spicy, don't you think? Spicy and sexy." She winked at him.

"Yeah, you're spicy alright. Like hot pepper sauce."

She cocked her head to one side and smiled. "So, you're saying I'm hot stuff? I'll take the compliment." She chuckled and slapped him on the arm. "Well enough of that shit. What brings you here?"

"I got a missing person—uh, make that plural—two people missing. Thought you might give me an update. I promised some people I'd check on it."

Tess nodded and walked over to the nearest desk. She sat down, grabbing the edge of the desk to roll her chair closer. After tapping a few keys and logging on, she glanced up at Colt. "What are the names?"

"Lauren Lamont and Tara—oh, shoot, I forgot her last name. That's okay, just give me something on the Lamont woman. My hunch is they're together."

Colt leaned in for a closer look and read the text on the screen: *No results found.* He straightened and frowned. "Are you sure you spelled it right?"

"Should be like it sounds—L-a-m-o-n-t. That's what I put in." She keyed it in one more time and got the same message. "The name doesn't ring a bell. Looks like no one has filed a report, Colt. When did they go missing?"

"Yesterday morning, I think." He ran his hand through his hair and gripped the back of her chair. "Thanks for checking."

He walked away but turned when she called his name. "If you find out the other woman's name, I can check that for you. But just to give you a heads up, we've got a high priority case everyone's working. Looking for a fourteen-year-old girl. You might have seen it on the news. She met some older guy online. The FBI's taking the lead."

"You guys must be swamped, but I'd appreciate if you could…I mean, first chance you get." He took a few steps toward the door and turned. "Thanks, Hooper. Let me know something."

Taking two flights of stairs up, Colt puzzled over why Marcus Gilliam lied to Lily Prather. He said he reported the women missing to police. Apparently, that wasn't true. Did the dude think his time was so dang valuable he couldn't make a simple phone call?

Colt checked back with Spencer to see if by some miracle Hondo was there. Spencer glanced up from his paperwork and glared at Colt standing in the doorway. "Told ya, Jessup. Your boy is a no-show. You gave him too much credit."

Spencer was right. Foolishly, Colt expected Hondo to do the right thing. Without saying so much as goodbye, Colt walked out, headed for his car. He pulled his phone from his pocket and called Samantha.

"Hey, Sam. Hondo didn't show. Can you find him for me? I'm on my way to meet with the task force. Otherwise, I'd do it."

"I'm in the middle of something, but okay. I'll see what I can do."

"Thanks, Sam. You're the best."

"I know, and someday I'll make you pay for all the favors I've done for you, Colt."

"Samantha Delano, there's not enough money in the world to make up for all you've done for me."

"True." She paused, then added almost as an afterthought, "Well, I promised your big brother I'd have your back. That's what I'm doing. Almost a full-time job."

Colt laughed. "You've got that right, and I appreciate it."

§

Isabella awoke to strange surroundings. After only a few hours of sleep, her mind was in a haze. It took her a minute to remember falling asleep on Landon's chest when they were curled up on the sofa in the home of someone named John. The morning light came in through the window. She sat up and slid off the sofa. The hardwood floor felt cool under her bare feet. She studied the room, giving extra scrutiny to the photographs of Landon's friend with family and friends. She picked up a framed photo from the end table, feeling a tinge of envy for the happy-looking family: John, his wife and two young boys.

She walked over to the windows. Four sections of paned glass spanned one wall of the room. She took in the view of a gray sky and a dense forest. An adult deer and two fawns nibbled on plants. The larger deer glanced up at the sky. Within seconds, a downpour of rain erupted. The deer scampered off, deeper into the woods. The storm quickly raged and slapped against the windowpanes.

A loud boom shook the floor. Thunder? No lightning preceded the sound. Not thunder, but what?

A creaking sound came from the direction of the staircase. Landon bounded down the stairs and into the family room to join her. Freshly shaven and showered, he looked as good as he smelled. His black polo shirt was tucked into his straight leg jeans. He looked sharp while she was a mess. She smoothed the wrinkles from her dress and ran her fingers through her hair. A touch-up of her makeup would have to wait.

"Good morning. I hope you got some sleep." Landon gathered her in his arms and kissed her.

"Good morning." Isabella placed her hand on his chest. "Yes, I did get some sleep. You know, I wasted good money on a hotel room, but I liked these accommodations better—*and* the company." She gave him a playful smile and tilted her head to one side. Seeing a trail of blood on his arm made her gasp. "What happened? You're bleeding."

He bent his elbow up and examined his injury. "Oh, I dropped my suitcase and the metal edge clipped me. I'll see if John has some bandages in the bathroom." He started back up the stairs and stopped. "When I get back, I'll fix us some breakfast. Then, we'll talk."

She laughed. "Are you kidding me? After last night, I can't believe we have anything left to discuss."

"It's about Brianna."

Her eyes widened. "Brianna? But we already talked about her death. Last night, we—"

"Something else. It's important."

"Gosh, Landon, you look so serious." She swallowed hard. "You're scaring me."

29

Colt glanced down at the speedometer and realized he was only doing thirty-five and the speed limit was forty-five. No wonder cars were passing him. He was oblivious to the rain slapping the windshield and the slick road ahead, only visible with his wipers on high speed. His mind was on Isabella. He worried the Burke guy might have done something terrible to her, like he suspected he did to her sister.

Rabbit called early to say Burke's phone was turned off or else he removed the battery. No signal. Colt called the number, but it went straight to voicemail. He checked with Isabella's family. No one heard from her. Tony and Jill were near hysterics and screaming at him to do something.

A load of troubles weighed on Colt's mind, dragging him down, taking him off his game. With no word from Isabella, it was a lousy time to meet with Roper and the other DEA agents on the task force. But he had no choice. Tomorrow was showtime. On his signal, police and agents would put the heroin shipment and its suppliers out of commission for good. That is, if all went according to plan.

He grunted a greeting to Special Agent Roper and plopped into a chair next to Geek. He slouched in his seat, his legs straight out and his arms crossed. He listened to Roper recap all aspects of the operation from the moment Colt would meet up with the drug gang until the takedown when agents would surround them in all directions. Their escape impossible if all went as planned.

At the end of his talk, Roper sprang up. At six-three and broad chested, he resembled a formidable commander ordering troops into battle. "Let's do a test run. Geek, you ride with Colt in case you need to tweak any of the equipment."

Geek frowned. "No disrespect, sir, but this isn't exactly the best time to do this. With the way the rain is coming down, we should wait just in case the tracker doesn't pick up the GPS coordinates and the camera lens gets wet or worse, shorts out."

"Nope. Now is the perfect time. Tomorrow's forecast is more of the same, so we need to know what we're up against. Saddle up, troops."

Colt had no choice but to follow Geek outside. It was the FBI's show, and he was just along for the ride. Although if it turned into a shitshow, it was his life on the line.

§

Nothing went right with the test run. Colt left Geek's side and sprinted to get in Roper's face. "I'm screwed!"

Roper responded with a shrug.

"What the hell, Roper? The camera lens was obscured by water droplets. You couldn't see shit. The audio was full of static. And the chip in my boot only picked up a signal half the time. Yet, you want me to go in there and hope to hell you can keep up with my movements and pick the right time to move in. Are you out of your mind?"

Roper stayed silent, looking past him as though Colt was not standing inches away, close enough to feel his hot breaths. Bouncing on his heels, Roper said, "Relax, Jessup. The weatherman said the front will move in later in the day. Geek will do some tweaking with the equipment, and you'll be fine."

"This is my life here! I need some kind of guarantee this isn't going to be a shit show with me ending up with a bullet in my skull."

With a half-smile, Roper tsk-tsked his remark, avoiding eye contact. "Always a pessimist."

"Not a pessimist—a realist. Worst case scenario, you guys have no clue where the truck is, and I'm left high and dry. If that happens, I'm unloading the goods and they end up on the street before the day is out. Is that what you want?"

"Not going to happen."

Colt turned his head sideways and spit. He had a sudden need for a smoke and pulled a pack of cigarettes from his pocket. "Okay, call me when you get your shit together."

He removed the drenched vest with the camera and mic hidden within its lining and threw it at Geek's chest. Soaked to the bone, Colt walked toward his car, cupping his hand around the end of a cigarette. When he couldn't get it lit, he threw it on the ground. He felt weighed down by more than wet clothing. He wished the rain could magically wash away his troubles. Instead, the downpour plastered his shirt to his chest, where a heaviness felt like an elephant plopped down. He tried breathing slowly to see if that would help. He needed a break, something to cheer him up. A phone call from Spencer did just that. "We found him," Spencer said. "Landon Burke just got picked up. He's on his way to the station."

"Is Isabella with him?"

"Nope."

The elephant was back on his chest.

30

The guy was too perfect. That was Colt's first impression of Landon Burke. He opened the door of the interview room in the criminal investigation division and found Burke sitting in the far corner, one arm resting on a nearby table, fingers drumming the surface. Square jaw, freshly shaven, no hair out of place. He wore jeans, not faded and torn at the knees like Colt's. The black polo shirt he wore looked brand new. Overall, his clothing barely qualified as casual wear. He sported a high-tech watch, the kind programmed to do much more than telling time. Colt glanced over at Spencer and raised his brows, sending a message: *Can you believe this guy?*

Colt took a seat. "I'm Detective Jessup." He nodded at Burke. "Tell us where Isabella Luca is."

Burke bowed his head. "I don't know."

Colt's hands tightened into fists. He fought the urge to knock the guy into the next century. Standing up and leaning forward, he placed his palms flat on the table. "What do you mean you don't know? C'mon, man, she was last seen with you!"

Landon scraped his chair backwards. He cleared his voice and said, "Do I need a lawyer?"

"Do you think you need a lawyer?" Colt didn't expect a reply. He looked at Spencer. "Did you read him his Miranda rights?" Spencer nodded. "Okay, then. Sure, Mr. Burke, you can wait for a lawyer, but what you should really do is help us find Isabella. Do the right thing, man."

"Sure, sure. I just don't like you thinking I did something to her." He rubbed his jaw and again cleared his throat. "This is what happened—I left her at Brianna's—her deceased sister's house—around noon. When I came back, she wasn't there."

Colt straightened and crossed his arms. He positioned himself close to where Burke sat and forced him to look up. "Let's see if I've got this straight. You got pulled over for speeding. You were in a vehicle registered to John Simmons of Waxhaw. The officer was alerted to the BOLO for you and brought you here. Got it right so far?"

Burke nodded.

"Be straight with me and we'll get along fine." Colt's hard eyes were a warning. "Where were you going and why wasn't Isabella with you?"

"I told you when I got back Isabella was gone. I was in a panic, looking for her everywhere," Burke said, blinking repeatedly. Maybe a sign he was lying. "When I was pulled over, I was on my way to her sister's house. I called her to see if she'd heard from Isabella. The two of us were going to search for her together."

Burke wasn't looking so perfect anymore. His worried eyes darted from one detective to the other, then to the floor. He rubbed his palms across the top of his thighs. One leg jerked up and down with intensity.

What Colt found odd was how Burke left the house. If Isabella was missing, why didn't he dial 911? Why go to the sister for help? Questions for later.

Colt scratched his cheek. "Were you aware that driving off with Isabella last night put everybody in a panic? You just took off. What the hell?"

"I wasn't aware of that until I called Kristen. I had no idea there was a problem. And for your information—Isabella *told*

Kristen she was leaving with me. So, I don't understand why there was such a fuss."

Burke combed his fingers through his locks, messing up his perfect hair. He blotted beads of sweat from his forehead with a handkerchief he pulled from his pocket. Now that he was perspiring, the scent of his aftershave wafted through the small room.

Even though Spencer cautioned him with a look, Colt turned on Burke, fire in his eyes. "If you know where Isabella is, then dammit, tell us now!" Colt slammed his closed fist on the table.

Burke grimaced. "I told you already. I don't know where she is. Why don't you believe me?"

Colt walked away without responding and faced the wall, aware of the prolonged silence. He needed a minute; otherwise, he'd lose his cool, and if that happened, Spencer would shove him out of the room and take over.

A scraping sound got Colt to turn around. Burke maneuvered his chair further back from the table. He repositioned himself in the seat and said, "Detective, I really don't understand why I'm being treated like I did something wrong. It's not a crime for me to come here to comfort my girlfriend."

"Girlfriend, uh? That's not what I heard."

"Okay, *former* girlfriend. We're working on a reconciliation. That's part of the reason I came here. That, and because of Brianna's death." Burke leaned back, and with eyes closed exhaled a deep breath. "Exactly what crime do you think I've committed? And why aren't you looking for her instead of wasting time on me?"

"Show me your phone log where you called Kristen," Colt said.

Burke tapped the phone's surface and turned it for Colt to see. Without asking permission, Colt took the phone from him and pressed the call symbol. When it rang, he walked out of the room and came back minutes later.

Colt gave a nod to Spencer. "Yep, she confirms what he said."

Colt dragged a chair over and straddled it backwards. He rested his arms across the top. "Where were you the night Brianna died?"

"I was flying back to New York."

"Here's the thing—we have an eyewitness that puts you at Brianna's house that coincides with the time of death."

"I *did* visit Brianna that night before I drove to the airport. She was fine when I left her. It was around seven-thirty or so." Burke's eyes darted again from Spencer to Colt. "I didn't harm Brianna, but I think I know who did."

<h1 style="text-align:center">31</h1>

Colt stared back at Burke, refusing to be the first to blink. Burke cupped his hands over his face and left them there until he finally looked at Colt. "Did you hear me, Detective? I think I know who killed Brianna."

"Do you now?" Colt stood and shuffled backwards out of his straddled position in the chair. He wandered over to the far corner, his fingers spread wide over his lower back. He turned around, looking first at Burke then Spencer. "Okay, I'll bite. Who killed Brianna?"

"Marcus Gilliam. He should be your prime suspect."

"The guy who honored her with a candlelight vigil. That guy?"

"Yes. With my help, Brianna found out he was stealing money from the organization. Lots of money. Thousands of dollars."

"Go on, I'm listening." Colt walked back to the chair, turned it around, and plopped down.

"About two months ago, Brianna called me out of the blue. I was shocked to hear from her. You may know this already—she and I, well, we had what you'd call a rocky relationship. When I left, she was still on drugs and making Isabella's life miserable. Anyway, what I was going to say is—she told me not to tell Isabella she contacted me."

"Stop right there." Colt held his hand up. "Why would she call you if you two weren't exactly tight? Doesn't make sense."

"Because of my profession. I'm a CPA and she wanted my advice. She thought her boss, and maybe his administrative director, were embezzling money from New Beginnings. I told her I was very busy—in the middle of a move—that I was leaving Seattle and moving back to New York. She was very persistent, so I promised when I got a chance, I would look over whatever she sent me. Two days later, I get a flash drive in the mail along with copies of bank statements."

Spencer cleared his throat and jumped in. "So, you're saying she came to you for help and never mentioned it to her sister?"

"That's right," Burke said. "She thought Isabella would be upset that she contacted me since—well, since we weren't together anymore." Landon sat straighter in his chair and brought his foot up, resting his ankle on the opposite knee. He tapped his hand on the side of his shoe. "Her suspicions were right. Money was used for personal expenses to the tune of approximately eighty-five thousand. It was mostly grant money and miscellaneous donations. And something else—money laundering, too. Bogus payments made to a specific company and then from that company paid directly to Lauren Lamont. A separate account at a different bank was set up to handle the bogus transactions."

"A secret slush fund—is that what you're saying?" Colt scratched his chin.

"Yes, that's exactly what I'm saying."

"And how did Brianna discover this?"

Burke sat up straighter and brought his foot down. He folded his arms over his chest. "She told me one day she was filling in for the receptionist and she got a call about an overpayment. When she couldn't find the journal entry, she did some digging and stumbled upon an Excel spreadsheet. That's where the overpayment was recorded. In a locked desk drawer, Brianna found bank statements. She made copies—about a year's worth—and included them along with the flash drive to my new address in New York. Once I got settled in, I looked over everything she sent. It was easy to see what was going on. Hidden in plain sight."

"You told Brianna what you found, huh?"

"Yes, of course. We talked by phone, but on the night she died, I went to see her. I was here on business, so I dropped by before I flew back to New York. I wanted her to get a clearer picture. I marked up and color-coded everything on the ledger and reports so she could follow the money trail."

Colt stroked the scruff on his chin, thinking. "And what was she supposed to do with the information?"

"Report it. What else?" Burke said, arching his brow. "I know someone at the state attorney general's office. I encouraged Brianna to call her." Burke tapped his hand on the top of his thigh, looking up at the ceiling, then at Colt. "I told her to be careful. If anyone knew what she was up to, she could be in danger. If you don't believe me, Isabella can confirm what I'm saying. I took her to Brianna's this morning, and we found where Brianna hid all the paperwork. We—Isabella and I—had a long discussion, and I told her everything, and I mean *everything*. By the way, she believes her sister was murdered, and we both agree it must have something to do with what Brianna discovered. Please don't waste any more time on me. Find Marcus Gilliam."

"Why didn't you call Isabella and tell her all this?"

"Believe me, I tried. When I couldn't get in touch with Brianna, I called Isabella several times. She wouldn't take my calls. I had to blindside her at the vigil last night."

Colt turned to Spencer. "Find out what car is registered to Gilliam and get a BOLO out for him."

He nodded and stood up. His scowl either meant he resented Colt ordering him around, or he was pissed his closed case just got reopened. Whatever the reason, Colt didn't give a damn.

Burke wasn't done. "I left Isabella at the house looking over everything while I went to pick up lunch. When I got back, she was gone. My first thought was whoever killed Brianna took her. Kristen and I planned to go looking for Isabella, but as you know, I got pulled over. And now, here I am."

§

Detectives Jessup and Spencer left Landon alone in the interview room. They said they'd return shortly, but he knew he had a long wait. They were going to Brianna's home to see for themselves.

As though it was a movie reel, his mind hit rewind and he replayed the morning's events. His first thought was reflecting on what Isabella said at Brianna's house.

She pressed her palms against her temples and said, "My head is about to explode. This is too much!"

She sat cross legged on the floor. "Help me up." She raised her arms and Landon pulled her to her feet. When her stomach growled, she laughed and placed her hand on her waist. "Yikes! I must be hungry again."

Landon covered a yawn.

She nudged him with her elbow. "I'm hungry and you're bored."

He put his arms around her and kissed her. "I think we need a break. You've been looking at that paperwork for too long. How about I pick up some lunch?"

She stared down at reports spread out across the floor. "Great idea. But not fast food. Something healthy."

"The other day, I discovered a little Peruvian restaurant with roasted chicken and fried plantains. Like the one near your apartment. Sound good?"

"Definitely." She ran her finger down his arm and smiled. "A man who knows what I want. I like that."

Thirty minutes later, Landon juggled take-out bags and a carton holding two drinks while he dug in his pocket for his keys. He tried to insert it in the lock on the front door, but it wouldn't fit. "What are you doing?" he muttered aloud. "This isn't your place."

And besides, the door wasn't even locked. He couldn't think straight. From the moment he reunited with Isabella, his brain was scrambled. Frankly, he was drained from their long, morning talk. After it ended, he brought her to Brianna's house.

He headed straight for the kitchen, calling out, "I'm back!" No response, only silence. "Isabella? I have our lunch." Again, no response. "Isabella? Where are you?"

Surely, she heard his booming voice. He walked down the hallway to see if she was in the bathroom, but the door was open. Next, he checked Brianna's bedroom where he left her examining the papers he discovered hidden in the closet. She lined them out on the carpet in a neat row. Now they were missing. Every damn page. The only thing left behind was her purse, still resting on the corner of the bed.

His heart pounded. Oh, God! Where could she have gone? What was she doing? Why not leave a note? Did someone take her? But who knew she was in the house? Questions came at him fast and furious, one after the other. Nothing made sense. Why would she leave in such a hurry she left her purse behind? And *how* did she leave? On foot? By car? He rushed to the garage and found it empty. But was there a car there when they arrived? He didn't know.

Distraught and confused, his breathing became labored, his chest heaving up and down. He took deep breaths to calm himself, but his heart continued to race. His legs felt like rubber. Leaning against the wall, he tried to think what to do. He had no time to fall apart. He had to find her—and fast before it was too late.

He rushed out of the house and bolted for his car. He pulled his phone from his pocket and realized it was turned off, maybe since yesterday afternoon. He punched Kristen's phone number at the same time he turned the key in the ignition switch.

"Kristen! Have you heard from your sister? She's gone!"

§

Landon reflected on how he got here, questioned like a criminal at police headquarters. When he realized Isabella was gone, he should have done the sensible thing and dial 911 on his phone.

He couldn't remember if he suggested it or if it was Kristen's idea. They decided to join forces and search for Isabella on their own.

He keyed Kristen's address into Google Maps on his phone and took off, flooring the gas pedal as he backed out of the driveway. He whipped the car onto the main road, tires squealing. He ignored the forty-five-speed limit.

Within five more miles of Kristen's home, he sped up. Minutes later, Landon glanced at the rearview mirror to see blue lights flashing.

"Shit!" He slowed down and eased the car over to the side of the road. He put the car in park. In the side-mirror, he observed the police officer slap the taillight with his hand and sauntered over to his side of the car. Landon rolled down his window and shut off the engine.

The young-looking officer had a buzz-cut and wrap-around sunglasses. He hooked his thumb over his duty belt and spread his legs wide. He gave Landon a once-over and swept his gaze over the entire interior of the car.

"Is something wrong, officer?"

"Do you know how fast you were going?"

"No, not sure. I was in a hurry."

"I clocked you at seventy. Well over the speed limit." He touched the frame of his sunglasses and said, "Can I see your license and registration?"

"Sure." Landon lifted one butt-cheek off the seat and dug into his back pocket for his wallet. "I'm not sure where the registration is. It's not my car. Maybe in the glove compartment."

"Is there a weapon in there?"

"What?" Lines creased Landon's forehead. "Not that I know of."

"Open it slowly, sir."

It was unlocked. Underneath the vehicle's operational manual and some repair service tickets, he found the registration card and handed it to the officer.

The officer took both pieces of ID and said, "Wait here. Stay in your car."

In his rearview mirror, Landon kept his eyes on the officer who got behind the wheel of his cruiser. Landon took a deep breath. His fingers tapped the steering wheel. His heart pounded and his chest felt tight. He repeated a pattern, first looking at his watch, then the rearview mirror. What was taking the officer so long? His anxiety built up almost to the boiling point. He wished he had bottled water to quench his dry throat. He waited and worried, anticipating the cop coming his way. So far, he stayed in the police cruiser. For a second or two, Landon thought of taking off. But it would only make the situation worse.

A second patrol car pulled in behind the first one. Now Landon understood the delay. The cop called for backup! What the hell for? The two officers ambled over to his vehicle.

The buzz-cut officer gripped the butt of his service weapon. "Sir, I need you to step out of the car. Hands on the back of your head where I can see them."

"What?" Landon's mouth fell open. "Why? What did I do?"

"Just do as I say!"

Landon slowly stepped out and raised his arms.

The officer's hand stayed on the butt of the gun. "Face the car!"

Landon did as he was told. Over his shoulder, he said, "There must be some misunderstanding, officer."

"Don't think so."

In hindsight, what seemed like a bad thing turned out to be a good thing. The cop brought him to police headquarters where Landon crossed paths with the detectives. They were his best chance at finding Isabella. He didn't have anything against Detective Spencer, but he put his trust in Detective Jessup. If anyone could find Isabella, it was that guy. At least, he wanted to believe it to be so.

32

At Brianna's home, Colt and Spencer discovered no signs of a disturbance or forced entry. The aroma of roasted chicken wafted through the air from takeout bags on the kitchen counter. They walked around inside, looking for clues to her disappearance.

As soon as they stepped into the master bedroom, Spencer stopped short of the bed, looking down, then up at Colt. "Why would she leave her purse behind?"

"She wouldn't."

A thorough sweep of the house produced nothing more. Back outside, Colt pointed to the house across the street.

"Now we go over there and speak with the old lady and see if she saw anything. She's our eyewitness on sighting Burke at Brianna's place the night she died."

Spencer jammed his hands in his pants pockets and shrugged. "Guess it's worth a try."

They walked up the front walkway, then stood on the porch, waiting for someone to come to the door. When it opened, a woman glared back at them with hard eyes. If she greeted everyone this way, the welcome door mat was all wrong.

She narrowed her eyes at Colt. "It's you again!"

"Yes, ma'am," Colt said, smiling. "Mrs. Abercrombie, I need to speak with your mother-in-law. Just for a minute. Please."

"What for?"

"She witnessed a suspect on the night of Brianna Connelly's murder, and she might have seen someone there today. Or perhaps *you* did."

"No I didn't. I mind my own business."

"Well—can we speak to your mother-in-law?"

The woman curled in her bottom lip, her front teeth biting down. In case she attempted to slam the door in their faces, Colt placed his foot on the threshold. To his surprise, she stepped back and allowed them entry.

Mrs. Abercrombie led the way to the front sitting room. With arms crossed, the woman stood in front of her mother-in-law's wheelchair. "Mama Bess, these men want to talk to you. They're police officers." She started for the doorway and turned around, narrowing her eyes at Colt. "Call me if you want me to ask them to leave."

The elderly woman placed her elbows on the arms of her wheelchair and interlaced her fingers. She looked up at the men and gave them the sweetest smile Colt had ever seen, the twinkle in her eye reminiscent of his dear grandmother.

"Gentlemen, welcome! Please—call me Miss Bess." She gestured to a love seat and adjacent chair. She followed Spencer's stare to her container of brownies. "Oh, I'd offer you one, Detective, but …How about something to drink? Sharon made a fresh pitcher of sweet tea."

"No, ma'am," Spencer said. "We can't stay long."

Miss Bess looked Colt up and down. She broke into a broad smile. "You know, Detective, if you got a haircut and a shave and dressed differently, you'd be a right handsome young man."

"Thanks, I guess," he mumbled. He frowned at Spencer who was on the verge of laughter, pressing his lips together to hold it in. Colt cleared his throat. "We're wondering if you saw a car over at Brianna Connelly's house today."

"Why yes, I did. Actually—I saw two cars. They came at different times though." She started to say more but stopped. "Don't just stand there, boys. Have a seat."

Colt's gaze at Spencer was meant to transmit a message: *Now we're getting somewhere.* He sat in an upholstered chair and angled his body sideways to face Miss Bess. Spencer plopped down on the sofa.

"Tell us what you saw. Start with the first car," Colt said.

"Well, the first car showed up before lunch." She pressed a finger against her chin. "Hmm, let's see. I think it was around eleven. No, wait, closer to ten-thirty."

"Can you describe it for us?"

"Yes, it was a light-colored sedan. I believe it was white."

Spencer locked eyes with Colt and nodded. "Sounds like the car registered to Burke's friend. The one he was driving." He turned back to Miss Bess. "How long was it there?"

"I looked out around noon and it was gone. Then the second car showed up. It was one of those big SUV things. Solid black. And the windows—well, they were black too."

"Tinted?" Spencer said.

"Yes, that's right. The windows were tinted."

"Did you see the driver?" Colt asked.

"Yes, a man got out. He had a head full of white hair. Pretty hair, a little bit long—you know, to his collar. Dressed very nice in his Sunday best. Tan suit, tie. Looked like a car salesman or a televangelist. Pretty much the same damn thing if you ask me." She chuckled. "I got a good look at him through my binoculars." She shook a crooked finger at Colt. "Now, young man, don't you go and judge me. Yes, I'm a little nosy, but what else am I going to do with my time?"

"You'll get no complaint from me," Colt said with a smile. "Was anyone else with him?"

"No, just him. He didn't stay long. He left with Brianna's sister, Isabella. I met her once when she came with that detective lady. Pretty girl. Anyway…gosh, I forgot what I was going to say. Oh, yes! Now I remember. When—when they walked out of the house, the man stayed glued to Isabella's side. His hand was gripping her arm. She didn't look very happy about it. It gave me a weird feeling like something was not quite right. I thought about calling Detective Samantha. I couldn't find her card though." She shifted her gaze from Colt to Spencer and frowned. "Something's wrong, isn't it?"

"We think the man took Isabella hostage and we need to find her," Colt said.

At first, Colt assumed she didn't understand, but then she brought trembling fingers to her thin lips. Her eyes pooled with tears. "Oh, my sweet Lord! Poor girl. I hope that man doesn't harm her."

"That's why we need to find her. Don't worry, we will." Colt's smile was as weak as his vow. "Anything else you can tell us would be a big help."

"That's all I saw. If there was more, I'd tell you."

Colt and Spencer stood up to leave. They thanked Miss Bess for her time.

"You boys drop by anytime. I don't get many visitors."

At the doorway, they turned when she called out to them. "I hope you find Isabella safe. I'll pray for her."

"Yes, ma'am. You do that," Colt said.

On their way to Spencer's car, Colt tapped him on the arm. "This matches with what Burke said. When we get back, let's cut him loose and meet with the captain. Get some support on this."

Spencer nodded and hit a button on his key fob. He grunted as he slid into the driver's seat. He turned the ignition and said, "I guess I had it wrong. This wasn't a suicide after all."

Ya think? Colt resisted the urge to say *I told you so.* He reached for his pack of Marlboros and tapped one out. "Mind if I smoke?"

"Yeah, I do." Spencer grimaced. "You know those things will kill ya."

"Oh yeah? I heard the same about eating rare steak."

§

Back at police headquarters, Spencer and Colt walked into the interview room where Landon Burke waited for their return. His eyes were glazed over, a characteristic Colt saw often on the faces of "secondary victims," one step removed from the primary victim. They waited and worried, carrying the stress of not-knowing about the welfare of their loved one.

"It checks out." Colt pulled over a chair near Burke. "What you said. We now have a witness who saw who we believe to be Gilliam leave the house with Isabella."

Burke ran his fingers through his hair and tilted his head up. "Oh my God! Is she okay? Did you find her?"

Colt shook his head. "No, the lady across the street saw them leave in a black SUV. It matches the description we have of the car registered to Gilliam. We have no idea where they went, but we're looking."

"What can I do to help?"

"The best thing you can do is go see her parents and give them an update. I'll let you know when we've got something."

Burke hunched over like a broken man, no longer exhibiting the straight posture from their first introduction. But Colt could think of nothing to say to give him peace of mind. He was a wreck himself. It soured his stomach thinking about Isabella's disappearance and wondering if something terrible had happened to her. Tony and Jill Luca already lost one daughter. He couldn't imagine the agony they were going through right now. He walked Burke to the elevator and arranged for a patrol officer to retrieve the car Burke borrowed from his friend.

Colt met up with Spencer in the corridor. "Ready to go see the sergeant and Cap?"

The three men assembled in Captain Meadows' office around a small conference table. As a petite woman with a sweet smile, Meadows gave the impression of a pushover, but she had the reputation of a ball-buster. In contrast, Spencer's supervisor, Sergeant Griff Taylor, was a gentle giant, at six-three and two-hundred and fifty pounds. He and Meadows listened intently as Spencer and Colt briefed them on the details of their case.

Meadows crossed her arms and addressed Colt. "And you think this guy…" She glanced at her notes. "Landon Burke. You think he's credible?"

"Absolutely," Colt said. "His story checks out. It matches up with what the witness told us. Are you in agreement, Spence?" After Spencer nodded, Colt turned back to Meadows. "We need to locate Gilliam before some harm comes to Miss Luca. We have a BOLO out on the car. We'll ping his phone and try to narrow down a location. Until we have something solid, we'll question people who can tell us where he might go. We think the other two women from New Beginnings are with Isabella. So, we're thinking three hostages at this point."

"And Marcus Gilliam is not at his office or his residence? Is that correct?" Taylor asked.

Spencer cleared his throat. "That's correct. We've sent officers to both locations and they confirm no sightings of Gilliam."

The thing about Captain Meadows was her ability to keep her thoughts to herself. She never made eye contact. While she mulled over the information, something was going on inside her mouth like she was sucking in her cheek and chewing on it with her molars. Finally, she brought her hands up to form a steeple and pressed her fingers against her chin.

Staring at a focal point behind Colt, she said, "Okay, let's get this rolling. I'll get Sergeant Blake to assist with additional officers. I'll get Sampson to get something out to the press. Keep me updated, gentlemen." Meadows stood and ushered the men to the door.

Colt walked with Spencer back to his desk. "Tell you what, Colt, you can initiate a ping triangulation and interview people at New Beginnings." Spencer sat down and rolled the chair backwards. It creaked with the additional strain on its mechanism. He rested the back of his head on his interlaced fingers and said, "Anders and I will go to Gilliam's home and see who's there. Maybe his wife."

Colt folded his forearms on top of the cubicle wall. "You know who she is, don't you?"

"Should I?"

"I've actually met her. We shared a bottle of wine at a bar." Colt smiled, savoring the memory of the gorgeous, sexy woman, someone he wasn't likely to ever forget. "Marcus is married to Kathleen Iverson, daughter of Robert Iverson who owns all that property around Lake Norman. I'm sure you've heard of him. The real estate developer."

"Oh, that guy. Damn!" Spencer grinned. "So, if Gilliam married into money, why not help himself to the Iverson money? Why embezzle?"

"Maybe he can't. He's involved in something illegal. Or maybe it has to do with another woman. Maybe Lauren Lamont is his mistress and she's high maintenance. Secret getaways, jewelry, the works."

Spencer grimaced and shook his head. "That's why I don't cheat. I couldn't afford a mistress."

"Oh, I thought it was because your wife would kill you."

"That too."

After checking the computer database for any information on Gilliam, Colt and Spencer went their separate ways. Just as Colt reached his car, his phone trilled. "What now?" He held it up to his ear.

"Colt, it's Sam. You better get over here. I found Hondo."

"So, he's stoned out of his gourd, huh?"

"No, he's dead."

33

In an upstairs apartment over a food market, Colt stood beside Sam and studied the body of Hondo who stared back with marble eyes. A rubber tube, needle, and empty syringe lay at his side. A strip of dried blood originated from a fresh track mark.

Colt shook his head and grimaced. "I pushed him and look what happened."

Samantha's eyes widened. "He was an addict, Colt. Don't put this on yourself. You didn't do this."

Colt ran his hand down his face and turned away. With his hands on his hips, he scanned the room. Although it was untidy, nothing seemed out of the ordinary. No forced entry and no sign of another's presence. A classic scene Colt and Samantha witnessed too many times. An addict ODs.

Deep down, Hondo was a good person outwitted and conquered by his demons. His life was a game of Russian roulette. Just a matter of time before his luck ran dry. His life snuffed out in a flash.

When the coroner showed up, Sam and Colt backed out of the room. Colt retrieved his cigarette pack and tried to hand it off to Samantha.

"You know I don't smoke!"

"Just thought it might be a good time for you to start."

"No, I might go to the shooting range later. That always helps."

"Yeah." Colt lit up and blew a plume of smoke. After only one puff, his nerves settled somewhat. "I've got somewhere to go. Want to come?"

"Where?"

"New Beginnings. See if I can get a lead on where that asshole might have taken Isabella."

"You sure you want to do this, Colt? Right before your big performance tomorrow? You've got an early start, you know. You'll get all out of whack over this missing person case and you can't get your head in the game on the work you're actually supposed to be doing."

"Don't start with me, Sam." He headed toward the door but stopped and turned. "Well, you coming? I can do this on my own, y'know."

Samantha exhaled loudly. "Alright. If you insist."

§

"Why, Marcus? Help me understand." Isabella sat rigid in the passenger seat. If her sight was a laser beam, he'd have a red dot on his cheek. He concentrated on the road ahead, ignoring her. A range of emotions coursed through her, one minute, rage and the next, fear. "Brianna admired you. She respected you. You didn't have to kill her."

He took his eyes from the road and smirked at her. "She chose her fate."

His words made her so angry, she didn't trust herself to respond. What would be the point anyway of yelling at him, calling him the worst form of human scum? He made her think of Scarpia, the antagonist and her tormenter in *Tosca*. If only she could do to Marcus what she did to Scarpia, put a knife through his heart.

He lifted two fingers off the steering wheel and shouted, "Don't you see? I had no choice. She was going to report me, dammit! If only she had come to me instead of sneaking around behind my back. I couldn't reason with her. God, I tried, but she wouldn't listen. Couldn't make her understand the repercussions of her actions. I offered her a cushy new position, more money to stay quiet. She refused—insisted she had to do the right thing." He let out a nervous laugh. "The right thing, my ass. She wanted to be the hero, taking down a powerful man, a leader of the community. That's bullshit."

"And Lauren?" Isabella stared down at her hands, her fingers intertwined and forming a tight ball. "She embezzled money right along with you. Was she in on the murder, too? How horrible for Brianna to be betrayed by both of you. I hope—oh God, I just hope she didn't suffer."

Marcus floored the gas pedal. The car veered toward the edge of the road. He jerked the steering wheel hard and despite wearing a seat belt, Isabella slid sideways. The gun alone was a threat, but his reckless driving might kill them.

His jaw was clenched tight, his teeth gritted when he yelled, "Enough! Don't say another word, Isabella! If you do, I might just shoot you right here and be done with ya for good."

He'd do it, too. His gun remained in his left hand, resting on his thigh, his finger near the trigger and pointed at her. She had more questions for him, but she knew better than to ask. She concentrated on the passing scenery out the side window. Nothing looked familiar. Directional signs to Davidson and Mooresville meant they were traveling north out of Charlotte. They drove by new construction of a mixed-use development with retail shops and townhomes. Eventually, the scenery changed to fields and pastures with rough-hewn fencing. The only sign of life was an occasional cow grazing to its heart's content. The countryside ended at the start of dense forests, mostly pine, maple, oak, and dogwood trees.

Marcus made an abrupt turn onto an unpaved road. He hit the accelerator harder, the tires spitting gravel. Trees as tall and rigid as toy soldiers cleared the way for a beautiful, story-book house. A for sale sign stood posted in the center of the yard. The house looked like the house where she spent the night with Landon. It too rested near a lake, only this one was much larger. According to directional signs along the way, the huge body of water was Lake Norman. In her youth, she'd spent many summers there boating and partying with friends.

Marcus parked in the driveway and came around to open her door. Once she got out, he poked the gun into her back and clamped his hand around her arm.

"Is that necessary? Where would I go? We're out in the middle of nowhere. No way I could run for help."

"Oh, you'd run alright. You're smart, Isabella. You know this won't end well for you. Just like your sister."

Her knees went weak. Maybe it was good he kept a grip on her to keep her upright. Her legs wobbled like jelly; her stomach tied in knots.

Marcus had a key to the front door. It creaked open. They stepped into a large foyer with an empty room to the right. The hardwood floors gleamed from the sunlight coming in. A panel of three tall windows lent a beautiful view of the lake. A speedboat skimmed the surface of the water some fifty yards away. Too far away to do Isabella any good.

"Now we go upstairs." Marcus waved the barrel of the gun toward the staircase. "You'll have some company. Won't get lonely." He snickered, gripped her shoulder hard and gave her a little push. "Now go on. Be a good girl and don't cause trouble."

At the top of the staircase landing, Marcus pushed her against a wall and pinned her there with his hand splayed across her chest. He tucked the gun into the back of his pants and brought out a ring of keys. He inserted a shiny silver one into a deadbolt lock. The door opened into a large empty room with an attached bath.

Marcus shoved Isabella inside. Seated on the floor and slumped against a wall, two women huddled together. Their heads were down, their hair covering their faces. The one with shiny chestnut hair hugged the other against her body.

"Hello again, ladies. Brought you a new friend." Marcus's voice sung out with cheerful glee.

Lauren Lamont swiped her locks away from her cheek and looked up. Although her companion kept her head bowed, Isabella recognized the pink streak of Tara Sanders's hair.

Tara met Isabella's gaze. Her eyes were glassy, her skin like a porcelain doll. Tara's chest heaved as she struggled for breath.

"You've got to let us out of here!" Lauren shot up and stepped within inches of Marcus's face. "Tara needs help. Now!"

"What's wrong with her?" Isabella's voice trembled.

"She's diabetic. Her insulin is in her purse, and Marcus wouldn't let her bring it." Lauren bent down and picked up a cup of water. She held it to Tara's lips. "Here, honey, take another sip." She looked up from her squat position. "If we don't do something, she's only going to get worse."

Tara's head hit the wall hard. Her eyes rolled back, showing only the whites. She moaned. "I feel sick. Oh, my stomach—hurts. It's hot. Thirsty. Oh, God, help me." She rubbed her abdomen before her hand fell limp at her side.

"Okay, okay. I can see she's sick. You think I'm blind?" Marcus rubbed his chin with his thumb and forefinger. "You worry too much, Lauren." His gaze shifted back and forth from Lauren to Isabella. "I have to leave, ladies." He smiled and said, "I'm getting a recognition at a community meeting today. Probably a tacky little plaque but so what? Finally, all my dedicated work at the center has paid off. About time."

His grin disgusted Isabella. She always respected Marcus for his commitment in helping recovering addicts. She never realized his real focus was on himself. *Wow!* The guy just might be the biggest narcissist Isabella ever met. Her sister said he was, and now she witnessed it for herself.

"I'll be back soon, and I'll bring food." He bounced the ring of keys in the palm of his hand. "That should make Tara feel better. She just needs to eat. Don't they just give diabetics some orange juice and then they're fine? I'll bring some."

"No, Marcus! You don't get it. She doesn't have Type 2. She has Type 1, too much sugar in her system. She needs insulin." Lauren ran her fingers through her hair. "Oh, God. She needs a medic. If she doesn't get help soon, she'll go into a coma."

Lauren patted Tara's arm and stood up. "If something happens to her, it's on you, Marcus. Haven't you done enough? You killed Brianna—and Shannon. Do you think I'm stupid? Thought I'd never put it together about what really happened that day? When is it enough? When will it end?"

Marcus's eyes darkened. The lines in his face deepened, his jaw set tight. The look he gave Lauren sent a chill up Isabella's spine. His hand trembled with rage. He swept his hand upward. Lauren closed her eyes and shielded her face, stepping backwards. He dropped his hand and didn't follow through with striking her.

In a gruff manner, he said, "Mistakes lead to consequences. You know that better than anyone. You—got—*careless*." Marcus pointed his finger at Lauren. "If Brianna hadn't talked to that person about an overpayment *you made* then—well, none of this would be necessary."

When he walked toward the door, Lauren called him back. "Wait! You're not going to do anything? You're gonna leave her like this?"

He exhaled a loud breath, shifted his weight from one foot to the other, and adjusted the knot in his tie. "I can't be late for this meeting. How would that look? I'm the guest of honor, remember? When I get back, I'll tell you ladies what we're going to do. Just enjoy the little time you have left." He smiled and winked.

As soon as he locked the door behind him, Isabella turned to Lauren. "I'm confused. I thought you were in on it. Brianna's death. The money laundering. The whole bit. So, why did he take you prisoner? And who in the hell is Shannon?"

34

"You have to go backwards before you can go forward."

Detective Tess Hooper's comment got no reaction from Colt other than a blank stare. He'd stopped by her desk to make sure the three missing women had been added to the database in the Missing Persons Division.

"Did you hear me, Jessup? You know what I mean—start at the origin of the abduction, then go from there."

She was right. His gut told him Tara Sanders and Lauren Lamont were taken from one of their homes.

§

The recovery center and Tara's home were in the same vicinity. Colt and Samantha stopped by New Beginnings first. They had a few questions for the missing women's co-workers. Side by side, they took the steep steps leading onto the porch. A brisk breeze caused the windchimes to clank noisily. Remembering his previous encounter with the art piece, Colt walked sideways, giving it a wide berth to do its thing. Samantha arched one brow, her typical *what-the-hell* look.

Inside, they were met by Lily at the reception desk. Colt introduced Samantha and explained the importance of retracing Lauren's and Tara's steps before they went missing. Since Lily displayed the most concern about their disappearance, he'd expected her to speak right up.

"We were hoping you could help us," Colt said.

Lily teared up, dabbed at her eyes, and traded a tissue for a ballpoint pen. She clicked it repeatedly. Colt waited and fought the urge to grab the pen away. She set it down on top of a memo pad and lined it up evenly, straight across. He wanted to say: *Spit it out, Lady.* Instead, he forced a smile and said, "Can you tell us anything, ma'am?"

"The day before Tara went missing, she left work early." Lily picked up the tissue and dabbed at the corner of her eye. "She seemed upset about something and in a rush. Then, not fifteen minutes later, Lauren tore out of here like a bat out of hell. Didn't even look back when I told her goodbye. I knew something was going on, but I didn't know what. But the next morning when neither of them showed up, well, I guess you could say I got this bad feeling. You know what I mean? Something in my gut." She placed overlapping hands over her chest. "I told Marcus about the two not coming in for work, but he just waved me away. Said they were just running late, doing errands. But I knew better. I wish I had just called the police myself. That's what I should've done."

Samantha stepped closer to the desk. "Is Marcus here?"

"No, I haven't seen him since the vigil. He hasn't been in all day."

"Well, does he have an assistant or someone who might know his schedule?"

"Yes, of course. That's Alisha." Lily pointed down the hallway. "That way. First door on the left. Uh, Detective?" She smiled nervously when Colt turned to face her. "It's past time for me to leave. After five o'clock. Do you want me to hang around a while longer?"

"No, that's okay."

Lily opened a drawer and removed her purse. "I sure hope you find Lauren and Tara. I've been so worried."

They caught Alisha just as she locked her office door. Her large handbag hung from her shoulder, bulging on the sides. She turned around when Colt cleared his throat. Her sour look told him she wasn't glad to see them.

"Alisha, hi, I'm Detective Colten Jessup and this is my partner, Detective Samantha Delano. I believe you were out yesterday when I dropped by. We'd like to talk to you about Marcus. We can't seem to locate him."

"He's at a community meeting downtown. He's getting a special recognition, or something like that. He won't be back. I imagine he was going home afterwards. You can catch him tomorrow." She took a step forward as if that concluded their business.

"Is there somewhere we can sit and talk?" Colt asked.

She exhaled an audible breath. "I was just leaving."

"Don't want to hold you up, but it's important."

Her nod was slow to come. She unlocked her office door, turned on the lights, and indicated two chairs facing her desk. She sunk into the large chair behind her desk and plopped her purse on the floor. It landed with a loud thud. She slouched in her seat and folded her arms over her chest, pouting. "Okay. What do you want to know?"

She claimed to have seen little of Marcus in the last day or so. Most questions she answered with a simple yes or no. But one thing she said set off alarm bells in Colt's head. He glanced over at Samantha, who perked up the moment Alisha mentioned Hondo's name.

"Let me see if I've got this right," Colt said. "You said Whit Drummond came by here yesterday?"

"Yes, that's right." Ashley ran her fingers through her long blond locks. "In the afternoon. I came back from lunch and there he was."

"Do you know why he was here?"

"Yes, Marcus called him. He wanted to thank him in person for doing the right thing and returning the watch he stole. The watch you brought by earlier."

"Did you hear any of their conversation?" Colt asked.

"No, I don't eavesdrop." She blinked a few times and added, "Well, maybe sometimes, but…"

"Anything you can tell us will help. It might seem insignificant, but you never know."

"Well, I heard them talking as Marcus led him to the door. Marcus thanked him again for returning the watch and then, Hondo held up a closed fist. He said, 'Thank you for this.'"

"For what?"

She shrugged. "I don't know. It had to be small, whatever it was. He clutched it tightly in his hand. Maybe Marcus gave him some cash. Only I doubt it since he's an addict. He'd spend it on dope. Never had any desire to get clean."

"Anything else you can tell us? Where we might find Marcus if he's not home?"

"No. By the way, he has more than one home. One in town and one at Lake Norman."

"His wife's family owns a lot of property up at the lake, don't they?"

"Sure. They have five building projects going on right now. It's amazing what they're doing. Condos, houses, retail, apartments. Lots of stuff."

"Impressive," Colt said with a smile. He stood up, as did Samantha. "Thanks for your help. Here's my card if you think of anything else." Colt handed it to her and walked out at a fast clip, several feet ahead of his partner.

Samantha quickstepped to catch up. "Hey, what's the rush?" She sidled up to him just as he scrolled through his contact list on his phone. "Who are you going to call, Colt?"

"The coroner." He headed for the car, holding the phone to his ear. "Marcus gave Hondo heroin. That's what he had in his hand. Smack laced with enough fentanyl to kill him ten times over. I'll bet you money on it."

"My God, you don't know that!"

His call went to voicemail. He grimaced and left a message. He stuffed the phone in the pocket of his jeans. "Think about it, Sam. I told Marcus we were looking for Hondo. He thinks Hondo witnessed him coming to Brianna's house about the time of her death. No way he knows Hondo didn't see who it was. He thinks he has to kill him to shut him up. Makes sense."

"Maybe. One thing is for sure, Hondo was careful about his dope—who he got it from. He didn't have a death wish. He was staying out of sight to stay alive ever since Big Jack was after him. That's why he went AWOL and we couldn't find him." Samantha rubbed her forehead. "I think we underestimated Gilliam. He's the devil personified."

Colt pulled out a flattened pack of cigarettes with only one left inside. "Damn. Our next stop is gonna be the 7-Eleven. I'm out of Marlboros."

Samantha pointed her finger at him. "You're just like Hondo. You've got an addiction problem."

"I can quit anytime I want. I've done it a hundred times." Colt chuckled.

"Don't go quoting Twain and think that'll make me shut up. There's nothing funny about heart disease or lung cancer. People die every day."

"Look at it this way, Sam. A bullet will probably take me before smoking does."

35

Spencer stood in the driveway of Tara Sanders's home.

"What are you doing here?" Colt asked him.

"Couldn't meet up with Marcus's wife," Spencer said. "She's out shopping. Her maid said she'll be gone for a while. I left my card. I figured there could be some clues at the women's homes. I went to Lauren Lamont's residence first. Her car was missing, so I came here, and voila." He pointed to a silver BMW sedan.

"We had the same idea." Colt said, sure to include Samantha although she stood at a distance with her back to them as she took a call.

Spencer hooked his thumbs over his belt. "Looks like we were both right. I just got here. Crime scene techs are on their way."

Colt's eyes roamed the area, taking it all in. He focused on the BMW. With hands in his pockets, he walked to the rear of the car. Seeing two suitcases in the opened trunk, he mumbled, "Uh-oh, not a good sign."

He ventured to the passenger side and cupped one hand on the window, blocking out the sun's glare. He peeked inside. Resting on the seat was a purse and beneath it, an envelope.

Spencer held up a cell phone with a hand encased in a latex glove. "We found this on the ground—driver's side. I was getting ready to check the phone log. Hey, Jessup, check out what's on the front seat. Boarding passes printed off a computer printer. Apparently, the women planned to fly to Boston."

"Boston? What's that about?" Samantha walked up and took a position beside Colt.

"Don't know," Spencer said. "Maybe one of them has family there. I've got officers canvasing the neighborhood. We're asking about the Boston connection." Spencer slipped the cell phone in an evidence bag. "Hey, did you see what's on the floorboard?"

Colt shielded his eyes to peer inside. "I don't see anything."

"Not there. Back seat. Another purse. Has a cell phone and a syringe and insulin. We might have a medical emergency on our hands. Better find these women quick."

Colt shook his head and grimaced. "That's the plan." His phone buzzed in his pocket. It was Captain Meadows calling. The head of criminal investigations only called for two things: Either he'd screwed up royally, or something extremely important involved him. He cleared his throat. "Jessup here."

"Jessup, I need you, Delano, and Spencer back at the station ASAP. Something's come up. I have Detectives Wagner and Crissmon in my office from the Asheville Police Department. They have a warrant that's just been issued for Marcus Gilliam in Buncombe County on suspicion of murder. They saw our BOLO on the wire and that brought them here. When you get to my office, I'll let them fill you in."

"Holy crap. You mean he iced someone else?"

"Just get a move-on quick as you can."

"Yes, ma'am. We're on our way."

§

Isabella stepped closer, hands on her hips. "I expect an answer, Lauren. What was your involvement in my sister's death, and who is this Shannon person you mentioned?"

"Shannon is the reason for everything that's happened." Lauren grabbed a washcloth from the bathroom and held it under cold water. "I hope we get some help for Tara soon. I don't know how much longer she can hold on."

Isabella forced a smile. "I know you're worried about her, but please…Were you there when Brianna died?"

Lauren nodded as she wiped Tara's face with the cloth. "Yes, but you have to understand, I didn't have anything to do with her death. I was the one who called the police the next day. I was there when she was found."

"Then what happened?"

Moving to the window, Lauren kept her back to Isabella. With both hands, she massaged her neck. "Marcus and I went to see Brianna. He suggested we bring over stuff to make drinks. You know—just to keep things cordial. And to celebrate."

Isabella put her hand on her hip and cocked her head to one side. "Celebrate? What are you talking about?"

"He offered her a promotion with a big salary and suggested a toast to that, but there was a catch. With the money and her new title, he wanted her silence. She couldn't tell anyone about what we'd done—the embezzlement of funds. But Brianna wasn't having it—said she was going to the authorities and turn us in. So, we went to Plan B." Lauren turned to face Isabella and leaned her back against the windowsill. "I thought that meant Marcus would add a roofy to her drink. You know—just to knock her out. Then, we were going to take her computer, search her place for proof of the funds we took. Then we'd leave her unconscious on the floor. I didn't know he made her drink lethal. No way I knew it."

Tears pooled in Lauren's eyes. She brushed them away with her fingertips.

Isabella pressed her lips together and shook her head. "Why, Lauren? Why did you embezzle money? Are you that greedy?"

Lauren narrowed her eyes. "No, of course not! It wasn't for me. It was to pay off the person blackmailing Marcus. I'm sure you don't know this, but Marcus and I were in a relationship—well, that is until recently. I broke it off." She turned to look out the window, refusing to meet Isabella's piercing gaze. "I knew he was married, but…He can be so charming you know. Like a fool, I believed him, fell for all his lies. Anyway…Marcus said some guy accused him of murdering his first wife, Shannon, and was blackmailing him or else he'd go to the authorities. He convinced me the man was just trying to get hold of some of his money after he found out he married into the Iverson family. Have you heard of them?"

"Yes, everyone's heard of them. I performed at the Iverson Center for the Arts in high school."

"I agreed to help him get the money to silence the blackmailer since he couldn't go to Kathleen—That's his wife." Lauren stepped back, tilted her chin up, and closed her eyes. "Oh, God, I was such an idiot for going along with his plan. There is no doubt in my mind that he killed Brianna and also Shannon. I see that now."

Isabella shook with rage. "Damn you! Why didn't you go to the police?"

"I was going to. I just—had to figure out some things first."

"What you did, Lauren, is *nothing!* You did *nothing* to save my sister! I can't even stand to look at you!" Isabella paced, her head down and hands in tight fists at her side. "How in the hell did you and Tara end up here?"

"Marcus thought Brianna told Tara everything. He and I had a huge argument about it in his office. That's when I made the decision to protect Tara. We were going to make a run for it. I realized my life was in danger too. I bought two airline tickets to Boston. That's where my brother lives. He's an attorney. I thought he could help me. At some point, I needed to turn myself in and talk to the police."

"Did Tara know anything?"

Lauren shook her head. "No, according to her, Brianna told her nothing."

"Did you lie when you told me my sister was back on drugs?"

"Yes. There was no truth to that. I just wanted you to think…Well, you know."

Isabella's mind was reeling, trying to make sense of everything. Lauren Lamont was no better than Marcus. She could talk all she wanted, make every excuse possible, but it didn't change anything. She contributed to Brianna's death. It took all the willpower Isabella could muster to keep from striking her. Every fiber in her body wanted to lash out, cause Lauren pain and suffering like she suffered. The emotional wounds, the hole in her heart, would never heal. But Isabella was done talking. Nothing good would come of it. Isabella could only take so much before she acted on the rage she felt. Enough!

A muffled sound came from outside. A barking. Isabella sprinted to the window and pushed Lauren away. A large dog, a golden retriever, trotted like a show-horse through the weeds at the edge of the forest. A woman ran behind him, holding his leash.

Isabella banged on the glass pane with the heel of her hand. "Hey! Hey! Up here! Help us!" She tried to force the window open, but it wouldn't budge. Sealed shut. She pounded on the glass. Maybe she could shatter it. Thrust her fist into it. But no, it was double-paned. She'd break her hand, not the glass. She turned toward Lauren. "Isn't there something we could use to break this window? God, I wish it was lower so I could kick it in."

Lauren scrambled away and returned with the metal cylinder from the toilet paper holder. Isabella didn't know whether to laugh or cry. Lauren thrust it forward into Isabella's hand, practically hyperventilating as she gasped. "This is all I could find."

The small object with a spring action was no more capable of breaking glass than Isabella's bare hand. It didn't matter. "Too late. They're gone. They went into the woods." She dropped her head and wiped a tear from her eye.

"Did she see you?"

"I'm not sure." Isabella focused on the dense area where the woman and dog headed. "I thought she looked up, but I don't know. Maybe not."

"She must have hiked here. There's no houses anywhere around."

Isabella pressed her lips together and nodded in agreement. The woman and the dog may have been their only chance at being rescued and now they were gone. Would their demise come soon? Or would Marcus keep them waiting, locked up, emotionally torturing themselves thinking about their ultimate end.

Isabella closed her eyes and pictured Landon. Poor Landon. He must be sick with worry. Their new beginning, the do-over Landon joked about, would never happen. Not now anyway. Last night, she fell asleep in his arms, thinking about their future together. She'd envisioned a happy life for the two of them. She'd miss his easy laugh, his big blue eyes, his strength when she was in his arms. But after she was gone, his life would continue. He'd eventually marry, have kids. She wanted that for him.

Lauren said something, dissipating her musings.

"What? What did you say?"

Lauren inhaled deeply. "Do you smell something?"

Isabella took a big whiff of breath. A chill rocked her body and her hand flew to her heart. "It smells like gas!"

"We're going to die!" Lauren covered her face with her hands and sobbed.

36

Spencer, Colt, and Samantha entered Captain Meadows's office. The captain introduced them to Asheville Police Detectives Wagner and Crissmon. Meadows suggested they go down the hall to the conference room. She didn't have enough seating for everyone in her office.

It was already late in the day, but the detectives from Asheville appeared crisp and sharp, unaffected by the two-hour ride and downtown traffic. Wagner, the senior officer and lead investigator, ran his hand down his silk tie and sat up taller in his chair. "As soon as we saw you were looking for Gilliam, we called. Thought we could join forces in finding this guy."

"So, you say he's wanted for murder?"

"Yes, that's right." The younger officer with slicked-back dark hair tapped a file folder on the table. "It's all here. We're not from homicide. We work in the Financial Crime Division. We brought in a suspect for bank fraud. His name is Frank Saluto. We conducted a search of his home and found information along with lots of cash which links him to your suspect. His attorney wanted him charged with a lesser crime instead of a federal offense in exchange for information about a murder he witnessed."

Crissmon stopped talking like that was the end of the story. Colt leaned forward, keeping his eyes on him. "Go on."

This time it was Wagner who spoke up. "We worked out something and listened to what he had to say. The suspicious death happened in our area, along a hiking trail, about two years ago. Saluto said he was taking a video of a hawk landing in a tree. He heard a shouting match between a man and a woman standing just below him. You see, he was standing on a cliff and hidden from sight by brush. He started filming the couple and then to his surprise, the man put both his hands on her shoulders and pushed hard. She went over backwards, screaming all the way down. He found out the next day the woman died. She fell sixty feet onto rocks in a creek bed. He didn't call authorities and report what he saw because there was a warrant for his arrest on non-payment of child support. The guy's a loser, what can I say?"

"Who was the woman?" Samantha asked.

"Shannon Locklear Gilliam. Marcus Gilliam's first wife. He was the beneficiary on her life insurance policy. We were contacted by the insurance company who suspected foul play, but we could never link him to anything. Her death was ruled accidental and the policy was eventually paid out."

"That's where you guys come in." Crissmon grinned. Wagner gave him a killer stare. Crissmon rolled his shoulders back and diverted his attention out the window where a window-washer scraped a squeegee across glass.

Wagner cleared his throat. "Saluto sat on the information for a while. He found out Gilliam remarried into wealth. That's when he contacted Gilliam and said he'd work a deal: his flash drive with the incriminating video in exchange for a hundred grand."

Captain Meadows leaned forward, elbows on the table. "I believe there's more to it than what you're saying. We're missing something."

"Yeah, there's more." Wagner leaned far back and tugged at his starchy shirt collar. "Saluto didn't collect all the money. Gilliam wanted to meet him somewhere so he could give him the remaining twenty thousand. But Saluto was scared to do that.

When Gilliam insisted on meeting somewhere secluded, he got a bad feeling. He thought Gilliam was going to kill him."

"Probably right about that," Colt said.

"Got any leads where he might be? You said he kidnapped some women?" Crissmon asked.

Spencer pushed his chair closer to the table and rested his elbows on top. "We're checking out the properties his wife owned near Lake Norman. That's where we think he took the women. We're also trying to get a signal from a cell tower but it's not pinging. Apparently, he has his phone turned off. Of course, every law enforcement in the county is looking for the car. When he abducted Miss Luca, he was still in his own vehicle. That was five hours ago. Of course, that could have changed by now."

Samantha bit down on her lower lip. "We better find him soon. There's no telling what he's capable of doing. Those women are in imminent danger. We need to move fast."

"She's right. He's going to kill them as soon as possible and then run. We've got no time to waste," Colt said.

Meadows nodded. "All right then. We need to reach out to law enforcement in counties to the north and to state patrol. Widen the net."

All agreed, but Colt had a different plan. One he needed to do alone.

§

"Where are you going?"

Colt put his hand on Samantha's shoulder. "Don't worry. I'll be back. I've got to visit a friend of mine. I think I've got an idea."

"What is it?" She tried to block his path.

"Damn, Sam, get out of my way. Look, I'd tell ya but I'm losing time. You gotta trust me."

"This better not be illegal, Colt. If it is, I don't have your back. I told you the last time if—"

She didn't finish. He was out the door, keys in hand, squinting against the low sun peeking in and out between buildings. He sighed with relief when she didn't follow him out.

He'd track down Mrs. Kathleen Iverson Gilliam at a bar. He'd seen her on numerous occasions at The Watering Hole when he worked undercover. The first time he saw her, he had no idea who she was. He took the barstool next to hers and said howdy. His shady appearance did not dissuade the wealthy woman from flirting with him. After her third glass of wine, she let loose, telling him who she was, who she was married to, and all about his lying, cheating ways. Now that he had time to think about it, he put two and two together and realized she hired Private Investigator Billy Fish to keep up with her husband's comings and goings. He should have made the connection sooner.

He remembered seeing the man in the New Beginnings parking lot trying hard not to be noticed. A direct call to Fish would get him nothing but a denial. But if he got Kathleen to admit to hiring him, maybe he could get her help and Fish's as well in locating the philandering husband.

But would she cooperate? That was the thing. She needed to know her husband went from fornicating with women to kidnapping them. Surely Kathleen would want him stopped.

On his way to The Watering Hole, he called Special Agent Jim Roper to see if the DEA and the rest of the task force had their act together yet. Since the failure of their morning test run with pouring rain and a repeat of bad weather expected tomorrow, Colt worried.

"How's it going, Roper? Everything working out okay?"

"Sure, we've got it covered. Geek fixed the transmitter and the mic. Should be good to go."

"Should be?"

"Okay, it will be. We've got our bases covered, Colt. This isn't our first rodeo."

"Mine either, but I've never had a bad feeling about a bust like I've got about this one."

"Then, come by. We'll do another test run. You'll see."

"I don't have time. I'm working a case right now. I'll have to take your word for it."

"We'll get you geared up at the staging ground. Make sure all the equipment works. So, come early. Allow for time." After a pause, Roper added, "One more thing."

"What's that?"

"Get some sleep so you'll be alert."

"I hope I get to sleep. It depends on when this other case gets resolved."

"Did anybody ever tell ya, you work too hard, Jessup? Chill, man. Just chill."

37

Before Colt reached The Watering Hole, he had time to make one more call. He didn't want to disturb his ex-wife, but the need to hear her voice was overpowering. What if something happened tomorrow and he'd never see her or Maddie again? He needed them to know how much he loved them. Even if Kate no longer had feelings for him, she should know how he felt. He smiled when she answered.

"Hi, Kate. How's it going?"

"Fine." He hated the long pause that stretched into awkwardness. "How about you, Colt? Are you okay?"

"Yeah, I'm good. On my way to check out something. Thought I'd call."

"I know that tone in your voice. Something's wrong, isn't it?"

"What? No. Hell, no. Can't I just call 'cause I feel like it? Wanted to see how you and Maddie are doing. I haven't seen her since her birthday. I thought she might call, but—"

"She's been spending a lot of time with her friends. When they get a certain age—well, you know how it is."

"Yeah, I get it." Colt let silence fill the air. He scratched his cheek and wished he'd lit a cigarette before he called. "You're a good mom, Kate. I want you to know I appreciate everything you do for our girl. She's lucky. To have you, I mean."

"You, too, Colt. You spoil her and I discipline her. Good cop, bad cop." She laughed. When he didn't join her laughter, she added, "Just a little police humor."

"Is she around? I'd liked to talk to her a minute."

"Sure. She's in her room. I'll go get her."

With the phone to his ear, he pulled into the parking lot and stared at a silver Mercedes-Benz sedan parked between a pickup and a jeep. A bag of dry-cleaning hung from a hook above the back-seat window, driver's side. The metallic beads on a dress sparkled from the last rays of sun. Could be Kathleen's car and her garment.

He heard voices in the background then Maddie's voice said, "Daddy?"

"Hi, angel. I miss you so I thought I'd give you a call. Did you have a good day?"

"Yeah. The best. Sadie and I went to the mall. We saw some guys from our school, and they invited us to go with them to the ice cream shop. I didn't get in any car with a boy. We walked over. Just so you'll know. I kind of like Zach. He makes me laugh—and he has good manners. Treats girls with respect. You'd like him, Dad."

"Yeah, I probably would." Colt always envisioned cleaning his gun in front of any guy who picked up Maddie. "You know, honey, you've got plenty of time for boys when you're older. Right now—"

"*DAD!*"

"Okay, okay. No lectures. I just wanted to call and tell you how much I love you. You know that, right?"

"Sure. Of course, I do. I love you too. You're not uptight and strict like some of my friends' dads. You're always fun."

"Thanks for the compliment. Well, I better go."

"Dad, there's something I-I—"

"What is it, sweetie?"

"I know Mom told you about the beer in my closet. I wanted you to know—it's not mine. A boy from our neighborhood asked me to hold it for him. He took it from his older brother's stash. After Mom found out, I gave it back to him."

"You did the right thing—giving it back, I mean. Well, I gotta go now. I just wanted to hear my sweet girl's voice and tell her I love her."

"Okay, Dad. Stay cool." She giggled and hung up.

§

Kathleen Gilliam sat alone at the bar. Her skirt, hiked up mid-thigh, put her long shapely legs on full display. Pink, polished nails tapped the side of her stemless wineglass. When Colt slid onto the stool at her side, her stare hinted at recognition.

"We've met before, haven't we?" She offered her hand. When he took it, her humongous diamond and ruby ring sparkled from the pendant lights over the bar.

"Yes, ma'am. Colt Jessup at your service. We shared a bottle of wine last time we met. Merlot, I think."

She laughed. "You don't look like the wine type."

"Well, I was that night." He smiled. "Good to see you again, Kathleen Gilliam."

Her laughter came from deep in her throat, thick as honey. "You remembered my name, but you got the wine wrong. It was pinot noir. Rich, full bodied."

"You talking about the wine?" He winked. "It makes me sad to see a pretty lady drinking alone. Mind if I join you?"

Her smile grew wider on pouty, red lips. "You're here, aren't you?"

He motioned to the bartender, raising a hand. "Whiskey. Crown Royal. Two fingers. No ice."

"Wow, I like a man who wants it simple. Straight whisky. No muss, no fuss."

"That's me alright."

He didn't mean to disengage their eye-lock. Before he knew it, she caught his stare sliding downward, landing on her neckline. He could tell she didn't mind. She leaned forward, exposing even more of her full breasts. A woman on the prowl.

But she made Colt nervous. Her tits, her eyes, her smile, and just about everything about her was a distraction, and he needed to concentrate on his next move. He let her go on and on about her latest trip to Tuscany and all she saw and did. He only half listened, working up a plan in his mind on how to get information from her. He didn't have a lot of time to waste. When she paused to take a sip of wine, he blurted out, "We have a common friend I believe."

She pursed her lips. "Sorry, I guess I bored you with all my talk about my trip. Okay, I'll bite. Who is this common acquaintance?"

"Billy Fish."

Kathleen aborted bringing her glass to her lips, instead held it suspended in mid-air. Slowly, she set it down. "How do you know Mr. Fish?"

"Oh, our paths have crossed. We're kinda in the same line of work. I'm a detective and he's a private investigator. Think you could give him a call for me? Ask him something?"

"Ask him what?"

"Where I can find your husband."

She uncrossed her legs, sat up straighter, and tugged at her neckline. She made him wait, picking up her wineglass and finishing the last sip.

Colt kept his eyes straight ahead and his voice firm. "I wouldn't ask if it wasn't important."

"Why would Billy Fish know where Marcus is?"

"Because you hired him to track him. Didn't you, *Mrs.* Gilliam?"

She ran her finger around the rim of her glass. "So, what if I did?"

"Ma'am, I don't give a diddly-squat about that. What I *do* care about is right now your husband is holding three women hostage, and I need to find them before he hurts them."

Her eyes widened and her mouth flew open. "That's preposterous!" Kathleen gave a nervous laugh. "He might be running around on me, but if he has a woman or women with him, it's consensual, I can tell you that. He's a real charmer. It worked on me." She frowned and picked up her glass. She tilted it back and forth, signaling the bartender for a refill.

"I wouldn't be here if I didn't have strong evidence to prove I'm right." He turned sideways with his elbow on the bar. He kept his attention on her, secretly enjoying her discomfort. "Kathleen, how would it look for your family if your husband is charged with the murder of three women? Think about it. You have a reputation to protect—a fine upstanding woman like yourself. Look, kidnapping is nothing compared to murder. A fancy lawyer might even get him off, who knows? But murder?" Colt clucked his tongue and screwed up his face. "I don't think so."

"I don't believe you, but I'll call Billy if it'll make you happy. He might be doing surveillance on my husband. I just don't know."

Kathleen reached into her purse and brought out her phone. She held it up to her ear and locked eyes with Colt. "Billy! Hey, it's Kathleen here. Are you tracking my no-good, lousy, cheating husband right now?" After a pause, she said, "You are? Where is he right now?" She listened and placed the phone against her chest. In a whisper, she said, "He won't tell me. Said it will be in the report he's bringing next week."

Colt snatched the phone and shot up out of his seat. He walked to the door and stepped outside. "Hey, Fishy, it's Colt Jessup here. There's no time to play games. I need to know where Marcus Gilliam is right now. He's holding three women hostage and probably planning to kill them. Tell me now or I'll bring you in on charges and we'll see how long it takes for you to lose your license. I'm talking jail-time too. Get my drift, pal?"

"You can't threaten me. Who the hell do you think you are?"

"I'm the guy who gave you a free pass. 'Member that drug incident with your buddy, J.J.? I could've brought up charges. I didn't. Now I'm calling in a favor."

"I don't owe you nothing, Jessup."

"I don't have time for your shit! He's going to kill them sooner rather than later, and if something happens to those women—I'm thinking—hell, I'll come up with something to charge you with."

"Okay, okay." He made Colt wait, cursing under his breath. "He's on Highway 21 southbound. Just past the Davidson turnoff."

"Good! I'm close by." Colt smiled. "You're doing good, Billy. Now, tell me if you saw him take women somewhere."

"Yeah, okay, I did. He took a woman to an unoccupied house on the lake. It's got a for-sale sign out front. I thought he brought her there for sex. Brought two others there yesterday for what I thought was a threesome. None of the ladies seemed under duress. Didn't act like they were there against their will."

"Well, chances are they had a gun at their back."

"You've got quite an imagination, Colt."

"Imagine I'm right. Now tell me, dammit, where's the house?"

"Wait a sec, I'll give you the exact address."

After Fish gave him the information, Colt said, "Keep following Gilliam. I'll call you from the road so you can update me on where he's at. This ends tonight."

The minute Colt hung up, he called Captain Meadows with the location of the house where the women were held and the last known whereabouts of Gilliam. He walked back to Kathleen and returned her phone.

"Would love to chit-chat some more, but I gotta be somewhere." Colt downed his whisky in one swallow and set the glass down hard. "Let me see your phone again. I got to key in Fish's number into my contacts so I can call him."

He entered the number and turned to leave, but Kathleen put her hand on his arm, keeping him there. "Don't harm my husband. I want to see the look on his face when I tell him I'm divorcing him. F-Y-I—he signed a prenup with a moral clause, and he's getting absolutely nothing from me. Nada."

Her strange, wicked smile stayed in his mind all the way to his car.

38

Under the cover of darkness, the SWAT team crept up to the house in groups of twos. No sound, no light, and no activity came from inside. A team member crouched below a front window and held up a mirror with an extended handle.

"Clear." Over his shoulder, he said, "You sure this is the right address, Sarge? The room's empty. No furniture."

"Yep, that's what the captain said." Sergeant Wilkes, the team leader, adjusted the strap on his helmet. "We're going in." He waved his arm in a forward motion.

The front door opened easily with a turn of the knob. A muscular team member, nicknamed Ox, shrugged and dropped the ramming rod into the grass.

"STOP! DON'T!" Wilkes held up his hand and shouted. Mouth hanging open, Ox took his hand off the light switch.

"Gas! Smell it? You turn on that light and this place goes up like a bomb."

The team rushed inside, busting every window with the butt of their guns. Four guys broke from the group to search for the source of the gas leak.

Wilkes held up his hand. "QUIET! Listen up!" A faint banging echoed through the room. Sarge pointed up. The team rushed upstairs. Two guys rammed their bodies against a door until it flew open, splintering the wood frame.

A woman fell limp into the arms of the man in front. She gagged and covered her mouth.

"What's your name, miss? Can you speak?" Wilkes asked.

"Luca. Isa—Isabella." She folded over, hacking, coughing, and pointing to the young woman lying motionless on the floor. "Hurry, help her," she wheezed. "She doesn't have much time."

§

Colt drove his Charger wide open, flooring the gas pedal, flashing his blue lights, and blasting his siren. Vehicles veered to the shoulder of the road. Some had the good sense to come to a complete stop. Speed shot up. Ninety—ninety-five—over 100 miles per hour. He steadied the quivering steering wheel with a firm grip. His other hand scrolled through his phone, landed on Fish's cell number.

"I'm still with him, Colt."

Colt put his phone on speaker and said, "Good! Hold on. Gotta radio dispatch."

"Dispatch, in pursuit of a black SUV Cadillac, Model XT6, license number NC Adam, Peter, Thomas 2-5-3-9. Do you copy?" Colt said. "10-9—Black SUV Cadillac XT6. Request assistance."

"Roger. Units 2430 and 2667 responding."

His heart hammered in his chest. Sweat leaked from every pore.

Pure grit spurred Colt to push on, not let up. Adrenalin heightened his focus on his target.

His car hit a bump in the road. He bounced up, hit his head on the roof of the car. Fingers to his forehead came back bloody. The force sent his phone flying. "Shit!" he yelled. Colt eased up on the gas. Bent sideways, he stretched his hand as far as it would go. "Damn, damn, damn! Hold on, Fish. I dropped my phone. Can't reach it. Can you hear me?"

Trying to peek over the dashboard while reaching the phone, he steered too far to the right. "Oh, shit!"

The right tires bobbled on the rough, uneven shoulder. Colt jerked the wheel left. His finger stretched, strained. It touched the phone, knocked it closer. He scooped it up and sat up straight. "Hot damn! Got it!" He wiped his forehead. "Fish, you still with me?"

"Yep. Just made a right on Gilead. You should be coming up to it soon."

Colt almost missed the turn. He screeched around the corner on two wheels. He turned off his lights and siren. No point letting Gilliam know he was closing in.

Fish's vehicle, a silver Audi sedan, came into view. Colt hit the steering wheel with his fist. "Now we're getting somewhere!"

Slowing down. Ninety—eighty-five—seventy.

He touched the cut on his head. His fingers came back slick with blood. He wiped them off on the side of his jeans.

"Hey, Fish, when we get into a straight stretch, I'll pass you and light up, try to pull Gilliam over. Got police up ahead, just waiting for the son-of-a-bitch."

"I can't see shit on this road! Except for his taillights. So damn dark. Hey, wait. Up ahead. Good place to pass but better hurry. It gets hilly real fast."

Fish slowed and eased over to the right. Colt took a deep breath, his heart still pounding. He passed Fish's car and sped up. Eighty-five—Ninety—Ninety-five.

Bummer! Marcus turned off on a two-lane road. Colt slammed on brakes, hit reverse, and made the turn. He caught up to the SUV and slowed.

"You don't even know I'm behind you, do you, asshole?" he shouted as though Marcus could hear him. "That why you're just cruising along in no big hurry? Time to make my presence known."

With one flip of a switch, Colt turned on his grill lights and flashers. Blue light pulsed and reflected off the back of Marcus's vehicle until he sped off, tires squealing.

"That's how you want to play?" Colt floored the gas pedal. "You're on, asshole!"

Marcus sped through a red light. His SUV clipped the back bumper of a delivery truck. The truck slid and skidded sideways, tires screeching and burning rubber. Colt steered around the truck, picked up speed.

The road became narrow, bumpy. Colt bounced in his seat. He tried to hold his radio steady.

"This is Officer Jessup, Squad 560," he said into his police radio. "Requesting a spike strip on McCoy Road, north of 485. Do you copy?"

"Roger. Do you have visual?"

"Yes, he's fifty yards ahead of me."

"Copy. Requesting Units 2430 and 2667 to activate spike strip."

Colt hung up. The SUV whipped onto the next road, streaming a trail of dust and gravel.

"Aw, shit!" Colt hit the steering wheel with the heel of his hand. He picked up the radio. "Dispatch, suspect turned off—Abbott Road, eastbound. Cancel spike strip. Need backup *stat*!" Colt swiped sweat from his forehead with the back of his forearm.

Marcus's vehicle slowed. Speed dropped to fifty, then forty. Its movement jerky, lurching. Shot transmission? If so, good news for Colt. He matched Marcus's speed.

At just the right moment, Colt mashed the gas pedal. The Charger clipped the back bumper, put the SUV in a spin. It rocked side to side, straightened, picked up speed, lost control, zigzagging on the road. It hit the shoulder and flipped. The car rolled, landed on its roof. On the far side of a ditch, it rested in a cloud of dust.

The Charger skidded to an abrupt stop. Heart pounding, Colt bolted out and raced to the SUV. The airbag deployed. The smell of burnt chemical was overpowering. Colt squeezed his nostrils using his index finger and thumb. A bloody hand stuck out through the broken driver's side window and gripped the dangling side mirror. Marcus was upside down inside the car.

Colt dropped to his knees and found a pulse on Marcus's neck. "You're alive, buddy! Gonna get you outta there. Hang on."

From his pocket, Colt pulled a knife. He cut the seatbelt. Blood spurted from Marcus's chin, trailed downward to his forehead.

Colt angled sideways. He slid hands underneath Marcus's armpits. Something blocked him. It was too dark to see what. He pushed the collapsed airbag out of his way. With eyes closed and blood continuing to stream down his face, Marcus moaned.

"Damn! I can't get you out. What's blocking?" All the pulling and tugging Colt did and nothing worked.

A hissing sound came from the rear of the vehicle. Colt stopped pulling and stepped back. He searched for the source. A flame ignited. The smell of gasoline grew pungent. A small blaze shot up, a flare of blue and gold near the wheel axle. It grew larger, bolder, coursing its way along a wire coming towards him.

He darted to the opposite side of the car and dropped to his belly, reaching inside. Marcus's leg was pinned beneath the steering wheel column. When Colt clasped the calf, Marcus screamed out. A bone protruded through the skin.

"Damn! That's gotta hurt. Sorry, dude," Colt said.

Flames inched closer, only a few feet away. From the rear of the vehicle, a stream of gasoline ran downhill.

Colt turned the leg to free it. Marcus twisted his face in pain, squeezed his eyes shut, and moaned before he lost consciousness.

"Sorry, bro. Know it hurts but gotta get you outta here." Colt gave a hard yank. Blood created a slick coating. Before the car exploded, Colt pulled Marcus out. He strained, using all the strength he could muster to drag his dead weight as far away as possible. Finally, at a safe distance, Colt released his grip on Marcus. His body hit the ground with a dull thud.

Colt bent over, bracing his hands on his knees and taking short, labored breaths. A big boom shook the ground. Colt jumped back, his heart racing. Flames shot up twelve feet high. Colt shielded his face against the heat. Seared particles and ash floated back to the ground.

Colt went to his car and called dispatch, requesting medical assistance and inquiring about his backup. Where in the hell were the units responding to his call? Five minutes later, two squad cars rolled to the side of the road and officers trounced through the weeds to where he stood.

"Welcome to the party," he said, gesturing to the display of twisted burning metal that was once a nice luxury car.

39

Colt paced, tapping his hand on the side of his jeans. He couldn't stay still. He'd smoked two cigarettes already and lit another. He waited at the scene for medics to show up. After that, he hung around waiting on the Asheville detectives. They finally arrived and became an audience for his animated, blow-by-blow run-down of the apprehension.

The detectives shook their heads and laughed along with Colt. "Man, oh man! Exciting night." Detective Wagner said. "We never get stuff like that. Well, not much anyway."

"If you guys don't mind, I've got a busy day tomorrow. Better get a move-on."

Colt headed for his car. On the way, his cell rang. He pressed the green call symbol and brought the phone to his ear. "'Bout damn time. Spence! Talk to me, bro!"

"We got 'em. The women are safe. I am at the hospital now. Isabella and Lauren Lamont seem fine, but we still don't know anything about Tara Sanders. The doctor said he'd come out and talk with us soon. Her parents are on the way."

"Have you had a chance to question them?"

"No, not yet. Gilliam left them to die. He turned on the gas and was planning on blowing up the place."

"I'm not surprised."

"So, I heard he's injured. That right?"

"Yep. He's in pretty bad shape, but he'll live. Face his day in court."

"Good. Hey, we'll touch base tomorrow. Go over some things."

"Sure. Right now, I'm going home and get some shuteye. I've got a big operation going down in about six hours. Gotta get a few winks."

"Good luck with that." After a pause, Spencer said, "You're alright, Colt. I think I had you pegged wrong."

"You're not too shabby yourself, big guy. Maybe we'll do this again."

"Yeah, maybe."

Colt laughed and hung up.

Thirty minutes later, he crashed on top of his bed, still dressed but minus his boots.

§

Not until Landon said a host of comforting words did Isabella feel truly safe.

He, her parents, and Kristen crowded around her. She sat on the side of a bed in the Emergency Room and felt Landon's hand stroking her arm. She was overwhelmed by their concern. The only words she could think to say were, "I'm lucky to be alive."

Her mother wiped a tear away. "Oh, honey, we were so scared. I thought I'd lose you too. First, Brianna and then…Are you sure you're alright?"

"Yes, Mom. I'm tougher than you think."

A doctor in scrubs cleared his throat and entered the room. Tall and handsome, he looked to be around Isabella's age. "Sorry to intrude, folks. I thought you'd want an update on Tara Sanders. She's stable now. Her blood sugar is normal. We're going to keep her overnight for observation. I spoke to her parents by phone. They'll be here in about twenty minutes."

Isabella brought her hands to her lips. "That's wonderful. I was so worried."

Sooner than expected, Tara's parents arrived. A nurse led Landon and Isabella's family to the lobby to meet them. Left alone, Isabella fingered the tie on the hospital gown just to have something to do. *Wish the doctor would bring the release papers, so I can get out of here.* She sensed movement at the door and looked up.

Two police officers stood on either side of the doorway as Lauren walked toward the bed. Seeing her made Isabella stiffen. What did she want? Lauren's eyes were red-rimmed. Tears left tracks through her makeup and smudged her mascara. An unruly section of her hair needed a comb. Her shoulders were hunched. Her walk and her posture lacked self-confidence. Lauren's looks were not so perfect anymore.

At Isabella's bedside, she clasped her hands together and bowed her head. "Isabella, I-I—well, I just want you to know I'm truly sorry for my role in Brianna's death. I was wrong to go along with..." She sighed deeply. "I will do my part in seeing that Marcus pays for what he did."

Isabella surprised herself by stretching forward to wrap her arms around Lauren. She wasn't ready to forgive her, not yet anyway but there was no point in staying angry. Nothing would ever bring Brianna back.

§

Landon drove Isabella from the hospital to her hotel. Even though they had been apart for so long, they fell back into a pattern of familiarity. As in the past, Landon conveyed his deep feelings for her in small ways: a kiss, an embrace, a smile.

With his hand on the small of her back, he led her through the hotel lobby and up to her room on the third floor. As soon as she entered her room, she kicked off her shoes and collapsed on the bed. Without a word, Landon stretched out beside her and wrapped his arms around her, kissing the nape of her neck.

"Just hold me. That's all I want—just to stay in your arms." She pressed up closer against him and closed her eyes.

He kissed the back of her head. "You're safe now, babe. I've got you."

She smiled; grateful he was there. They got under the covers and stayed in a spoon position until a peace carried her into a deep sleep.

Around two in the morning, Isabella startled awake. She sat up in bed, disappointed what she experienced was only a dream. She felt Brianna's hand on her arm. She saw Brianna's big smile. She heard Brianna's voice. "I am fine. I am happy. Be happy too."

The dream left her with a hollow feeling. A realization. Brianna wasn't alive. She was gone. Isabella wiped away a tear. Why must the euphoria at seeing Brianna be short lived? *Brianna, come back. Return to me. Please.*

Landon rolled over and rubbed sleep from his eyes. He placed his hand on her arm. "Are you okay? You were moaning."

"I'm fine." She gave him a reassuring smile. "Go back to sleep."

She turned on her side and pulled the sheet up to her chin. But her eyes remained open. Her mind twisted into a jumble of thoughts, and she was too wired for sleep. It wasn't just the dream. Everything about the last fourteen hours left her numb, emotionally and physically. When would she feel normal again? When would she allow Landon to make love to her? When would it feel right?

After revisiting her perilous ordeal, Isabella exhausted herself into sleep.

40

Colt's alarm sounded too soon. He stumbled out of bed and splashed cold water on his face. He didn't like what he witnessed in the mirror; a face beaten down more by life choices than aging. So, what if he was sleep-deprived and looked like hell? He had a job to do and if he did it well, he'd live to see another day. But if he screwed up, well, his daughter would be without a daddy, and he'd be damned if he'd let that happen.

The torrent of rain didn't come. The weatherman's inaccurate forecast of a downpour put a big smile on Colt's face. Even Special Agent Roper grinned when Colt pulled into the staging area. He extended his arms and strolled over to Colt. "See? Clear skies. We're gonna be fine." He slapped Colt on the back and said, "Let's get you suited up. Geek wouldn't let you down. You know that, right?"

But Roper's optimism did not dismiss the sick feeling in the pit of Colt's stomach. He attributed it to both the spicy beef jerky he ate and his nerves on edge. *Let's get this over with*, his internal thought, expressed as a scowl instead of words.

The rest of the team stood by and watched him slip on the denim vest wired with audio and video capabilities. In silence, they gawked, thinking who knows what, while Colt sat on a tree stump and switched boots, making sure the transponder was hidden deep inside.

Seated in the driver's seat of a borrowed truck, Colt let the door hang open. He nodded to Roper. "Well, time for me to roll."

Roper patted him on the shoulder. "Good luck, Jessup. We've got your back."

Colt nodded without conviction.

Twenty minutes later, he arrived at the gravel lot next to an abandoned building. Relics of its past remained. A busted-up neon sign hung from a pole. The only letters left intact in the word *HAPPY HOUR* were the *H* and the *R*. A large paneled van quivered from its engine idling. A sign on its side read *Ray's Industrial Supplies*. Standing around, kicking gravel, and trash-talking were a motley crew of misfits, armed to the gills.

Colt hadn't seen Rake since their game of pool. He stared wide-eyed as Colt approached. "You subbing for Scooby? He didn't make bail?"

"Yeah, that's right," Colt said. "You're stuck with me."

A guy known by his high school jersey number, 52, leaned against the van near Rake. Fifty-two was a hefty figure with long stringy hair. He bore imaginary holes in Colt's skin with his hellfire eyes.

Boone hitched his chin in Colt's direction. "Well, lookee who crawled out from under a rock. Ready to do this shit, Rowdy?"

For a second, Colt froze, then it hit him. He was Rowdy now, the badass drug dealer from Northside. "Sure, Boonie, let's do this. Where's the shipment? Close, I hope."

"Not far. You're riding with me, Pug, and Rocky. Rake's gonna drive the van. Fifty-two's with him." Boone's brows knitted as he studied Colt's face. "What the hell happened to you? That's a nasty cut on your head, dude."

Colt put his hand to his wound. "Got in a bar fight last night with some asshole."

"Who looks worse, you or him?"

"He does."

Boone laughed. "Good."

Pug came up behind Boone and pounded on his back like he was playing drums. "Okay, Boonie, we're in the lead just like we talked about. Rake will follow with Fifty-two. In the rear will be those guys." Colt followed Pug's gaze to four men grouped together. Guards, judging by their artillery. They'd form a perimeter around the operation and stand lookout as the drugs were unloaded. The task force prepared for this. Resistance and firepower. If all went as planned, the gun guys would be contained before the first shot was fired.

About ten miles down the road and off I-85, the entourage pulled into a secluded wooded area where a tractor-trailer was parked on a gravel road. The smell of diesel fuel hung heavy in the air. Colt strained in the darkness to study the lay of the land and determine the best entry point for the task force's assault.

Boone backed up the van to meet the rear of the tractor-trailer. The van was still rolling when Pug tried to hop up into the truck. "Hey, asshole! Put the damn thing in park. You tryin' to kill me?"

Pug laughed along with the others. Rocky hit the brakes hard. Pug jumped onto the edge of the trailer and sprang to his feet. He pulled back a heavy tarp and used a crowbar to pry up a cut-out section of wood in the faux flooring. He stared down at a storage hole, retrofitted into the undercarriage of the rig. Inspecting the product, he stood knee deep in the hole, then traded places with Fifty-two. Weighing well over two hundred pounds, mostly muscle, he was better suited to lift ten-pound bags of heroin.

In assembly line form, the unloading began. Soon beads of sweat dotted everyone's face and half-moons formed on their armpits. The threat of daylight made them work furiously, not slowing down for any reason. Grunting and swearing took the place of conversation.

Colt's heart raced. Every second led to the summation of six-months embedded with lowlife criminals. The only thing standing between him and them was his signal to the task force.

The last hidey-hole was uncovered with its stash. Colt stomped the flooring back in place. Pug huffed and puffed as he dragged a heavy tarp over it.

Fifty-two grunted when he jumped down from the trailer. He exchanged a look with Rake who nodded. From that moment on, Fifty-two became hinky, his eyes darting from one direction to another. What the hell? No one else noticed, but Colt did. Fifty-two and Rake walked toward the front of the van. What were they up to?

Their absence made Colt nervous. Sweat formed on his forehead. His heart raced. Were Rake and Fifty-two plotting something? Would it screw up the takedown? He tuned out the chatter around him and focused on the new development. As time ticked by, he waited, watched, and debated if he should send a distress signal to the task force. All he had to do was speak the magic word that would send the team swarming in with guns drawn. Tension built up inside him, an artery in his neck pulsed. His heart continued to race. What if he went up front to find them, see what they were up to? Of course, he'd have his finger on the trigger of his Glock just in case. Boone would be no problem if he had to take him out. Sure, he was a whizz at pool but not exactly a sharpshooter. But Fifty-two was the unknown. They were strangers until today. If Colt was going to do something, the time was now. But just then, the two returned. They held up automatic assault weapons, chest-high and pointed at the other guys.

"Nobody move!" Rake shouted, his spittle landing on his arm. "Can't argue with an assault weapon, boys." He gestured to

Colt, Boone, Rocky, and Pug. "Set your weapons down—nice and easy."

Pug placed his gun on the ground and stepped forward. "What the hell are you doing, Rake?" He raised his arm as if he'd take Rake's weapon from him but then dropped it.

Rake jutted the barrel forward. "I said—stay back! Fifty-two and I are leaving with the drugs. Don't even think of stopping us." He looked at his partner who did a sweep with the barrel taking in everyone in his sights. "C'mon, Fifty-two, let's go."

Two of the look-out guys charged forward, firing their guns, and missing. A spray of bullets mowed them down. In one burst, dozens of shots fired. The carnage was brutal. Blood gushed from the chest wound of one man. The femoral artery of the other spurted up like a geyser. The metallic smell of blood permeated the air, thick with smoke and gunpowder.

Pug, Rocky, Boone, and Colt crouched behind the trailer for cover.

In the six months that the task force met, the possibility of automatic weapons was never discussed. Among the drug guys, the preferred weapon of choice had always been semi-automatic pistols with extended magazines. Assault weapons had never been part of the game-plan. If the feds rushed in now, outgunned, and unable to return fire, they'd be easy targets. Colt speculated the team was adjusting to the new development before they dove head-first into an ambush.

But Colt knew what needed to be done. Shots to take out Rake and Fifty-two had to come from the thick brush on the opposite side of the road, not out in the open. He guessed Roper's team was not in position to terminate the threat. Most likely, they trounced through the brush on the opposite side. Could they take the kill shot without exposing themselves?

Rake yelled out. "Anybody else wanna try to stop us? Huh?"

With more bravado than good sense, Rocky took a step forward. "You ain't doing this. Those drugs belong to all of us!"

Rake open fired, hitting Rocky multiple times. His body jerked with each shot. He fell to the ground. Blood coated his chest, his pants, and his face. His dead eyes glazed over. Standing less than ten feet away, Colt trembled, his nerves shot. Had Rake not stopped, he'd have been dead too. He felt a sting and glanced down to see a bullet had grazed his leg. From a tear in his jeans, Colt spotted blood. Still, he counted himself lucky.

And just like that, multiple shots came from the woods. Rake and Fifty-two went down hard, their torsos ripped with bullets, blood coating their bodies. In the fog of smoke, the team pounced from their hiding spot.

At last, Colt could breathe normally. His heart rate came down as a DEA agent slapped cuffs around his wrists and shoved him forward with Pug and Boone.

Two agents led Colt over to a team of medics. They treated his gunshot wound and wrapped it in sterile gauze.

Roper said something to another agent and walked over to Colt. "You okay?'

"Yeah. Just a scratch."

"You did good, Jessup. Real good."

"Because I managed not to get killed?"

"Get in the van. The guys will take you out of here." Roper put his phone to his ear. "See you later."

"Hey, wait a minute. When is someone going to take the cuffs off me?"

Roper laughed. "As soon as your drug buddies are taken away."

On the way back to the Drug Enforcement Agency's building, Colt mindlessly stared out at the passing scenery but none of it registered. He hoped the agent seated beside him didn't notice his eyes watering. Not a sign of allergies and not a sign of weakness. Thoughts of his daughter made him emotional. He defeated death and lived to see another day, to see his precious Maddie.

<h1 style="text-align:center">41</h1>

When Isabella awoke, the digital clock beside the bed showed ten o'clock. Landon was already up, freshly shaved and dressed in jeans and a dark polo shirt. He slouched in a chair in front of a desk, staring at his cell phone screen. The minute she mumbled good morning, he rushed to her side. He eased down on the mattress and reached over to kiss her.

"Good morning. How do you feel?"

"Fine." A lie, but wasn't it the response most people were programmed to say?

"No, you're *not* fine. Too much has happened. But I promise you this—I will do everything in my power to be here for you. To help you through this. I should have been there for you from the beginning—when Brianna..." He closed his eyes and shook his head.

Isabella sat up and reached forward to hug him. "Don't. You didn't know. I should have called you." She rubbed the side of his face with her thumb. "Landon, let's not play that game, regretting what we did or didn't do. Let's focus on the present."

"You're right. So, tell me—"

He stopped speaking the second her phone trilled. She grabbed her cell from the bedside table. "Wait. I have to take this call." She swung her legs off the side of the bed, the phone to her ear. "Hi, Kiki. So glad you called. I have so much to tell you."

"Tell me later, Bella. If I don't tell you the good news, I'll explode. I swear I will."

Her agent's jubilant tone made her laugh. "Okay. You go first. What is it?"

"Stuart Milford just called. You got the role, Bella! You will be singing the lead part at the Houston Grand Opera this coming season! Isn't that wonderful? Wow! We have so much to do, so much to talk about. When are you coming back to New York? Soon, I hope."

"Yes, soon." Isabella's eyes locked with Landon's, knowing he'd heard every word. "That's great news, Kiki. Thanks for making it happen. I'm so excited. It's a wonderful opportunity."

"It's huge, girl! This will lead to more starring roles. You're on your way, Bella. There's no limit to what you can do now."

In the end, Isabella didn't tell Kiki any of her news. No need to dampen her spirits.

Isabella tossed her phone onto the mattress and smiled at Landon. "I said I wanted to focus on the present, but I also want to think beyond that."

Landon raised one brow expectantly. "Go on."

"Do you want to have a future with me in New York?"

He brought her into his arms and gave her a crushing kiss. When he released her, he looked deeply into her eyes. "You know I do."

§

Colt knocked twice before Kate answered the door. She hastily tied the sash around her short, silky robe. Her surprised look made him regret not calling first.

"I shouldn't be here," he said.

She ran her fingers through her hair. "No, it's fine. Come in."

He stepped inside and kicked the door shut with the heel of his boot. Despite wearing no make-up and being torn from her bed at a late hour, she still looked pretty. He gave no warning when he pulled her into his arms and pressed against her. She stiffened and two-handedly pushed him away. He dropped his hands to his sides and stepped back.

"Sorry." Colt bowed his head and rubbed his thumb against his nose. He forced himself to look up. "When I said I shouldn't be here, it's not what you think. What I mean is—I shouldn't still be alive."

Immediately, he regretted saying it. Why didn't he keep his big mouth shut? It was Special Agent Roper's fault. After the bust, Roper said, "No one can believe you weren't killed, Jessup." Then, he added, "One of those bullets should have taken you out. I mean, holy shit! That guy shot—oh, I don't know—maybe fifty or sixty rounds in less than a minute. You were standing right there! Rocky took four shots to the chest, three in the gut, one in the thigh, and one through his hand. And you? Just a nick on the leg. How is that even possible?"

"Just lucky, I guess."

"Lucky? Hell!" Geek interjected. "We're talking a miracle, bro. How many lives do you have anyway?"

"It wasn't my time, that's all."

How could he explain any of that to Kate? She stood before him with the same anxious look she'd worn many times over the years. He had a habit of showing up unannounced like a psych patient in need of therapy. She'd always been quick to remind him he had a family to take care of. She asked him more than once, "Why not find a career that doesn't require getting shot at?"

He'd made her uncomfortable, hugging her like that. She smoothed her hair in place. When he brought her into his arms, the panels of her robe fell apart. She pulled them together, covering up. He could no longer see the swells of her breasts.

She cleared her throat. "What happened, Colt?"

"Nothing new. I got shot at. Only this time was different."

"Different? How?"

"It was the first time I'd been shot at with a fully automatic assault rifle."

She bit her bottom lip and leaned against the wall, leaving a prolonged silence between them. "But you're alright, aren't you?"

"Yeah, I'm fine. I shouldn't be. Should've taken a hit. Don't know why I…" He glanced up at the ceiling and sighed. "The guy next to me had about a dozen GSWs. Me? One bullet grazed my leg, that's it."

"That should tell you something, Colt. You can't keep doing this. *Please.* You have a daughter. Stop doing undercover work, I'm begging you. Maddie loves you so much. If something happened to you, she'd be crushed."

"I hear ya. I'm thinking this is the last time."

"I've heard that before."

"Well, this time I mean it."

"Are you quitting the force?" Her eyes brightened.

"I don't know. Maybe." He paused to consider the possibility. "Being a cop is all I know, Katie-girl."

Katie-girl. When was the last time he called her that?

He didn't expect her to step closer and run her finger along the side of his face. It felt nice. "Think about it, okay?"

He nodded and returned her smile. "I'll go now. It's late. But before I do, can I have a hug?"

She laughed softly. "Sure."

He brought her into his arms and held her tightly. His lips kissed the side of her head. The feel of her soft skin, the warmth of her body, the quick rush of pleasure emboldened him. He placed a finger under her chin and aligned her lips to meet his. He kissed her. At first, lightly. Then he kissed her long and hard, not wanting to come up for air. She responded eagerly, her fingertips digging into his back. Her heartbeat thumping against his chest. But then, she pushed away, sending a mixed message.

Colt stood as still as a statue; his thoughts trapped in a mesh of confusion. This time he wouldn't say he was sorry. He wasn't. In the heat of the moment, it felt right. He wished she wanted to give him another chance. To be honest, she'd given him more chances than he deserved. He took both her hands in his and squeezed. "I better go. I'll call in a day or so and make plans with Maddie."

"Sounds good. She'll be excited to see you."

What she said jarred him. It made him realize if he stood a few inches closer to Rocky, he'd be dead. And Maddie would be fatherless.

Is my job worth it? Someday leaving that poor girl without a daddy.

§

The months of undercover work and the task force operation were over. Rake, Fifty-two, Rocky, and two of the lookouts were dead. Everyone else, including Pug and Boone, were in jail, pending trial.

The investigation into Brianna's death was also wrapped up. All that was left was the paperwork, the thing Colt hated most.

He sat in his car and read over the initial notes on the investigation. He scanned the pages twice, wondering if he'd missed something. To get clarification, he called Spencer. "Hey, Spence, what about Hondo's death? I don't see it here. Are you telling me, the DA is not gonna charge Marcus with that?"

"Nope. I met with him and begged, but he said it's all circumstantial and he can't prove it in court. Hondo willingly did the drugs. Looks like an overdose."

"But the dose was lethal. Marcus planned it that way."

"So? He's gonna deny it as long as the sun shines and the cows come home. Besides, we can't prove he gave the drugs to Hondo. Look at this way—the Asheville police have a solid case—more than enough to charge him with capital murder. And of course, there's Brianna's death. We have his prints on the glass at Brianna's home, and the Lamont woman has agreed to testify against him. He might end up with two life sentences, so be happy with that, my friend."

"Yeah, yeah, I hear ya. I just wish there was justice for Hondo. He wasn't such a bad guy, just messed up."

"Gotta go, Colt. I got a meeting with my sergeant. Just got assigned two new cases."

"Okay, Spence. Keep in touch."

Spencer mentioning his sergeant reminded Colt he needed to meet with his and talk about his next assignment. He'd put him off with a lame excuse. But the truth was, Colt hadn't made up his mind if he wanted to stay in vice and work undercover. What Kate said kept popping into his head. She hit him where it hurt most, saying, "If anything happened to you, Maddie would be crushed."

With his future uncertain, Colt frowned and glanced at the clock on his dashboard. "Holy shit! I'm supposed to take Isabella and Landon to the airport."

He started his Charger and screeched out of the parking lot behind Police Headquarters.

§

"I'm serious, Songbird. You send me tickets and I'll come."

Colt took his eyes off the road and glanced in the rearview mirror. He wanted to see Isabella's reaction to what he said. Seated in the front passenger seat, Landon said, "Insist on box seats, Colt. Do it up right."

"Yeah, I want box seats. Two of 'em. I'll bring my daughter so she'll get a taste of high class living. Learn to appreciate opera. Hell, I might even get a haircut and a shave at some fancy salon. You won't even recognize me, Songbird."

"Okay, Colt," Isabella said, smiling. "I'll hold you to it. If I send tickets, I expect to see you there. Or if you like, you can come to Houston. I'll be performing there as well."

"Nah, we'll come to New York. I wanna show Maddie around. Broadway. Times Square. The Statue of Liberty. All of it. She's never been. Hell, we might even take a carriage ride in Central Park."

At the airport, Colt followed the signs for departures and got in the far-right lane. He rolled to a stop, put the car in park, and popped the trunk. He placed their suitcases on the curb and said, "Well, Isabella Luca, I guess this is it. Until I see you in New York."

She gave him a hug and a peck on the cheek. "Bye, Colt. Thanks for everything."

"You bet." Colt extended his hand to Landon. "We got off to a rough start, but now that I've gotten to know you, well, you're alright, bro. You two make a fine couple. Take good care of our girl. She's special." Colt looked over at Isabella, pleased she caught his quick smile and wink.

A police officer gave Colt dirty looks for parking too long curbside, prompting Colt back inside his car. He drove off and followed the exit signs. Just as he merged onto Billy Graham Parkway, his phone rang. It was Samantha.

"Before you say anything, listen to me," she said. "I heard through the rumor mill that there's a new opening in homicide. You'd be perfect, Colt. I already floated your name around and got some positive responses. What I'm saying is—the job's yours if you want it."

"You sure they'll take me? What about my reputation? I don't always play by the rules, you know."

"It doesn't matter. Well, it does matter, but they might cut you some slack, especially if you solve cases. You need to get out of this undercover work before you get yourself killed. I've kind of grown fond of you, dumbass. So? Will you talk to them?"

"The pay and the hours are just as lousy."

"You're not doing this for the money. None of us are. Will you at least think about it?"

Colt reached for his cigarettes and pulled one from the pack. He placed it between his lips, then removed it, remembering his pledge to cut back.

"Colt? Are you there? Answer me, damn it."

"Yeah, I heard ya. I'll think about it."

"Good. Where are you headed now?"

"The shooting range. Wanna join me? I've got ten bucks that says I'll score higher."

"You're on, Jessup. There's nothing more satisfying than a girl beating a guy."

He laughed. Maybe he'd let her win just for the hell of it. And maybe he'd stop smoking. Go cold turkey. *Just maybe.*

ACKNOWLEDGEMENTS
I could not accomplish publishing a book without the help, support, and encouragement of others. The following people have made this book possible:

- My husband, Ron, for his love and his willingness to put up with my obsession with this project.
- My daughter, Christina Arethas, for her consultation and expertise on the opera segments of the book.
- Tim Barber of Dissect Designs for his remarkable cover for ROCK BOTTOM.
- Jenifer Ruff and Dennis Carrigan for editing and making the book more polished.
- My Mystery/Suspense Critique Group made up of awesome fiction authors: Reita Pendry, James Boatner, Jenifer Ruff, Alex Whitney, and Dennis Carrigan.
- Special acknowledgement to Cindy Henderson for winning the STREET NAME FOR UNDERCOVER COP. Congratulations! Rowdy was the perfect choice for my lead character, Detective Colt Jessup.
- To ARC readers Sharon Rice, Fran Howe, and Cyndi Wannamaker

THANK YOU!

Dear Reader, thank you for reading ROCK BOTTOM. I hope you enjoyed the story. If you did, I would appreciate your help by posting a review on Amazon and/or Goodreads. Also, please visit my website, join my *Readers in Suspense Group* and subscribe to my blog. Lastly, tell your friends if you think they would enjoy a fast-paced suspense novel with a twist of romance.